To Corinne

Many thanks for

April 2014

THE BOOK

by

R A Jarman

www.thebook.me.uk

First published in Great Britain in 2014

Typeset in Bookman Old Style and printed by Short Run Press, Sowton, Exeter.

ISBN: 978-0-9927179-0-2 (hardback)

THANK YOU

To my parents, for inspiring in me a love of books, not least by naming me after a fictional character

To Mike Walker, Heritage Officer of Tuckers Hall and a fount of knowledge on the Incorporation of Weavers, Fullers and Shearmen, for his generosity with his time and for reading and commenting on an early draft

To Julian Nowill of the Devon & Exeter Institution, for similarly reading an early draft and for providing helpful comments

To the Devon & Exeter Institution, those who founded it and those who work for no financial reward to keep it alive

To Rob Gliddon and Short Run Press Exeter, for their support and professionalism

To my former employers, who unexpectedly provided me with the time to complete this project

To friends and family, for their love and encouragement

To all who pledged support through Kickstarter to fund the printing of the first edition of this book. For their names, see the End Notes

To my best friend, most supportive critic, most loyal conspirator, and truest love, Sylvia – for everything

PREFACE TO THE BOOK

Hallo.

Can I begin by saying I am both grateful and surprised that you are reading this?

This makes you a Reader (with a capital R) and, in some sense, it makes me an Author (with a capital A). You see, up until you started reading this, I hadn't thought of myself as an Author. I don't honestly think I wrote this book – it kind of wrote itself. It emerged out of a lifetime of experiences, snatches of song, chance encounters, a love of words, books, and libraries and above all, the magnificent city of Exeter and its rich history. All I did was copy out the words in my head. It's only now, as you are reading them, that I really qualify as an Author, don't you think?

The second thing you should realise is that this is a book about history. About personal history, economic history, social history, financial history, it is about the nature of historical truth. And the key word in that last sentence is 'about'.

What this is not about is actual history. None of this happened, really – it is a STORY. There are places and names and events and explanations and people and causes and consequences that you might recognise (or think you recognise) BUT –read my lips – this is a story.

So please don't write to me and say that the houses in Southernhay were actually finished a couple of years after someone is supposed to have moved into one. I *know* that, but I've tweaked things a bit because it suits my purposes.

And if you work in one of the organisations I mention or your name or personality resembles any of my characters and especially if it looks like I've made out that you, or someone like you, or someone in your family or that you know or have heard of might have behaved badly, just stop there. Don't sue me – please?

I made this all up. It's a story. I enjoyed it and I really hope you enjoy it, but don't believe it is true. It isn't – it's meant to be fun.

Finally, just to put you in your place, you are invented too. When this project started, you didn't exist. You only exist now, as you are reading this preface. So think about that. Ask yourself what is real, what is true, what constitutes you, and whether you exist outside your own perception of yourself.

Then tell me this is pretentious twaddle, take a sip of good wine or tea or whatever you fancy, turn the page and – please – enjoy The Book.

Roger Jarman, the Ides of March MMXIV

For me, writing a book (or anything) is not a one way process. I really want to hear back from you, the reader, about the bits you liked, the bits I could have done better, the bits you would like to see more of.

I would be thrilled if you were to give me feedback of any *sort that will help me become a better writer and will give you a better read next time.*

So please email: IveReadTheBook@gmail.com

Thank you.

Thursday 28 March 2013

Chapter 1

There is a saying that – for those who find accountancy too exciting – there is always auditing.

Much the same could be said about being a solicitor and conveyancing, thought Nathaniel Barton, not for the first time. But, as he gazed through the window of his office on the highest floor of 14 Southernhay, Exeter, Nathaniel felt more than a little dissatisfied.

He was 56, divorced, living alone and, as he well knew, he contributed a significant amount to the profits of Kennaway & Partners. Over the past decade or more – ever since, in fact, he and Sally had split up – he'd schooled himself into a quiet and undemanding routine.

Today, as every weekday, he had arrived at 8:45, walked in through the front door of number fourteen and nodded a silent greeting to Sophie. As every weekday, he had resolved he would walk up the four flights of uneven, coarsely carpeted stairs without pause. And, as every weekday, he had paused on the third landing.

From here he could see the low door to his office on the landing above, opposite the archive store. These two rooms, he supposed, would have been the home of the servants in the grand house during the eighteenth century. Now it was the preserve of the Kennaway & Partners drudge. Where, in earlier times, the occupants would have spent their nights in a deep sleep after carrying out the household chores, now it was the home of Nathaniel who carried out the repetitive tasks of establishing title, granting encumbrances, and scanning deeds.

Today, as every weekday, he had hung his lightweight coat on the back of the door, placed his briefcase on the floor by his chair and turned on his PC. While it booted up, he had plugged in his kettle and popped a fresh teabag in his mug. Now, seven hours later, the contents of his Outlook Inbox had been dealt with and it was only quarter to four.

He still had to draft a couple of instructions for searches yet to be started; and the Thursday afternoon before the long Easter weekend was not really the time to address a task which might only take twenty minutes but could easily take four weeks or more.

It was the more challenging searches – poring through seventeenth century manuscripts, peering at faded maps of long-vanished streets – that Nathaniel now enjoyed the most, though he knew full well (and was often reminded) that it was quick and easy that turned the prettiest penny.

And along with a well-established legal practice in the heart of one of England's finest cities, Charles Kennaway – CK to employees and competitors alike – had inherited a fine regard for profits.

Unaccountably, Nathaniel was feeling somewhat dissatisfied. Yes, it was the last working day of the week and yes, he could look forward to four days away from the office. But that wasn't normally something that excited him. After all, as a man of few friends and even fewer hobbies, a Bank Holiday was little more than an opportunity to read a few more murder mysteries, drink a little more beer than he permitted himself during the week, and perhaps engage in a rambling and ultimately unsatisfying phone conversation with his brother in Italy.

It was now four o'clock. He really didn't feel up to attacking his pending tray and, to be honest, there was nothing that couldn't wait. Solicitors already had a reputation for moving with glacial speed and no client would expect any frenzied activity in Easter week.

So, sod it. The sun was shining and, as far as Nathaniel was concerned, the sun could legitimately be said to be over the yard-arm. The Cathedral Close was a bare five minutes away and Nathaniel could already picture himself at a table outside the Royal Clarence, a glass of chilled white wine in one hand and a few smoked almonds in the other. Grabbing his briefcase and coat, he almost skipped down the back stairs of the Southernhay office and left through the side door. No point in alerting Sophie (and, through her, CK) to this unexpectedly early departure.

Entering the close under the Victorian iron bridge, Nathaniel picked his way over the uneven cobbles. It was not just the early departure from work that was lifting his spirits. Every time he walked down this ancient back street, he was conscious of a rich history, of the unchanging but ever-changing solidity of the city where he lived and where countless generations had lived before him. The bridge he had walked under had been installed in 1814; the wall which supported the bridge on either side was Roman; and the street itself was clearly mediaeval. A plaque on his right commemorated the death of an eighteenth-century governor of Ontario; and ahead, he could make out the corner of the (largely) fourteenth-century cathedral.

As he turned into the close, Nathaniel realised that there was something of a chill breeze. Bright as the day had looked from his fourth floor window, the prospect of sitting outside became increasingly less appealing.

No worries. Next door to the hotel, the Well House beckoned. Recently refurbished, it had ceiling to floor windows overlooking the close; more importantly, it kept a fine and varied cellar. Nathaniel's unusually early arrival meant he was able to secure his favourite window seat.

Armed with a pint of Bays Gold and a bag of pork scratchings, he gazed idly out at the late afternoon bustle. Ahead of him was the statue of a seated Richard Hooker, calmly reading a book. Further on stood the north side of the cathedral, a magnificent if slightly tired building, possessing (as Nathaniel had learnt during various solitary wanderings) not only the longest mediaeval vaulted ceiling in the country but also Britain's first wooden representation of an elephant in the form of a carved misericord.

That imposing building had impressed Exeter citizens for over six hundred years, and before then, mused Nathaniel, the forum and baths of Roman Isca would have done much the same.

His attention shifted as a stunningly beautiful woman strode past the window talking animatedly into her iphone. His eye landed upon his empty glass so he returned to the bar for a refill. Resuming his window seat, he picked up a slightly tattered copy of the *Express & Echo* to while away the time.

He skipped past the ever present articles on failed rubbish collections, the photos of winsome tots in school productions and the correspondence on (alleged) council malpractice. His attention was caught by a double page spread headlined 'Snow started a rot at our Tudor gem'. The article began:

'*It is only one of a handful of Grade I listed properties in Exeter and it needs your help. The sudden heavy snowfall of December 2010 took a heavy toll on the Devon & Exeter Institution in the Cathedral Close.*'

Nathaniel looked across from his seat and there indeed it was – an unobtrusive white door set in an unassuming red stone wall. Founded in 1813, the Institution now had a library of some 40,000 volumes plus other memorabilia of Devon history. The more he read, the more fascinated Nathaniel became. He had worked just round the corner from this building for three decades and had never known of this 'Tudor gem'.

He gazed up from his paper, took a sip of his beer, and thought back to his time at Oxford. Although he had so often found himself a fish out of water – a provincial estate agent's son surrounded by the gilded scions of England's wealthiest families – it was his only experience of life outside Exeter and it had left him with many fond memories. In particular, he had become attached to Duke Humfrey's Library, the oldest surviving part of the great Bodleian (founded, by happy chance, by another – rather more illustrious – Exonian). Here, he had been happy to while away afternoons and evenings in the company of some of the country's oldest books as if he could, by some form of osmosis, absorb the wisdom, knowledge and pure quiddity they contained without the effort of actually reading them.

Despite his apparent indolence, young Nathaniel had gained a respectable second, and had returned to Exeter to what looked at the time to be a promising position in a well-established legal practice. Now, nearly four decades on, what had he achieved? What had he become? Could this long-established but newly found Institution offer him some sort of solace in what had to be seen as his declining years? Just as Duke Humfrey's had nourished him as a youth, might not the Institution take his mind off the dullness of his daily round?

On a sudden impulse, he gathered up his coat, briefcase and the newspaper and hurtled out of the pub's front door.

Chapter 2

Faith Codrington paused for breath outside the Well House, and switched her mobile from her left hand to her right. Her mother took the all too rare opportunity to get a word in.

'Hush now, Faith, you've been talking non-stop for the past fifteen minutes! I've got the message that you've arrived and that you're excited. I take it Exeter, England is every bit as fascinating as Exeter, Ontario?'

'Fascinating doesn't cover it, ma. On my left is the oldest hotel in the UK, ahead of me is a sixteenth-century coffee house, and on my right is a mediaeval cathedral. When your home town is less than 200 years old, you've got to agree that this is pretty mind blowing.'

'That might be so, but I'd better love and leave you now, my dear, lunch service is building up and it looks like pa will need a bit of help out front. Can I call you later this evening?'

'No problem, ma. I haven't felt this high since getting into the Panthers cheerleading team. I've still got lots of exploring to do. Catch you later.'

Faith slipped her phone back into her shoulder bag and sat on the low wall surrounding the cathedral lawns. This close was pretty amazing. It looked like a random collection of buildings from every period of the city's history and Faith knew that beneath her feet were the remains of the Roman forum. Yet it was strangely harmonious.

What particularly impressed her was that this was not some carefully preserved but sterile assemblage of monuments. This was the beating heart of a living city.

Yes, there was the occasional and inevitable crocodile of tourists following their red jacketed guide. But there were also students (both university and college) lounging in groups on the grass. Here a family with a small child jumping up and down the stone steps around the statue of Richard Hooker; there a couple of shoppers laden down with carrier bags from the spring sales in Princesshay.

Faith was a historian and it was her postgraduate thesis that had brought her here from New York Uni. Born and brought up in Exeter, Huron County, Ontario, Faith had, from a young age, taken an interest in her home town's namesake in Devon. It was the wool trade that had first brought riches to Exeter in the fifteenth century, and it was the history of the wool trade that was the topic of Faith's work in her postgraduate programme in New York.

And there was a darker thread that tied Faith and her family to Exeter and to the cathedral behind her.

Faith was black and her surname, Codrington, originated from the notorious seventeenth-century sugar estate on Barbuda in the Caribbean. Nine generations ago her six times great grandpa had borne the brand of the Society for the Propagation of Christian Knowledge.

When the British Parliament voted to abolish slavery, compensation was duly paid – not to the 665 slaves on the Codrington Estate, but to their owners. And it was the Bishop of Exeter, Devon and his 'business associates' who had pocketed nearly £13,000 in 1834 – equivalent to around one and half million pounds sterling in 2013.

Most of those 'liberated' stayed in the West Indies in ill-paid jobs and in living conditions little better than those on the plantation. Faith's forebears had been made of more enterprising stuff and had worked their way across the Caribbean and up through the United States, ending up in the new settlement of Exeter in Canada in the early 1850s.

Faith's parents still had that same dynamism that had driven the first Codringtons, and it was their small chain of Bob's Jerk Shed and Bistros that had funded the studies of their only daughter.

Summa cum laude at South Huron District High, a first in History from Toronto, and now in the final year of her postgraduate programme at New York Uni.

Her thesis covered the changing role of Exeter's Guild of Weavers, Fullers and Shearmen through the centuries and she was currently heading to the Devon & Exeter Institution where some of the Guild's papers were held.

As she started to get up from the wall, a middle-aged man holding a briefcase and newspaper barged into her and then ran on without a word of apology.

'Jeez,' muttered Faith under her breath, 'what happened to old-fashioned English courtesy?'

Gathering herself and taking another long gaze round the close, she resumed her stroll towards the Devon & Exeter Institution. She was, she thought, heading towards the last stage of her education, the doctorate which would unlock the universities of the world to her, where she could teach and research and learn and be happy.

Looking back on this March day, Faith would recall that feeling of unworried calm and optimism, and wonder at how she could have been so naive.

Chapter 3

Nathaniel, breathless, arrived at the imposing white door of the Institution to find it locked. If only that damn woman hadn't blindly stepped into his path, he'd have made it before the five o'clock closing time. What was she thinking of?

Automatically Nathaniel checked his watch, which told him it was still five minutes short of five. He then noticed the brass button labelled 'Press Me' and was reminded of Alice in Wonderland. Feeling that he was indeed about to enter a fantastical other world, he pressed the button and heard a dull click from the white door's lock.

When he pushed hard, it swung open but he found himself confronted by a woman built along much the same proportions as the door, except that she favoured a covering of tweed rather than blistered white gloss

'Yes?' she barked. Trying not to feel too much like an eight-year-old in front of the headmistress, Nathaniel enquired: 'This *is* the Devon & Exeter Institution?'

The woman rolled her eyes heavenwards, but Nathaniel was unsure whether this was her natural response to imbeciles or she was simply indicating the brass sign above her head.

'Well, I've just seen the article in the Express and Echo, and I saw you were appealing for more members and I...'

A ghastly grimace spread across her face and, taking Nathaniel's forearm in a painful martial arts hold she dragged him into the hallway. 'You should have said so, dear boy. Sorry that we're closing up right now, but here you are, take these away, have a read, fill in the form and pop back in on Tuesday.'

With a bundle of papers thrust under his arm, Nathaniel found himself spun on his heels and projected back through the door, which closed behind him with a firm thud. Well, thought Nathaniel, if ever a Hunt Ball needed a bouncer, they need look no further.

As he was propelled back into the close, he found himself face to face with the young woman who had stepped into his path earlier. It was only a deft side step from her that avoided another collision. As she opened her mouth to speak, Nathaniel heard himself saying, 'We must stop meeting like this,' before flushing bright red.

Mortified at his unaccustomed levity, Nathaniel strode back towards the Well House before his new acquaintance could respond. He went back to his table, more in hope than expectation that his half empty glass would still be there.

'I'm sorry, we thought you'd gone for good,' said a slim young Goth with a tray full of dirty glasses. 'Can I get you another? Bays, wasn't it?'

Her polite tones were so at odds with her warrior princess appearance that Nathaniel found himself saying yes.

In a rather less tranquil mood than when he first arrived at the pub, Nathaniel began running through the positive stream of uncharacteristic things he had done that day.

Bunking off far too early from work, check. Two – no, make that one and a half – pints of best bitter before the sun had genuinely crossed the yardarm, check. Bumping into the same person twice without apologising on either occasion, check. And what on earth was he doing, at his time of life, deciding to join the bloody Devon and bloody Exeter bloody Institution?

Morosely, he sat down, removed the now slightly damp papers from under his arm, and addressed his pint. Smoothing down a glossy black and white leaflet, Nathaniel began to read:

'The Devon & Exeter Institution was founded in 1813 by some two hundred gentlemen of the country and city for promoting the general diffusion of Science, Literature

and Art and for illustrating the Natural and Civil History of the County of Devon and the City of Exeter.'

It seemed that the building these liberal gentlemen chose to occupy had been the town house of the Courtenay family, who still lived at nearby Powderham Castle on the Exe estuary.

The leaflet went on: '*The founding fathers demolished the old hall and kitchen and in their place and on the former courtyard built two lofty libraries lit by domed lanterns, each library with its own gallery, glazed cupboards and extensive shelving.*'

Nathaniel drained the last of his Bays Gold and relished the phrase '*two lofty libraries lit by domed lanterns*'.

He rather thought he would like the Devon & Exeter Institution.

Chapter 4

Faith stood calmly for a moment, resisting the temptation to scream. Who *was* this man who had taken it upon himself to bump into her at every opportunity? Was it just her, or was the idiot just indiscriminately dashing up and down, bumping into random bystanders? Where was he going in such a hurry, and in opposite directions?

Breathing more slowly, she unconsciously repeated Nathaniel's sequence of trying the door knob, spotting the brass button, and then ringing for attention. But this time the response was rather less helpful. The tweed-clad concierge emerged with a large handbag and smaller dog with a matching tweed waistcoat.

'Sorry, Miss, we're closed now for the weekend. I would have gone earlier but for some idiot who rushed in here just as I was about to lock up.'

'Tell me about him,' muttered Faith under her breath.

'Are you one of the uni students?'

'Post grad. I was told the Institution held the papers I need for my thesis. From the Guild of...'

'...Weavers, Fullers and Shearmen? You must be Miss Codrington. I was told to expect you earlier. Sadly, with funding what it is, we don't exactly keep long hours. Apart from the Librarian' – Faith could hear the capital letter – 'and the housekeeper, the rest of us here are all volunteers. But if you come back Tuesday – yes, I know, Easter weekend – I'm sure there'll be someone here to help you.'

As Faith ruefully recalled her over-long conversation (or was it monologue) with her mother, her brief acquaintance spun round and Faith watched the two tweed-clad bottoms wobbling away over the cobbles of the close.

Somewhat deflated after her earlier enthusiasm, Faith decided she needed a cream tea. With a sixteenth-century coffee house only a few steps away, this was a wish more easily satisfied than her plan to scope out the Institution's library. With a pot of Lapsang Souchong and a warm scone in front of her, Faith's natural good humour was almost restored and she could begin to reflect more positively on the reasons for her choosing an obscure Exeter guild as the subject of her study.

Through what were called the middle ages, society became less agrarian and more urbanised. There was less dependence on farming and the feudal structures that supported it; trades, services and manufacture became more important. Men (and it was *always* men, grimaced Faith) grouped together to form guilds, and there was a long running academic debate on those guilds' roles and functions.

Some argued that guilds were little more than protection rackets, literally closed shops that controlled entry to a profession so as to keep prices high. Others agreed with Marx that they were organs of the bourgeoisie, testing the power of the land-based aristocracy. Yet others saw them as precursors of trades unions, designed to protect the rights and privileges of workers.

There was also ongoing research into the relationship between guilds and the established church. Whereas members of the national faith – whether Roman Catholic or Church of England – expected and received access to funding, influence and business contacts, more marginal groups needed their own networks and resources. Guilds could provide alternative structures for businessmen wanting to get on, especially if they were Jewish, nonconformist or immigrant.

Over time, guilds had become so powerful, politically and financially, that autocratic monarchs felt they needed to be eliminated. Charles II, in particular, had been determined to remove the privileges of all guilds nationwide, except for those in the City of London on whose support he could depend (and that he could oversee more effectively).

Even the mighty Exeter Guild of Weavers, Fullers and Shearmen had been required to surrender their privileges to the Crown, but they were then saved by the untimely and unexpected death of the king from an apoplectic fit in 1685.

No real mystery there, but Faith had been intrigued by the fact that, when the Guild's independence had been challenged, they had called a series of meetings where, unusually, one set of minutes had remained unpublished.

Faith wanted to see those secret minutes, to understand the tensions and arguments of the time, to get inside the minds of those early capitalists.

That was why she was here in Exeter, that was her mission and no clumsy oafs or punctilious volunteers would get in her way. Filled with new resolve, she delicately wiped the last traces of clotted cream from her lips, paid her bill and set off back to her university accommodation. The weekend ahead would be for exploring the streets of Exeter and relaxing.

It would be her last relaxing weekend for some time.

Tuesday 2 April 2013

Chapter 5

Weekends disagreed with Nathaniel, Bank Holiday Mondays even more so. When Easter came round each year with its four long ponderous days and nights,

Nathaniel genuinely didn't know what to do with himself. Holidays were one thing; ten days in Paris, a long weekend in Prague, something new to see, new foods to try, the occasional romantic encounter. But what to do, on your own, in an Exeter back street, in the place you had lived for almost the whole of your life?

Tuesday could not come quickly enough. Arriving at the office at 8:15, he walked in through the front door of number fourteen and past Sophie's empty desk. As every weekday, he tried to walk up the four flights of uneven coarsely carpeted stairs without pause; and, as every weekday, he paused on the third landing.

He hung his coat on the back of the door, placed his briefcase on the floor by his chair and turned on his PC. While it booted up, he plugged in his kettle and popped a fresh teabag in his mug. Within minutes, he had sent off emails to Sophie, CK and a couple of random clients.

He pulled his completed Devon & Exeter Institution application form out of his briefcase and virtually skipped down the stairs, this time without pause.

Slipping out through the side door and then in to the close, he arrived at the anonymous white front door at exactly the same time as a rather random assembly of sideburns and knees covered in what seemed to Nathaniel to be the identical tweed to that worn by his previous acquaintance at the Institution. Was this some kind of uniform?

Turning to greet a slightly out of breath Nathaniel, the tweed individual enquired in a reedy voice 'Can I help you?' Before Nathaniel could frame his reply, the door was unlocked and he was ushered in. 'Of course, Dolores told me we had a new applicant at the end of last Thursday.'

Dolores? Nathaniel struggled briefly to reconcile the exotic name with the burly termagant who had shown him the door last week.

'Yes, I've filled in the form, but I'm a bit stuck for a suitable referee.'

'Well, in addition to being the librarian I'm also the admissions secretary – Lionel Simpkins. And you're a decent looking chap in a suit and tie so I'm more than happy to sign you in.'

'Oh, is that it? Does that mean I'm now a member?'

'Not that simple, I'm afraid,' said Simpkins. 'Your form goes on the notice board for a month, at the end of which the Committee has to confirm your membership. Any member can lodge an objection during that time, and one vote against is decisive.'

Seeing Nathaniel's downcast expression, Simpkins reassuringly patted him on the arm.

'The last time an applicant was blackballed was back in 1983. We're not that kind of organisation. And of course, you can start using our facilities immediately. Would you like me to show you round now?'

'Afraid not,' said Nathaniel, conscious of the stewed tea awaiting him back at the office. 'But can I pop back later today?'

'Of course. But you *do* know we close at five? Nine till five, Monday through Friday.'

This was not what Nathaniel had been hoping for. He had, if truth be known, been looking for a refuge where he could perhaps while away empty evenings and even emptier weekends. Still...

'Yes, I'll be back this afternoon.'

'I'll expect you,' said Simpkins.

As Nathaniel walked briskly back to the office, his mind was racing. Why was he acting so impulsively? What was the attraction of this fly-blown, fusty

Institution with its ridiculously unhelpful opening hours? How was he possibly going to find time to use its facilities during the working day, particularly this afternoon when, if his memory served him, he was meant to be visiting a client?

Without thinking, he walked back into the office through the main entrance to receive a withering glance from Sophie. Something of a fixture at Kennaway's, Sophie had been a scrawny, disobliging young blonde when Nathaniel had joined the firm; over thirty years later, only the hair colour had changed.

'A little late today, Mr Barton?'

'Have you not had time yet to check your emails? I've just popped out to drop an urgent package into the Post Office. As you know, they don't open until after *I've* arrived at the office.'

A small and unworthy victory, but a victory nonetheless.

Nathaniel set off on the climb to his top floor office and actually made it without the customary pause on the third landing. The tea was, as expected, stewed and cold, his PC desktop was indicating incoming email, and Nathaniel reluctantly sat down to face the day.

Before doing anything else, he checked his Outlook Calendar, and found to his chagrin that he did indeed have an appointment that afternoon with a software company based in Exmouth. So much for popping back to the Institution.

With a heavy heart, he then went to his Inbox where he found an urgent email from that same software company. Copious apologies, but could he reschedule for next week?

There *is* a God, thought Nathaniel, as he quickly composed a reply. Yes, despite the late notice (sniff), he *would* be able to defer the meeting until a week today. Here were a couple of suggested times.

The remainder of the morning sped by. Searches completed, a couple of files closed, and Nathaniel shut down his PC at one o‘clock with something resembling a warm glow.

'Out again, Mr Barton?' queried Sophie with a raised eyebrow.

'Check the Calendar. Client meeting in Exmouth,' riposted Nathaniel, with a strong sense of playing truant. With an unaccustomed sense of liberation, he strode purposefully into the Well House and ordeed a pint of Bays and a rare roast beef sandwich.

Thirty minutes later, he was pressing the buzzer next to the big white door of the Institution. The tinny tones of Simpkins through the intercom confirmed the door was unlocked and he walked in.

Chapter 6

For Faith, the four day Easter break was not really long enough. It seemed as if she had spent every daylight minute walking the streets of central Exeter.

Starting with a guided tour of the line of the city walls to orient herself, Faith had then crisscrossed the patchwork of churches, alleys, hills (so many hills!), inns and bridges that made up the fabric of the old city.

Everything she saw vindicated her decision to leave the glamour and buzz of New York to continue her research in the place where it had all happened. Despite extensive bomb damage in the Second World War and the subsequent depredations of speculative builders and developers, Exeter remained very much a single entity bound together with strong threads of time and experience, of lives lived, battles fought, and victories hard won.

It seemed to Faith that the stones could indeed speak to her, whether she stood in a turret of the Roman wall, sat on a simple wooden bench at the back of the Gothic cathedral, or walked around the home of the Guild of Weavers, Fullers and Shearmen itself, the magnificently restored Tuckers Hall with its panelled rooms, beautifully laid out exhibits and slightly incongruous display of sixteenth-century armour.

The Upper Hall on the first floor was a magnificent room, lit by mediaeval windows and topped off with a barrel-vaulted ceiling. Faith saw in her guide book that this room was a late addition to the building, having been installed in the sixteenth century when the Guild's former chapel was converted to its main meeting place.

She smiled to herself on reading that a 'recent addition' had been over one hundred years old by the time that her little home town of Exeter, Ontario was founded.

At the far end of the room there was mounted a carved and painted coat of arms of Charles I. This seemed a little ironic to Faith, as her reading had led her to believe that the city of Exeter had let the Civil War and the subsequent Commonwealth simply wash over them without ostentatiously taking sides.

For wool merchants and manufacturers, life had been all about business, whatever was happening in the worlds of government and politics. The city's motto 'Semper Fidelis' – ever loyal, presumably to the throne – was more of a PR job in Faith's eyes, and represented an attempt to persuade the restored monarchy to look kindly upon the city's business activities.

That the ruse hadn't actually worked, that Charles II had sought to remove the Guild's privileges, was central to Faith's research project. All the more interesting for her, then, that the Upper Hall also held a coat of arms for the new king, although in a rather odd place.

A large fireplace dominated the left-hand wall of the room; behind the grate was a black, cast iron plate which bore the insignia of the restored monarch, Charles II.

'Strange,' mused Faith, 'not the clearest declaration of loyalty.'

She jotted down some thoughts in her notebook, along with the irreverent observation that there might be some concealed message – 'may you burn in hell, your majesty', perhaps.

The weekend flew by too quickly, Tuesday morning duly arrived, and Faith was seated patiently outside the office of her supervisor for the summer semester, or term, as she now knew she had to call it.

Professor Sir Stephen Duntze, MBE – he insisted on all his titles, in the correct order – had a global reputation as *the* authority on the mediaeval wool trade in Europe. The fact that he himself was a direct descendant of one of the leading merchants of the eighteenth century lent a certain aura to his status, and he was never backward in referring to it. What had somehow been overlooked in the rush to acclaim his intellectual prowess was that he had used his privileged access to family archives to supply the material for his constant stream of academic papers and prestigious international lectures.

John Duntze had arrived in Exeter from Bremen in Germany in the 1720's. He was already a wool merchant with connections, wealthy enough to marry in the Cathedral and then to establish the Exeter Bank. His son became a Devon MP and was awarded a baronetcy in 1774.

But Faith was far from impressed by even the most august of academics using their authority to keep a humble postgraduate student waiting twenty minutes beyond the time of her appointment. As she cast yet another despairing glance towards the pale-faced secretary outside the closed door of the great eminence, a discreet buzzer sounded.

The secretary got to her feet, tottered uncertainly to the door on ludicrously high heels and pulled it open with what Faith thought was an unnecessary flourish.

On entering the office, the first thing to catch Faith's eye – as it was clearly intended to – was an immense, heavily carved desk which made her think immediately of the altar in Exeter cathedral. Raising her eyes, she then saw the true object of veneration in this office, the massive bulk of Professor Sir Stephen Duntze, MBE.

Rather irreverently, Faith's first thought was of Sidney Greenstreet in his classic role of Signor Ferrari in *Casablanca.* All her supervisor lacked was a fez and a fly whisk. There was the crumpled white linen jacket, the loosely knotted cravat, the fleshy lips and the piggy eyes. And, good grief, the voice...

'Do take a seat, Miss Codrington,' lisped Duntze, gesturing towards a chair some inches lower than his own. 'Are you in any way related to the Gloucestershire Codringtons?'

This struck Faith as a particularly crass way to discomfort her. Last time she looked, Canada was some way from Gloucestershire and, hey, had he not noticed the colour difference?

'Only indirectly,' she responded rather waspishly.

'Ah well, Exeter University is all about rigour and attainment, Miss Codrington. Family and privilege count for nothing here.'

As if that's not how you became Sir Professor MBE, reflected Faith.

'Nor do, so-called, disabilities,' continued her supervisor. 'As you will know, I lost my sight last year, but this has, paradoxically, helped me to focus so much more on the essentials of my work without visual distractions.'

Faith felt the blood rush to her face in embarrassment. Who was being crass now? She was oblivious to the next few words but was able to pick up the threads when she heard him refer to the Guild.

'...Fullers and Shearmen, which as you know has been central to my own studies for several years. I understand you have a particular interest in the events of 1684 and 1685?'

Relieved that the professor's blindness prevented him seeing her earlier alarm, Faith was able to reply with confidence.

'Absolutely, sir. The continuing story of the London guilds is well documented, and I've read a number of monographs on the older provincial guilds, most of which no longer exist. What fascinates me is how and why Exeter is on a very short list of cities outside London that possesses a trade guild that has been able to survive and thrive.'

'I think 'thrive' is a little disingenuous, Faith – if I may call you so. Compared to the power it exercised in its heyday, I think you will find the Guild a shadow of its former self. Heavens, they even allow women members these days!'

As Faith shifted uncomfortably in her seat, Duntze divined he had perhaps gone a little too far for the sensitivities of the modern woman. He tried to lighten the mood.

'So, digs in order? Finding your way around and so forth?'

'Sure thing. The rooms I've been given are first class and I feel like I've trodden every sidewalk in the old city. I can sense the antiquity of this place, how its history is woven into its buildings and bones. I'm really looking forward to digging into the detail.'

Duntze's sightless eyes stared above her head and he wiped a drop of spittle from his lower lip. As if to himself, he said softly,

'Yes, to many of us who are Exeter born and bred, this is our little world, our universe entire...'

He fell silent, and the silence stretched on until Faith began to wonder whether Duntze was asleep and she should perhaps tiptoe out.

With a sudden snort, the vast bulk before her shook itself.

'One more thing, Faith. I must introduce you to Marcus, who will be showing you the Guild papers you need for your research.'

He flapped vaguely over his left shoulder, reminding Faith once again of Signor Ferrari and his fly whisk.

Looking up, she was startled to see, standing in the far corner of the office, a thin figure, clothed entirely in black, who seemed to be gazing out of the window. Slowly, as if it was causing him immense effort, if not pain, he turned to face Faith who, not for the first time on that fateful day, felt a metaphorical rug being pulled from beneath her feet.

If she had expected a Peter Lorre to partner Sydney Greenstreet, she would have been disappointed. Instead of a curly headed and dissipated cherub, Marcus gave the impression of being taller than he actually was by virtue of his almost skeletal thinness. His head was totally devoid of hair – he even lacked eyebrows – and from just above his left eye, across the bridge of the nose and down to the chin there ran a perfectly straight scar, silver white against olive skin.

His eyes seemed to be all pupil, a deep coal-black, devoid of brightness or any apparent feeling. Faith had to pull her gaze away and she felt a sudden chill in the room.

'Marcus is an officer of the Guild, but also a friend of this University. I hope he will also be a friend of yours. He will be your guide through the archives which, as you know, are held in the Devon & Exeter Institution. Have you signed up there yet?'

'I'm afraid I just missed out last Thursday,' replied Faith, keeping half an eye on the stranger in the corner whose presence she found somewhat unnerving.

'Well, get along there sharpish today or tomorrow. I'll expect that to be done before our first session this Friday.'

With that, Faith was concerned to see ripples forming in the large stomach across the desk from her, which then ran up the chest and over the shoulders and contorted Duntze's face as he rose slowly, a mighty cumulus coming into view above a mountain peak.

He extended a limp hand in Faith's general direction, which she felt obliged to shake in a desultory fashion. Later, she remembered the sensation as being like trying to pick up a dead octopus.

Mysteriously summoned, the secretary held the door open and Faith left, with a promise to return on Friday.

It was only as she was walking back across the campus that she realised that her new friend Marcus had not spoken a word.

Chapter 7

The lobby of the Institution was perhaps ten feet square and reminded Nathaniel of nothing more than a hallway in one of the lesser properties maintained by the National Trust. A carpet that had seen better days covered an uneven flagstone floor and what was clearly an original Georgian barometer was mounted on a wall that showed more plaster than paint.

'It's Mr Barton, isn't it?' came a voice from his right, and there emerged from the Librarian's office the elderly mix of whiskers and tweed he had met earlier. Mopping his brow with a handkerchief, the figure continued.

'Lionel Simpkins. Damn hot, don't you think?'

Nathaniel couldn't really agree, but from politeness nodded his assent.

'Well, you've chosen a jolly good time,' said Simpkins. 'No more acquisitions to catalogue today, and only a couple of other members in, so I'd be delighted to show you round myself.'

'Well, if it's no trouble...'

'Not at all, old chap, not at all. First up, behind me here is our notice board and look! Here's your application, pinned up with all the others. And, before you ask, I'm absolutely sure you'll go through on the nod like everyone else. It's a formality, but these days, formality is sometimes all we've got, don't you think?'

Nathaniel had a momentary rush of panic. Was this world of old chaps and doddering tweed-clad officers the right one for him? He was only 56, goddammit. Did he want to become embalmed in an institution that was – literally, if the *Express & Echo* was to be believed – crumbling before his eyes?

He need not have worried. Simpkins ushered him though an arthritic pair of double doors to reveal a two-storey high, galleried room, lined from floor to ceiling with multitudinous shades of brown leather books. It may not have been his beloved Duke Humfrey's Library, but it came damn close.

To one side was a row of brass-handled file drawers holding, Nathaniel imagined, the keys to this array of treasures. And in the centre, there stood a huge leather-bound map table with rows of shallow drawers beneath.

Nathaniel closed his eyes momentarily and inhaled the dust of history. When he reopened them, he was then hit by the incongruity of four huge scaffolding towers, one in each corner of the room, supporting a latticework of wooden beams, self-evidently supporting the roof above.

Catching the flicker of distaste across Nathaniel's face, Simpkins remarked 'You know, this always reminds me of that ghastly Gothic chapel...'

'...bang in the middle of the Grand Mosque in Cordoba,' continued Nathaniel.

'Absolutely!' cried Simpkins, 'I *knew* you were the right sort of chap for this place. Come on in, and I'll give you the sixpenny tour.'

The next hour was pure bliss for Nathaniel. Simpkins patiently talked him through the chequered history of the Institution and walked him first round the Major Library.

'For many years, this was the only room with books,' continued Simpkins. 'The other room was for objects – stuffed animals and birds, Roman coins, that sort of thing. Luckily, we were able to offload all that to the Royal Albert Memorial Museum when that was opened in 1868.'

Nathaniel loved the proprietorial way that Simpkins spoke, almost as if he had personally cleared the room nearly 150 years ago.

Simpkins paused in front of an impressive phalanx of beechwood cabinets, housing numerous small, brass-handled drawers

'Well before Dewey Decimal, of course, so we've got our own indexing system. See there, at the top of each cabinet, a golden letter. They're in order of importance, and obviously you don't get more important than God. So A here is theology, ecclesiastical writing and so on. Yards of sermons which, if you ask me, have never been read since they were written. B, over there, is History. C is Geography in which we include travel writing, diaries of big game hunters, that irritating Freya Stark female. It is all, I must admit, a bit random. Back in 1914 there was a long argument about whether Herodotus should be filed under B or C. Fortunately, the Great War came along and put a stop to it.'

The Minor Library was much the same, though a little smaller and without any scaffolding towers. There was no card index ('All covered in the Major Library,' according to Simpkins) and, instead of map drawers, there were racks of bound newspapers, including the *Exeter Post-man* and *Trewman's Exeter Flying Post.*

'And one of our prize collections takes up part of this room. Exeter's Guild of Weavers, Fullers and Shearmen has a unique collection of documents going back to the fifteenth century. When a leading guildsman was our President back in 1877, he arranged for it to be stored here.'

'What are those little pink slips?' asked Nathaniel.

Every now and again, there were gaps on the shelves, where books had been replaced by fluttering pieces of paper.

'Well, if you're a full member – not an associate or student – you are allowed to borrow books, to read here or to take home for study or enjoyment. The pink slip has the details of the member if we need to know who has the book. And now, on to M...'

Privately relieved that he wasn't taken through every last letter of the alphabet, Nathaniel eventually found himself taken back through the Major Library, up an uneven carpeted staircase from the lobby, and into a pair of high-ceilinged rooms with fine views of the Cathedral Green.

'These are the reading rooms. On the left is where we hold two copies of every daily newspaper for the convenience of members.' Nathaniel noted that, in the Institution, the term 'newspaper' did not include any of the red tops.

'And on the right is what *used* to be the smoking room, but which then had to be given up when ladies were admitted to membership.'

Nathaniel wondered idly where non-smoking women were meant to go, but Simpkins interrupted his reverie.

'Time, I think, for the cup that cheers.'

Simpkins led Nathaniel back through the two libraries into a cramped little room at the back of the building with, Nathaniel was impressed to see, a perfectly intact ornate Jacobean plaster ceiling.

'Used to be part of the original town house of the Courtenays,' said Simpkins, 'Now, what's your poison?'

At the back of the room was an electric kettle of an indeterminate vintage, a motley collection of willow patterned Wedgewood and two or three tins of uncertain provenance. Indicating these, Simpkins talked him through the options.

'Breakfast, Earl Grey or Red Bush – though frankly I'd rather drink pencil shavings than *that* abomination. No milk, I'm afraid as it's Polly's day off; same goes for biscuits.'

Lionel Simpkins, Nathaniel could see, was of the generation that felt that shopping for domestic requirements was physically impossible for any human in possession of a Y chromosome.

'Earl Grey, I suppose,' he replied, and was surprised to find himself longing for the rather more generous provision he had made for himself back in the office.

Over tea, the two chatted about how each had arrived at their present positions. Nathaniel was pleased – but not surprised – that Simpkins was also an Oxford man, though of a couple of generations before him. He had spent much of his professional life as a librarian at

Exeter University, and would have retired had he not been given the post at the Institution.

'And never regretted it. May seem a bit of a backwater, but it keeps me busy and I don't think pottering around the garden and daytime TV would have been for me. And of course, there's Dolores...'

Simpkins attempted a roguish wink but only succeeded in displaying the signs of a small seizure.

He led Nathaniel back through the Minor and Major Library and was about to take him into the lobby when he caught sight of a black-clad figure studying the notice board.

'Ah,' said Simpkins, visibly growing pale. 'Why don't I show you *this* way out?'

Reaching for what looked like another case of books, Simpkins pulled towards him what was revealed as a door, covered in the spines of deceased books.

'Through there, sharp left, open the outer door and you're back in the close,' barked Simpkins and suddenly he was gone.

Although bemused by his companion's sudden change of tone, Nathaniel realised that he had already given generously of his time to someone who was not yet a full member.

Turning the handle of the door to the close, he absentmindedly walked through – straight into the back of the woman he had twice bumped into in the previous week.

Chapter 8

Faith had found her first meeting with her supervisor disconcerting in more ways than one.

First, when she had thought she'd detected some politically incorrect irony in Duntze's initial enquiry, he'd trumped her race card with his own blindness.

And then there'd been that business with Marcus.

'Weird looking dude' didn't do justice to the way he'd made her feel. Shivers up the spine were all well and good for adolescents at drive-in horror movies, not for postgraduates in university studies.

As a girl brought up in the back of her parents' restaurant, Faith's instinctive source of comfort was always food. Beginning to feel like an Exeter native, she headed once more for Mol's Coffee House in the Cathedral Close and again ordered the classic Devon cream tea.

'A gal could get used to this sort of thing,' mused Faith, blessed with a metabolism that meant that, however much she ate, she never seemed to change the proportions of her trim figure.

Glancing at her watch, she realised this was as good a time as any to sign in at the Institution. A box well and truly ticked before visiting Professor Sir blah blah blah again.

This time round, there was no rush, so she strolled towards that big white door for a second time, glancing around her at the gilded youth of Exeter sprawled in various positions on the cathedral lawns in the unseasonably pleasant sunshine.

Her mood was shattered as, bursting through an unremarkable wooden gate, came her double nemesis of the previous week. The same coat and briefcase, the same hangdog expression, but this time no escape as Faith, a good two inches taller than her antagonist, peppered him with some of the coarser insults she had learnt during her time at NYU.

When she paused for breath, the little pipsqueak (of uncertain parentage and even more uncertain sexual habits) looked her straight in the eye and spoke.

'Look, I know I seem to be making a habit of this and I do recall making a rather stupid remark last week, but on both occasions I *was* in a hurry and this time I'm not, so please can I buy you a cup of tea to say sorry properly?'

Fortunately for the flustered Nathaniel, his breath lasted until he had finished the sentence – just.

If she had not been so determined on going to the Institute, and if she had not just that moment drained an excellent pot of Lapsang, and if she had not wanted to retain at least some of the moral high ground, Faith would – probably – have yielded to a perfectly reasonable and perfectly phrased apology.

But, though you can take the girl out of Ontario, you can't take Ontario out of the girl; so, turning magnificently on her heel and with only silence as a parting shot, Faith continued on her way, leaving a frustrated and slightly diminished Nathaniel in her wake.

Faith bent to press the bell on the Institution door but had to step back sharply as the mysterious Marcus strode past her without any acknowledgement.

'What is it about me?' asked Faith. 'All of a sudden I seem to be remarkably attractive to men, though only in a gravitational sense. None of them seem to stick around long enough for love to blossom.'

She instantly realised this was a *little* unfair to her most regularly orbiting satellite as, on this occasion at least, he had offered to buy her tea. When she looked back, though, he had disappeared; so she carried on through the still open door.

Before her stood a visibly shaken Lionel Simpkins, so pale that Faith thought he might be on the verge of fainting. But within a moment, Simpkins drew on his years of public service, straightened his back, essayed a weak smile, and asked how he could help the young woman.

As a university student, Faith had a claim on immediate membership of the Institution, which she was able to secure with a few entries on a printed form.

When Simpkins offered to show her round, she politely declined. All her requirements, she expected, would be met by Marcus. In any event, she was genuinely concerned that, in his present state, the librarian would lack the energy to complete his mission.

Simpkins gratefully said his farewells and retired to his office, closing the door behind him and pulling down the blind. Faith let herself out of the door, decided to let matters academic go hang for the rest of the day, and went off in search of some serious shoe shops.

Wednesday 3 April 2013

Chapter 9

After his brief introduction to the delights of the Institution, Nathaniel found his daily round even more tedious.

On Wednesday, as every weekday, he arrived at 8:45, walked in through the front door of number fourteen and nodded a silent greeting to Sophie. As every weekday, he resolved he would walk up the four flights of uneven coarsely carpeted stairs without pause; and, as every weekday, he paused on the third landing.

As every weekday, he hung his coat on the back of the door, placed his briefcase on the floor by his chair and turned on his PC. While it booted up, he plugged in his kettle and popped a fresh teabag in his mug.

If it were possible for a keen eyed observer to have noticed the subtle gradations in enthusiasm with which Nathaniel followed this daily routine, they would indeed have recorded an increased listlessness in his movements, a marginally greater delay between keystrokes, and longer periods spent gazing through the window, towards the ceiling, or at nothing in particular.

And this was something that Nathaniel himself recognised. He had doggedly and, as he was open enough to admit to himself, selflessly dedicated himself to a mind numbing routine that, frankly, had given him little satisfaction. For over thirty years he had done this – twenty eight of those as a single man following his miserable divorce and the effective loss of his son.

He had operated as an automaton, doubtless at great profit to Kennaway & Partners but with precious little benefit to himself. His only prospect was more of the same for another ten years before he was packed off with an inscribed watch and an all too modest pension.

Now he was becoming consumed by an obsession with a clapped out organisation in a decaying building stuffed with mouldering tomes. Why? Was this a manifestation of that dreadful cliché, the mid life crisis?

As he sat there on that April day, Nathaniel, for the first time in an extremely long time, was reminded of his father.

Johnny Barton had been everything Nathaniel was not – boisterous, outgoing, clubbable. Too young to enlist in the Second World War, Johnny had married young and then volunteered for the army rather than be conscripted into National Service. With a talent for languages, he'd served in the Middle East in the early fifties, apparently with some distinction, although he'd never spoken much about it in Nathaniel's hearing.

Johnny returned from Jordan in '53 or '54 to take over his father-in-law's estate agency, an already successful business which continued to grow under his stewardship. Johnny in his loud suits and red Jag had the gift of the gab and an eye for a bargain. He was always the first to buy a round in the golf club bar, and if the brassy blonde on his arm was no longer the increasingly plump Mrs Barton, so what?

Johnny was the lad, the fixer, the man to get you a silly price if you were selling and an even sillier one if you were buying. Yet he always seemed to turn a handsome profit.

Nathaniel felt that his larger than life father had never understood the bookish son who read law at Oxford and then returned to Exeter for a lifetime of conveyancing. Johnny had always been more at ease with Nathaniel's younger brother, David. This perhaps explained why, after some 'accounting discrepancies' at his stock broking firm, David had found himself in self-imposed exile in Italy.

In a way, reflected Nathaniel, it was a kindness that Johnny had died before David's disgrace came to light.

In 1981, Johnny had handed over the reins of Milford & Barton to his general manager and said he needed to go 'out East' for a while. Nathaniel's mother, by now a fully signed up member of the Mayfair gin and bridge circuit, seemed oblivious to the impending departure. And Nathaniel himself, safely ensconced at Kennaway & Partners, married and with a child on the way, was not moved to ask the purpose of this trip, let alone raise any objection.

When Johnny returned to Exeter in the October of 1981, he seemed somehow deflated. He showed no signs of wanting once again to take up the reins of the estate agency which had entered into something of a decline without the driving force of his flamboyant personality. He had always, as people said, liked a drink. Nowadays, in the way of all alcoholics, he no longer *liked* his drink, but he spent a lot more time with it nevertheless.

Nathaniel couldn't recall a time after that fateful trip when he did not see his father in some stage of inebriation. And the memory of the very last time he saw him before his death could still bring tears of genuine loss to his eyes.

It had been a cold December evening, a few days before Christmas '82. The central heating was on full blast in Nathaniel's house but the atmosphere between himself and his wife, Sally, was very definitely frosty. Still, they were decorating a Christmas tree together 'for the sake of the boy', though what a two year old's expectations were would have been hard to say.

When he first heard his mother's slurred voice on the phone, Nathaniel thought that she was the drunk who needed assistance (again). But once he had pieced together the words 'father', 'floor', 'head' and 'blood', he had driven as quickly as he could through the intermittent sleet to his parents' home in St Leonard's, one of Exeter's smarter areas.

As he had half expected, when he arrived there were no corpses to be found. His father was slumped in an armchair nursing a cut head and a large scotch while his mother flapped aimlessly. Reluctantly assuming the role of man of the house, Nathaniel packed his mother off to bed, inspected the cut (which was superficial rather than life threatening), sat in the chair opposite his father, and did his best to assume a stern expression.

Before Nathaniel could say anything, however, his father jerked out of his torpor and fixed Nathaniel with the gaze of a stuffed trout.

'Nathaniel, my boy, my dear boy, I've never understood you, have you, sorry, no have I? And I don't think I've, no damn it, you – I don't think *you* have ever understood *me*. But we've got along, haven't we?'

As Johnny's eye noted that the scotch glass was now empty, one of his legs attempted to lift him out of the chair while the opposite arm flailed impotently towards the sideboard. At this stage, Nathaniel felt that a welcome unconsciousness would be a state more easily achieved than temporary sobriety. So he generously filled his father's glass from the litre bottle of malt standing near at hand.

'I've always done my best for your mother, for you, and for little Davey...'

So far, so familiar to Nathaniel who had heard these maudlin sentiments before. Now Johnny was off on another track, travelling to a place that Nathaniel couldn't follow him, at least not then.

'... and I've always done my best by them, the bastards. Yes they paid me, in good gold coin and plenty of it, but for services rendered, my boy, for services bloody rendered.'

Pause for another draught of malt.

'Now the business is going down the toilet, should never have left that numpty in charge, I really need the moolah, but where *are* the buggers? Like the bloody banks – only give you an umbrella when it ain't raining. So I said, you cough up now, or I cough to the auth..., the thorit,..the police, the papers, whoever. Then where would they be?'

Johnny was visibly slowing down now, and it was clear to Nathaniel that he wasn't going anywhere and that he would be best left to sleep it off. He gently placed the half empty bottle of malt at his father's right hand, shouted a farewell up the stairs to his unconscious mother, and returned home to find his wife too had gone to bed, leaving a forlorn half decorated tree.

When the police called Nathaniel at his office the next day, he was not surprised. To his continuing shame, he was rather relieved at the news that the body of his father had been fished from the River Exe at 9:15 that morning. His blood alcohol level was four times the legal limit for driving and indeed Nathaniel was privately amazed that Johnny had had the capacity in his drunken state to walk the 450 yards to the river bank.

It had never occurred to Nathaniel at the time that the death was anything other than misadventure.

Though it was possible Johnny had wilfully killed himself, the coroner, who had recently sold his late mother's home through Milford & Barton at a price well above the odds, was minded to be kind to the family.

The curious footnote to the whole affair, Nathaniel recalled as he sat at his desk, was that it was only when making the arrangements for the funeral that he learnt his father's given name had also been Nathaniel. He'd always gone by his second name, John. It might have been, Nathaniel thought, to distinguish himself from his grandfather, another Nathaniel.

So here he was, the third Nathaniel Barton in a row, with a dead end job and a dead end life.

As he audibly groaned, his office door opened and Sophie walked in.

'Not pleased to see me then, Mr Barton? It's a long climb up those stairs to be greeted by a poor impression of a sea lion.'

'No, no, sorry Sophie – I was thinking of a case.'

Now was not the time for negative feedback to get back to CK, not when he was preparing to distribute the annual bonuses to staff.

'No offence taken, then. I'm here In Person at The Request of Mr Kennaway himself...' Nathaniel could hear the capital letters '... to let you know that he requires all offices to be vacated by 14:30 pee em this Friday to permit the full refurbishment of the office computer network over the weekend. You will need to make the appropriate arrangements and apologies for the short notice.'

With that, Sophie slipped back out of the office as silently as she had arrived. She immediately put her head back round the door and chirruped.

'And CK expects that you *will* be making up the lost hours next week.'

What a surprise, thought Nathaniel.

Still, in earlier weeks (or years) his response to such a peremptory request would have been irritation, if not despair. Now of course this impromptu half holiday was an unexpected opportunity to do some thorough fossicking around in the Institution.

Friday's interruption to office work could not come soon enough.

Chapter 10

Faith still hadn't really come down to earth after arriving in Exeter. All the books she had studied had failed to prepare her for the experience of walking genuinely old streets, seeing ancient buildings, touching their stones and appreciating their complex patterns and interrelationships.

Not to mention that gorgeous pair of shiny scarlet stilettos she'd been able to pick up in a sale. This was going to be a good week.

Now she was in the sleek new University library, preparing for her first supervision with Sir Professor Moby Dick MBE. It could not have been a greater contrast to the Institution.

There, the furniture was hard and unyielding; here, bean bags and squishy sofas were the norm. There, there was an antiquated and occasionally impenetrable card index system; here, you just googled what you wanted.

There, you popped a decaying teabag into a cracked cup; here was a sleek coffee shop, offering everything from an austere ristretto to a full on cinnamon-infused cappuccino with chocolate and caramel sprinkles.

But while the University library was a glittering information machine that decanted data as readily as it did coffee, Faith appreciated that the holy grail for historians – the hand ground coffee from the boutique estate, if you like – was original source material. That was what the Institution would give her, and that was why she had travelled the best part of four thousand miles to get here.

Her last thought before settling down to her research was to recognise what the Institution and the University had in common – they both provided libraries. And libraries were so important.

She recalled what a high school teacher had once told her: 'if you want a thousand answers, go online; if you want the *right* answer, go to a library.'

Now, she had to pull together some background, some context for her supervision on Friday. So with a double macchiato on the side table and her ipad to hand, she settled down to some serious work. Joyce Youing's classic 1968 book '*Tuckers Hall, Exeter*' had still to be bettered, and Faith returned to it as to an old friend.

Some hours later, outside the library windows, the campus was shrouded with gloom. Faith logged out and stretched her arms and legs. As so often before, she had lost track of time when carrying out her research. And as before she had arrived at the same dead end.

'...the next Hall met on 7 January [1685] and whatever business was transacted, the record of it was carefully erased and is no longer legible...Clearly there had been some panic measures but in the circumstances almost anything was justified...There was another Hall on 26 January but no Minutes were entered by the Clerk.'

It was that most unsatisfactory conclusion that had led Faith to Exeter with the hope she could lay to rest the uncertainty about what was decided at that mysteriously unrecorded assembly of Exeter's great and perhaps not so good.

The big picture was reasonably clear. The Guild had grown over centuries as the wool processing industry itself had grown. Its power and influence enabled it to survive repeated dips and reverses, that is, until Charles II had sought to remove its privileges and monopolies.

The king's timely death (timely for the Guild at least) removed the immediate threat of extinction. But the increasing use of mechanical looms in Lancashire and Yorkshire was ultimately to destroy the Devon industry.

What the Guild seemed to have done, however, was to move effortlessly into other areas of money-making activity. Banks were founded, investments were placed, strings were pulled, and fortunes were made. Ultimately, all of this success followed that unminuted meeting in 1685; Faith was determined to find out exactly how.

She turned off her ipad, popped it into her shoulder bag and strolled slowly back across the campus to her rooms. She should have been hungry, but she lacked appetite. A glass of water and a few black grapes were enough before she slid into her bed.

Though she quickly slipped away into a dreamless sleep, by midnight she was tossing and turning, while the silent black eyes of Marcus burnt into her very soul.

Friday 5 April 2013

Chapter 11

A long thirty minutes into her first supervision with Sir Professor Stephen Duntze MBE, Faith was, for the first time in her relatively short academic career, beginning to flounder. The session had started well. The door had opened promptly enough and Faith's supervisor had acknowledged her presence with a wave of his imaginary fly whisk. Faith had been pleased that on this second occasion there had been no Marcus lurking in the background.

As requested, she had launched into her account of the formation of craft guilds in mediaeval England. She had addressed the history of the Exeter Guild of Weavers, Fullers and Shearmen and briefly outlined their role in the dynamically expanding social and economic life of the city through the fifteenth and sixteenth centuries.

Throughout her discourse, the professor's sightless eyes had flickered aimlessly around the room. Every time Faith paused for breath or to turn a page of her notes, the fleshy lips would part and emit a slow sibilant yeeesssss...

After half an hour of this verbal version of Chinese water torture, Faith had had enough. She slammed her notepad on to the desk.

'Prof – what's going on? I'm revving the engine here, but the wheels don't seem to be getting any traction.'

For a brief moment, Faith felt she should be phoning the airline for a return ticket to New York now. But then the behemoth quivered and spoke.

'Miss Codrington, you have just been serving me a perfectly acceptable TV dinner. Two minutes in the microwave (or in your case two days in the library) and ping, there it is. To be fair, it's more than perfectly acceptable. I can see that you bought it in one of the more upmarket stores, Marks & Spencer perhaps, or Waitrose. Even so, this is the sort of pre-digested barely warmed through mush that I would have expected of a first year undergraduate. Or is that the level of attainment that gets you a doctorate in the colonies these days?'

Before an indignant Faith could respond, he went on. 'I can find no real fault with anything you have said. That is precisely what is wrong with it. A scientific hypothesis that cannot be tested is not a scientific hypothesis. A piece of historical writing, which is what I assume we are trying to produce here, has to be capable of being contradicted if it is to say anything worthwhile.'

Duntze's keen ears caught the sound of Faith's chair being pushed back. She was determined to leave before he could hear her sobbing.

'Don't go, my dear. Allow me to make three points to you.

First, if you can manage to stay here to be criticised, you have passed the first test. Criticism is the harshly rushing water that powers the mills that weave the good strong cloth of scholarship.

Secondly, you may not appreciate that I supervise very few students personally these days. You come highly recommended, and while what you have told me so far would not set the world alight, I believe you have the capacity to do much better.

Thirdly, since losing my sight, I must confess that I now have quite a taste for microwave meals. My housekeeper stocks the fridge for me. For the containers on the first shelf, I must use the first setting on the timer; for those on the second, the second setting; and so on.'

With that conciliatory speech, Duntze seemed to have temporarily exhausted himself. He sipped slowly at a glass of iced water and ran his finger round the inside of his stiff collar.

He continued: 'I am sure that what will add the seasoning to today's rather tasteless offering will be the papers that Marcus will show you. Has he contacted you yet?'

'No – should I give you my cell number?'

'Your cell? Oh, you mean your mobile phone – no, *he* won't need that. Let's allow you both some time to start on those Guild documents. Can we agree that I see you back here at ten of the clock on Monday 15th?'

Faith left her supervisor's study with a clamour of voices in her head.

Little Faith was asking her why she was bothering with all this crap; why didn't she just go back to New York? Big Faith was muttering 'Screw him and his doctorate – I need a good gin martini.' And Pedant Faith was asking impishly how Sir Professor Stephen Duntze MBE was in any condition to *see* her same time a week Monday?

A short walk across the campus took Faith back to her room in Duryard Hall. As she opened her front door, she saw on the floor a cheap black and white postcard showing the front door of the Institution. Turning it over, Faith saw inscribed in impeccable calligraphy:

LIBRARY VII post meridiem M

Mentally giving the finger to her supervisor, Faith felt able to apply her critical skills to this all too brief communication and came to the conclusion that the mysterious Marcus wished to see her in the university library in just over two hours time.

That was inconvenient to put it mildly. As usual, Big Faith had won the internal argument and the early evening was pencilled in for a wander to the Phoenix Art Centre to check out the cultural scene and a couple of serious drinks. If she didn't dawdle, it would only take her an hour to get dressed and made up. Now she would have to kick her heels for a while, so what could she do?

Quickly doing the math, she reckoned her mother would be finishing up lunch in one of the restaurants back home. So, grabbing a coke from the fridge and pulling out her iphone, she settled down for a session of maternal TLC.

At five to seven precisely, an impressively coiffed, perfectly made up, sweetly scented Faith in a too too perfect cocktail dress and the killer scarlet heels she had been able to find on Tuesday presented herself in the central atrium of the University library. The hour on the phone with her ma had boosted her confidence as usual and, with the cash in her clutch bag alongside a nude shimmer lipstick, she was good to go. She just had to keep the appointment with her new 'friend' and then – look out Exeter!

Momentarily lost in thought, she did not see or hear the slim black clad figure approach her until he was within touching distance. He gestured to a nearby sofa, but Faith felt incapable of sitting down; she felt as if it would be an admission of weakness, of submission.

'Ah. We shouldn't take long, should we? As you can see, I'm aiming to hit the town soon.'

Faith was bemused. She might not be a Vogue model, but, in her finery as she was, she was unaccustomed to a dead, glassy stare in response. Somewhat inappropriately, she wondered if Marcus was gay. But then she recalled Darren, her flatmate in New York, who took great delight in her outfits and make up, even borrowing the odd item for an evening when he thought she wasn't looking.

'Then I will be brief.'

While Marcus' skull-like head had led Faith to expect a sepulchral groan straight out of a horror flick, his voice was light and high pitched, with a trace of an accent that she thought might be Italian.

'You require access to Guild papers, privileged access, no?'

Faith nodded but remained silent.

'This is an unusual request, but it is possible. I will however have to ask for something in return.'

'Within reason,' said Faith.

Perhaps this ambivalent figure was of a more heterosexual persuasion than she had first thought and was working his way round to requesting something indiscreet.

'It is a small service that should cause an intelligent and,' he paused, 'attractive woman such as yourself little difficulty. You are a member of the Institution?'

Faith nodded again, increasingly unsure of where this was leading.

Earlier in the week, the University library had seemed a place of life and fun, of colour and activity. Now, apparently alone in the building with a man who looked like a leading light in the Spanish Inquisition, it seemed cold, charmless, and slightly threatening.

'There is another member of the Institution. I want to find out what he is doing there, what he is reading, what is his purpose.'

To Faith, this sounded like a line from a bad film.

'Why do you need to know? And why not ask him yourself?'

Marcus caught her gaze with his dead, black eyes and Faith did her level best to stare back.

'This is a private matter, of little consequence. It does not concern you in the slightest. Of course, if you have no wish to study the Guild documents I will be able to show you...'

Faith knew that if her mother had been beside her she would have quoted Matthew Chapter 16, verse 23.

But Faith's mother was not an up and coming academic, Faith's mother was not a young woman caught between the rock of Professor Duntze's disapproval and the hard place of Marcus' stare. There would be no 'Get thee behind me, Satan' on this occasion.

'OK,' she gulped, breaking the stare. 'I'll do it. How will I let you know what I've found out?'

Marcus passed her a sealed envelope. 'I will contact you.' With that, he turned and walked stiffly and silently away.

Faith took a moment to gather her thoughts. They all ended with the same question – what had she gotten herself into? With the edge of the glossy French manicured nail on her left thumb, she opened the envelope Marcus had given her. Inside was a four by six colour photograph, a head and shoulders shot of the man who she had, literally, bumped into three times already. Turning it over, in the same immaculate script as the postcard summoning her to this meeting, she read the name 'Nathaniel Barton'.

Chapter 12

For Nathaniel, Thursday passed in the usual blur of searches and correspondence, and Friday morning was much the same. By contriving to take a late lunch break, he was able to leave the office for good at 1:30pm, pursued through the door by an intentionally audible sniff from Sophie.

With a light packed lunch in his briefcase, he was able to walk straight to the Institution where he was greeted by Simpkins as a long lost friend.

'Dear boy, how splendid to see you again and so soon. I'm a little tied up at the moment. Some new journals in, you know, and I find it best to index things straight away. When I think of the disarray when I first joined...'

'No, don't worry,' responded Nathaniel with a smile (this new cheerfulness on his own part he found very pleasing). 'I thought I'd have a rootle round first to see if anything takes my fancy.'

Back in the Major Library, Nathaniel quickly found the card index and bagged a chair at the map table. Truth be told, there was little competition for seats.

In an armchair in the far corner, a figure of indeterminate gender in a large overcoat appeared to be asleep, while three chairs down from Nathaniel an elderly woman with a magnifying glass was closely scrutinising a volume of bound newspapers.

Without knowing quite what he was looking for, Nathaniel thought a random approach would serve best, and as he riffled through the meticulously handwritten five by three index cards, he realised that the system for cataloguing books was every bit as quirky as the Institution itself.

'*Artichokes: their cultivation and culinary purposes*' sat between '*Arthurian iconography in the railway stations of Cornwall*' and '*Articula Gynaecologica – memoirs of an eighteenth century surgeon.*'

With no interest in gardening, railways or obstetrics, Nathaniel wondered rather perversely if there might be anything on conveyancing. '*Combe House – a gentleman and his snuff boxes*' caught his eye. The place was now a fine country house hotel where he'd had a number of excellent lunches over the years.

Flicking through the drawer of close packed cards, Nathaniel paused. The cliché 'the hairs stood up on the back of my neck' had always seemed just that to Nathaniel – a cliché. But that was a perfect description of the sensation he was experiencing now. In his right hand, he was holding a card which said: '***Commonplace Book of Nathaniel Barton Esq.***'

Underneath the strong black italic of the title, a different hand in pencil stated: *{fol. 128pp Leather bound (Florence?) No later than 1767? Manuscript, largely blank, ref. M IV 1}*.

Still clutching the card, Nathaniel slumped in his chair. This was the most extraordinary coincidence. A Nathaniel Barton of the eighteenth century? Could this be a relative, an actual ancestor even? He recalled his father in one of his expansive moods proclaiming that Bartons had been 'an ornament of Exeter' – he would pause for dramatic effect – 'since time immemorial'. While aware of his father's natural talent for exaggeration (he had been an estate agent, after all) it could well be the case that there was a genuine family connection between a Nathaniel Barton of 1767 and the Nathaniel Barton of 2013.

Taking a deep breath, Nathaniel checked the reference on the card again and, without thinking, slid it into his top jacket pocket. This was his way with anything from supermarket receipts to parking tickets.

He remembered from his tour with Simpkins that M, by a happy chance, stood for Miscellaneous, and could be found in the Minor Library. There was indeed a fourth bookcase in this section and Nathaniel assumed that 1 indicated the top shelf. Unfortunately, this was three or four feet above his reach.

Nathaniel wasn't quite sure of the correct procedure. When he was a student in the Bodleian, you filled out a green slip and handed it to one of the ever present attendants who would duly deliver the requested volume to your desk. Nathaniel was aware that Simpkins seemed to be the only member of staff on the premises and he was still, presumably, indexing the new acquisitions in his office. So Nathaniel looked around to see if there was any random piece of furniture he could use to gain extra height.

Well of course: a sturdy looking set of library steps on wheels, complete with hand rail and an ornate heraldic carving on either side presented itself, and it was the work of a moment to manoeuvre it into position. Checking that he wasn't observed, Nathaniel climbed up until he was able to reach out and pull the book off the shelf.

At the very instant at which he grasped the spine of the commonplace book, a muscular spasm ran the length of his right arm. There was an acrid smell of burning, and Nathaniel was flung backwards at some speed. Although the reading table broke his fall, he lost consciousness briefly, though not his grip upon the book.

His next memory was of the name 'Nathaniel Barton, Nathaniel Barton, Nathaniel Barton' being endlessly repeated in a dull monotone while he was sitting in a leather chair in Simpkins' office. The old librarian was wiping his face with a cold flannel and looking anxiously into Nathaniel's eyes.

'Oh dear, oh dear,' said Simpkins. 'You really should have called me, you know. Those steps can be treacherous if you don't know how to use 'em.'

Nathaniel started to protest that it wasn't the steps, but then (without quite understanding why) thought better of it.

'I don't want to be a bother. I'm sure I'm fine.'

'You've got a bump on the back of your noddle the size of a goose egg, and a man who's been unconscious can have all sorts going awry. I remember our young Mr Laine. Fell off his bicycle, next thing you know he'd run off with the vicar's wife. With Health and Safety how it is, I shall have to record this in our accident book. And *you*, Mr Barton, will have to promise me to pop in to your GP's on the way home. I insist upon it. Here's the telephone now.'

More out of concern for the old man, who was now looking rather pale himself and mopping his own brow with the flannel, Nathaniel dialled the Barnfield Hill Surgery and was able to secure himself an appointment that same afternoon. While he believed that the stiff walk to the surgery would be enough to restore his spirits, Nathaniel had to admit that at this *precise* moment he still felt a bit groggy.

And what was also worrying was the exact nature of the phenomenon that had floored him. Regardless of Simpkins' quite natural deduction, it wasn't a matter of the library steps moving or even of him losing his footing. It felt very much like an electrical shock. Given the antiquity of the building and the likelihood that it was shifting on its foundations, it was entirely possible that there was some damaged wiring of uncertain age that had shorted out when he tried to tug the book from its moorings.

He wondered whether he should share this theory, but saw that by now Simpkins was washing down a couple of tablets with a cup of tea and looked, frankly, in worse shape than Nathaniel. Promising himself he would raise it on his next visit, Nathaniel sincerely thanked his elderly first aider for his prompt and effective action and set off for what he expected to be a cursory doctor's visit.

From the low doorway, an observer would have seen only the tops of two heads in armchairs arranged either side of the strikingly carved wooden fireplace.

Two plumes of cigar smoke eddied upwards, catching the light from fitfully guttering candles.

'A rather strange event occurred at the Institution this afternoon...'

'How so?'

'A chap fell backwards off the library steps and had to be revived by Simpkins.'

'Strange indeed – well done, Simpkins.'

'That wasn't the most striking feature, though. The chap who fell was called Nathaniel Barton'

'There's a name I didn't think we'd hear again.'

'Quite.'

There was a barely audible hiss from the doorway, but when the two companions turned as one to see who was there, he was gone.

Chapter 13

Faith paid off the cab driver as he dropped her at the end of Gandy Street. As she began to pick her way over the uneven cobbles, Faith momentarily felt the choice of four inch heels was mistake. But the admiring gazes of other more conservatively shod women passing by confirmed her original selection.

With the buzz of an Exeter Friday night on a warm spring evening around her, Faith was easily able to overlook the protests from her ankles as she made her way up the steep slope to the Phoenix.

After her bizarre encounter with Marcus, Faith had almost had second thoughts about a night out, but she was not prepared to waste the investment of time (and money) that she had made in her look for the evening. Going up to the bar, she ordered her first (and hopefully not her last) drink.

'Classic Martini, Mayfair gin, no peel, one olive.'

She'd got the taste for the quintessentially English spirit when she'd first arrived in New York. She loved the hints of angelica and orris that cut through the icy chill of a well-made Martini, and she sure felt like she needed this one.

The bartender was giving it the full Tom Cruise, pouring the gin from above head height, wiggling his cute little ass in time to the cocktail shaker, and then inserting a perfectly speared olive with a final flourish. She let him keep the change and didn't have the heart to make it clear that that was *all* he would get out of her that evening. She took her first, slow, exquisite sip.

'Anything good on tonight?'

'Depends on what you fancy.'

Now Faith wished she had been a little more unsubtle with him, and gave him the Hard Stare #3.

Blushing, the bartender continued.

'There's a reggae poet on in about ten minutes, but...'

His voice trailed away, and he turned to some complicated task under the counter involving fruit and a sharp knife.

Faith took a seat in a corner and reflected on the subtle incidents of racist behaviour she had experienced since coming to England. You could not blame the people of Exeter for the contrast with the many colours and shades and races of her beloved New York. But every now and again while walking round Exeter she would see someone staring at her in frank surprise – my lord, you would think she had three heads. And now here was this young barkeep tying himself in knots because he had fallen into the stereotypical trap of assuming that, simply because she was black, she would want to listen to a reggae poet.

As it happened, she *would* like to listen to him, thank you all the same. It would be interesting to see how some arty type in an English back street would compare to the raw power she had once felt in a Trenchtown bar or the energy in a TriBeCa basement she used to go to every two or three weeks. So she took her martini through to the little studio behind the bar to see what she would find.

The steeply raked seating was almost full, but Faith was able to squeeze into a single empty seat near the entrance door. The low stage in front of her held two huge speakers bathed by a single bright spotlight. Slumped in the shadows to the far side sat a dreadlocked figure, head bent.

The first bass notes emerged from the speakers, so profoundly deep that Faith felt rather than heard them. Soon the familiar rhythm was there, with its sudden stops and starts, reverberating echoes and uncertain timings. Slowly it all began to make sense, the insistent pounding of the music, the vibration of the floor, the moulding of the audience into one gently swaying, sympathetic force. And then the poet began to speak.

His words, in an almost unintelligible patois, wove their way in and out of the pulsating beat coming out of the speakers. If the rhythm was a finger of black smoke pointing in accusation at the heavens, the words were autumn leaves blowing in and out and around the darker core.

The poet spoke of loss, of pain, of degradation, separation, death – but also of life, joy, hope and togetherness. Looking back, Faith felt she had both lost and found herself in that thirty or so minutes.

Gradually, the voice faded and stopped, the bass ceased to pound and when Faith looked up, the speakers were still there but the poet had gone. She realised her fingers were aching where she had been gripping the stem of her glass. While she had been immersed in the performance, she had not drunk a drop.

She was first out of the studio and the young man behind the bar looked at her with the expression of a puppy expecting to be kicked.

'What did you think?'

Faith sipped slowly at her drink.

'I was impressed. It was a good call.'

She felt she owed him this titbit, which he gratefully acknowledged by – virtually – wagging his tail.

Before he could start licking her face, Faith asked: 'Who *is* that poet? He was fabulous.'

'Name's Natty B – local guy, bit of a painter, I think, comes here two or three times a month. We never know when, but luckily we don't have to advertise. Word gets around. The studio's always full when he's here. Don't know where that reggae stuff comes from – he's whi... well, I mean he's not from Jamaica.'

Affecting a broad Jamaican accent, Faith tickled him under the chin.

'It ain't where you're from, honey, it's where you're bound.'

Putting her half consumed drink down on the bar, she left and headed for the nearest taxi rank. She no longer felt like a night on the town. The performance she'd just witnessed had eased her soul and – almost – wiped out the memories of her earlier unpleasant encounters. She would relax over the weekend, and then start her new career as a private eye on Monday.

Monday 8 April 2013

Chapter 14

Nathaniel's weekend passed in a haze of lethargy, remorse and self doubt. It was true that Friday's fall had taken it out of him at first, and he had still felt rather rough when he saw his GP. But he had to admit to himself that he had then rather laid it on with a trowel and he recognised that a complete week's rest from work was a somewhat excessive prescription. To be honest, there had been many days during his time at Kennaway's when he had been able to drag himself into the office while feeling considerably worse than he did now.

But there it was. Rather by accident, he had a quite legitimate reason for spending a whole week (if he wanted) nestled in the Institution, and so he had grabbed the opportunity (and the sick note) with both hands. A voicemail message for Sophie describing his ailment in appropriately pathetic tones, and bingo – the Institution would be his oyster, for a week at least.

It struck him how quickly the place seemed to have claimed him as one of its own. His agitation and sudden mood swings of the past few days had left him, to be replaced by a quiet calm. He decided he couldn't usefully speculate on where these feelings came from or what it was about the Institution that almost made him feel as if he had found a second home. Throughout his whole working life he had, in his former wife's annoying phrase, 'gone with the flow'. Although, to continue the metaphor, the flow might have changed direction in a way he could not predict, he was still content to go with it.

That Monday morning, the weather was a little cooler, but Nathaniel still stepped out in his shirt sleeves. The walk into town was the usual random Exeter mix of downhill and uphill, and he knew a brisk pace would keep him warm. It was only as he was about to enter the Cathedral Close that he realised that he was of course only a few steps from the office.

What if he was observed at large when by rights he should be languishing at home, feebly clutching a sick note?

So what, he rapidly concluded. The GP was only required to pass judgement on fitness for work. Nathaniel was not required to cower behind drawn curtains all day with a glass of tonic wine.

And now he had a mystery to solve.

Who was this Nathaniel Barton whose commonplace Book had somehow found its way into the Institution? Nathaniel smiled, and pressed the brass bell for admittance.

'Come in, come in, come in,' said a smiling Simpkins, leading Nathaniel by his arm into his office.

Guiding Nathaniel into the same chair where he had been revived, Simpkins attempted a feeble wink.

'Looks to me as if you've got yourself signed off work for a couple of days, eh?'

He may appear a few sandwiches short of a picnic hamper, thought Nathaniel, but he's still got his wits about him.

'The whole week actually. I was rather keen to get my hands on that volume I was trying to retrieve from the top shelf.'

Reaching down to a drawer in his desk, Simpkins continued, 'Quite. I didn't want any more accidents, so I put it by for you. I also took the liberty of checking its provenance in our Acquisitions Book, and it's all rather interesting. Indeed, it didn't have to travel far to get here. Do you know those big Georgian houses in Southernhay, round the corner?'

'Absolutely. In fact, I work in one of them.'

'Well, then, you'll also know that they were built as private properties originally, for people with rather more money than you or I have. But these days, the posh money tends to move out of the city, and it was in 1968 that a local solicitor, Geoffrey Kennaway, had one of the old houses fitted out as offices for his legal practice.'

'Good Lord,' exclaimed Nathaniel, 'number fourteen?'

'Number thirteen, actually. Do you know it?'

'All too well. If I wasn't here now, I'd be working there.'

'Well I never,' said Simpkins, mopping his forehead with the ubiquitous handkerchief. 'Quite a coincidence.'

'No more so than this book belonging to my namesake,' Nathaniel remarked thoughtfully.

'Anyway, this book was found wrapped in sacking under the floorboards of what was probably a servant's bedroom. It was handed to old Mr Kennaway. His family have been members of the Guild from way back. Seventeen times, I believe, a Kennaway has been Master. So naturally, with their association with the Institution, he was happy to donate it to us.'

Almost reverentially, Nathaniel gazed at the brown leather covered volume before him. The binding was simply stitched, almost crude. To Nathaniel's eye, it looked home made. The edges of the pages were a yellowish brown and wrinkled; there didn't seem to be a straight line anywhere. There was no lettering on the covers that Nathaniel could discern, simply a small white Institution label on the back cover with its reference number.

Seeing the number, Nathaniel remembered popping the matching index card into the top pocket of his jacket. Realising he'd left his jacket at home that morning, he felt it would be wiser not to admit to his inadvertent theft until he could return the card on another occasion.

'Well I suppose that's the good news, as it were,' continued Simpkins. 'The bad news is that you ain't going to need a whole week to read it. I've skimmed through it, but it looks like only the first few pages have anything written on them, and that's mostly illegible.'

'But I can look at it now, can I?'

'Of course, young fellow, only to read here though. You won't be taking any books out of the building until your membership's confirmed.'

'Understood,' said Nathaniel and reached out to take the book from Simpkins.

As he grasped it, he felt another jolt in his arm, not as powerful as before, but still disconcerting. Trying as best he could to avoid breaking into a run, he strode out of the office towards the Major Library.

That thrill running up his arm on this occasion could not have been any sort of electrical shock. What was it about this book, or was he just imagining things? Never one to speculate too long on questions he could not answer, Nathaniel filed the matter away in a corner of his brain and took his seat at the map table.

Monday seemed to be a much busier day in the Institution than Friday. The same torpid figure occupied the armchair in far corner. Next to him (or her?), two military types from central casting were bent over a large map of Afghanistan in animated discussion. A clergyman was collecting a variety of small volumes from the Theology section while next to the card index was a small group of university students who seemed to be noting down references on their phones and tablets.

Nathaniel realised he might want to take notes too, so retraced his steps to Simpkins' office where he left what in his own mind he was now calling 'The Book' with the ever helpful librarian.

Ten minutes later, Nathaniel was back, armed with a small black notebook and couple of cheap pens, purchased at a nearby stationers. He collected The Book from the office, and once again a small tremor ran up his arm, less powerfully than before but still noticeable. He resumed his seat at the map table.

The two military gentlemen were still earnestly refighting one of the innumerable Afghan campaigns but the students were gone, and Nathaniel was able to address The Book in an atmosphere of relative calm.

The front cover opened stiffly and it seemed to Nathaniel that this was not the finest example of the bookbinder's art. Even making allowances for its antiquity, The Book seemed poorly put together, a cheap as well as a commonplace book.

Simpkins had been spot on when he said the handwriting was largely illegible, to the average reader. Nathaniel, however, was not the average reader. Through his work with old title deeds and correspondence, he was well versed in deciphering documents going back well before the eighteenth century. It was his eye and his experience that time and again had confirmed his value to Kennaway & Partners. Nathaniel's interpretation of a difficult text had often explained away a discrepancy or smoothed a transfer of a property, skills that Nathaniel considered remained undervalued by his employers.

So what would, to the lay person, have appeared as an unintelligible scrawl was, after a few minutes close study, as clear to Nathaniel as the front page of that morning's Daily Telegraph.

'In the 47th year of my life I am today blessed with a boy child, my 1st wife having perished in childbirth some 25 years ago and my only having taken a 2nd wife this year past, I am now resolved to use this Commonplace Book to provide a record for my son (how sweetly that sounds) of significant events in his family, his city, his country and the world in the hope and expectation that when he too becomes a father he will have a legacy of information to pass to each succeeding generation. In the furtherance of God's greater purpose this day of the 3rd of December in the year of our Lord 1767.
Nathaniel Barton Esquire'

So, this was the voice of an earlier Nathaniel Barton, born nearly four hundred years ago, speaking to the Nathaniel Barton of today. The sentiments were as fresh and recognisable as if they were spoken yesterday.

The Nathaniel of 2013 could sympathise. He too had produced his first – and, as it happened, only – child within the first year of his marriage.

A warm summer evening in 1986, too much cheap white Burgundy, an unexpectedly ferocious bout of lovemaking on the living room floor with both caution and contraception thrown to the winds, and their child was conceived. Some nine months later, their son was born, and Nathaniel, holding the violet-tinged, squealing homunculus in his arms, felt truly blessed, much as that earlier Nathaniel clearly had.

That, however, was probably the point at which their marriage began to die. A scant two years later, in the month after his father died, Nathaniel had returned to work to be greeted by sly sideward glances and muttered corridor conversations that stopped as he approached. When he had confronted Sophie, the self appointed traffic manager of all the office's streams of gossip, she had at first played dumb. But when Nathaniel persisted, she responded with a question of her own. Why was it, she enquired with an air of faux innocence, that he appeared to be the only person in the building that was unaware that Kennaway's would be handling the divorce proceedings of Sally Barton?

Red faced, Nathaniel had retreated to his office, not daring to turn and see Sophie's expression of triumph. It wasn't the knife thrust of the divorce itself that hurt – Nathaniel had to admit that the end of his marriage had been long, too long, in the making. It was the sheer cruelty of using Kennaway's to twist the blade.

Despite the humiliation, a combination of alimony and inertia had kept Nathaniel at Kennaway's. Over time, Sally's financial demands had shrunk as her gallery grew ever more successful and then disappeared entirely when she married the only son of a Gloucestershire aristocrat. But by then Nathaniel had neither the will nor the energy to move on from Kennaways. His one huge regret was that he had seen so little of his son.

Sally had quickly plucked her new partner from the artistic crowd he had always thought of as failed hippies and Tristram had been a more than adequate father for the growing boy. For many years now, 'contact' had only been one way. At first, books on birthdays and at Christmas; later, just cards with the obligatory folding money enclosed.

Nathaniel was surprised at the small tear in the corner of his eye. 'Come on,' he admonished himself. 'Stop worrying about the recent past and let's read about the old Nathaniel. Looks like life was looking up for him.'

It soon transpired that both Nathaniels had been far too optimistic.

'Bumped into Kennaway last night.'

'How's he doing?'

'Well, you know... Anyway, thing is, one of his junior partners is our friend Barton.'

'I thought he was dead – drowned in a bottle, didn't he?'

'No, that was his father – this is the son. No longer one of ours, of course.'

'So he was the chappy who came a cropper in the Institution, then?'

'Indeed.'

'Should we be worried?'

'Wouldn't have thought so.'

'I think you'll find Marcus disagrees...'

Chapter 15

Nathaniel took a deep breath and gazed around the Major Library. This was not a dream; he was not going mad. It's simply that there had been a chap with the same name, let's call him Nathaniel #1, living in 1767. He'd just had a son; what happens next?

When Nathaniel #1 said he would note down 'significant events', he had at first been true to his word. Without having any particular purpose in mind, Nathaniel began jotting in his notebook some of the events that the earlier Nathaniel had recorded for the benefit of his son.

1769 saw the demolition of the old North Gate, the laying of a foundation stone for the Assembly Rooms, and the founding of the Exeter Bank. Mrs Barton visited an acquaintance and was granted the tasting of a pineapple.

Louis XVI succeeded to French throne in 1774. Three years later, the eighteenth century Nathaniel recorded his discomfort at the recent events on the North American continent. Apparently, previously loyal subjects of the crown had aspirations to write their own constitution, somewhat after the example of the regicidal French. Where would it all end?

Nathaniel had to smile at that. No provincial solicitor from the eighteenth century could have predicted the global power that the United States of America had now become.

Back to more parochial matters. 1778 saw a stone pavement laid in High Street, the building of a sturdy new bridge across the Exe and the foundation, just down the road from the new home in Southernhay that Nathaniel #1 had been able to purchase, of the Devon & Exeter Hospital.

Reading of that new home, Nathaniel reminded himself that that splendid new home of the 1770s was the same building that he trudged to every weekday for work. Just one of an increasing list of coincidences that might prove significant.

The commonplace book was just that. Not everything in there was of huge historical significance. Old Nathaniel had written down some doggerel daubed on the wall of the Exeter Theatre after a performance of one of Mr William Shakespear's Roman plays.

'The Queen of the Nile (who washes in milk)
Her Antony constantly urges:
Don't bring me those bolts of Chinese silk
But lengths of Exeter serges.'

Taking another moment to reflect, Nathaniel gazed around the Major Library. It was not just a matter of names. He guessed that if he googled 'Nathaniel Barton' back at the office, he'd pull up dozens of others. No, it was that *physical* connection that Simpkins had pointed out, that Nathaniel #1 had actually lived in the very building where he now worked.

There was then a short passage which struck Nathaniel as so out of character that he transcribed it word for word in his notebook. From the random jottings that had entertained him for the past two or more hours had emerged this striking new tone:

'Attended a Hall, and was most perturbed to observe sundry persons blabbermouthing in corners against me, who has been a loyal servant of the Guild for thirty years and more. There are dark whisperings of another Nathaniel Barton having committed some heinous crime, and I am determined to search it out, whatsoever the consequence.'

This was dated 2 July 1780, and when Nathaniel turned to the next page, it was blank.

Nathaniel sat silently for a moment. He had just read, and been intrigued by, the various ramblings of

Nathaniel #1 and had strangely come to like this person not unlike himself. A straightforward enough man, with a love of family, placing the need to support that family above his own satisfaction and, by and large, making a decent fist of it. Nathaniel supposed that in the eighteenth century your ordinary professional person didn't tend to go in for divorce.

And that was it. The story stopped.

Nathaniel was consumed with an urge to discover more, but how? His mind turned to the old newspapers stored in the Minor Library. Perhaps if he checked the editions for July 1780, he could learn more of Nathaniel #1 or of the 'heinous crime' of which his fellow Guild members seemed to be accusing him.

Taking The Book with him in a rather proprietorial fashion, Nathaniel walked through the double doors to the Minor Library. Like the room he had just left, this library too was lined floor to ceiling with books in every shade of brown, except at the far end where there were bound volumes of local newspapers. The issues of Trewman's Flying Post were embossed in clear gold lettering, year by year from 1763 to 1917. Nathaniel went straight for 1780 and heaved it up on to the reading table.

He opened the collection at July and paused. This was the reason he had wanted to join the Institution, the opportunity to be with books and documents of a previous age. The print on the paper was his direct link with another intelligence. Through the miracle of writing and reading, the barrier between Nathaniel and the eighteenth century journalist's thoughts was, literally, paper thin.

He smiled, briefly, and began to scan the dense type. It did not take him long to find the first reference to that earlier Nathaniel. The edition of the Flying Post for 7 July 1780 (Volume XVIII, number 855) had a short but poignant entry.

'On Monday Evening, about ten o'clock, the following melancholy Accident happened: a Lawyer of Exeter, Nathaniel Barton, fell from the new Exe Bridge into the river and was unfortunately drown'd before proper assistance could be procured. Mr Barton was reported as taking gin at the Bishop Blaize Inn in the company of a lean companion with a distinctive scar on his face. The Mayor and Alderman have requested that this gentleman present himself at the office of the Sergeants-at-Mace to give his account of the Incident.'

Nathaniel smiled at the mention of the Bishop Blaize. He had supped more than one good pint of Bays there in his time.

But he had to confess he was puzzled. Nathaniel had to concede to himself that he might be reading a little too much into the entries in the commonplace book. But the older Nathaniel, a God-fearing middle-aged lawyer with a new wife and child to support, did not appear to be the sort of man who would get himself drunk and commit suicide.

There was a faint possibility that the discovery he had made in the Guild's records was so unspeakably appalling that suicide was the only way out. But what seemed far more likely was that he had been silenced by person or persons unknown, quite possibly by his drinking companion from the tavern.

Nathaniel sat back in his chair and reflected further. The Bishop Blaize was on the western side of Exeter, just outside the old city wall. To get back to his Southernhay home near the cathedral, Nathaniel #1 would have had to walk up hill and eastwards, not along the river bank and southwards over the bridge. If he had truly wanted to kill himself, the inn was but a few steps from the rushing waters of the River Exe. So what, or who, had led him so far out of his way, and then to his untimely death?

Nathaniel read on. Perhaps he would discover the identity of the 'lean companion with the distinctive scar'.

The next edition of the Flying Post had no further news of enquiries into the death of Nathaniel #1, hardly surprising at a time when law enforcement was something of a free-for-all with no professional police force. There was, though, one small item of interest.

'Advertisement. On Monday 3 July, at ten o'clock of the Evening, Nathaniel Barton Esq untimely drown'd in the river by the New Exe Bridge. A Reward of 20l. is offered to any who witnessed this grievous accident and who can present themselves to Mrs Mary Barton of 13 Southernhay in the City of Exeter.'

The following edition, for 21 July, had three entries of interest, which taken together told a sorry tale.

'Advertisement. To Be SOLD, for a Term of Seventy Years absolute, from the 1st Day of August, 1780 TWO FULLING-MILLS, near the Quay, in Exeter, called the QUAY-MILLS, now rented by Messrs. Kennaway and Barton (being One Wheel and Half), held by Lease from the Chamber of Exeter, under a small reserved Rent.

The Premises are now let for 69l.15s, per Annum.

A Survey or Auction will be held, for Sale thereof, at the Oxford Inn in Exeter, on Saturday the 12th Day of August next, at Two o'clock in the Afternoon. In the mean time, Application may be made to the Tenant, Abraham Kennaway II, who will shew the Premises.'

Nathaniel smiled ruefully at the thought that, three hundred years before, a Kennaway and a Barton had apparently been in business as partners together while now a Kennaway was a Barton's employer. He went on to the next entry, immediately below the first.

'Advertisement. To Be LETT, ALL that elegant and convenient DWELLING HOUSE, belonging to Mr Abraham Kennaway II, desirably situated in the most healthy and pleasing place, being N° 13 Southernhay adjacent to Cathedral Close, Exeter:

The Premises consist of a Hall, two Parlours, Kitchen, Pantry, and Brewhouse; a neat Dining-Room with a Dressing-Room on each Side; seven good Bed-Chambers, with Closets; a Laundry, and large Room for drying Cloaths. There is a back Stair-Case with four good Servants Rooms; three Cellars with good Wine Vaults; a Court, in which there are two Pumps, the one producing hard, the other soft Water, from a Reservoir containing forty Hogsheads. The Whole is fit to receive a genteel Family, without Expence or Alterations, having lately been fitted up with neat Marble Chimnies, Papers, Locks, Bolts, Bells, &c &c.

Enquire of Mr Frederick Hirtzell, Beadle, Tuckers Hall in Fore Street, Exeter.'

But surely that address, 13 Southernhay, was still the home of Mary Barton, widow of Nathaniel #1. Was she moving so soon? It made no sense when, only the previous week, she had asked for information on her husband's accident to be brought to her there.

Two more pages on, Nathaniel found the answer to the riddle.

'Obituary. It is with extreme regret that we have to announce the death of Mary Barton (nee Kennaway) in the 52nd year of her age, which melancholy event took place at Southernhay, in Exeter, on Sunday the 16th instant, to the irreparable loss and great affliction of her near Connections and of a large circle of warmly attached Friends.

Recently widowed, Mrs Barton is believed to have died of grief at her tragic loss. She leaves a son whose Estate, as a minor, will be administered by his Uncle, Abraham Kennaway II.

This Notice is placed at the Instruction of the Guild of Weavers, Fullers and Shearmen to whom Nathaniel Barton was ever a devoted and loyal Servant.'

These were the last references Nathaniel could find; he completed his handwritten notes, closed the huge volume with a heavy heart, and returned it to its place on the shelf.

The sequence of events was now becoming clear to Nathaniel. Three centuries ago, a Nathaniel Barton was a lawyer who, it appeared, had worked for or been a member of the Guild of Weavers, Fullers and Shearmen. He had also operated a fulling mill (Nathaniel wasn't quite clear what that actually was) in partnership with his brother in law, Abraham Kennaway.

All had seemed well in his world. Nathaniel #1 had had a happy second marriage and a young son, until he learned of some dark event in his family history involving the powerful Guild of Weavers, Fullers and Shearmen. Shortly afterwards, both he and his wife died in quick succession and in unexplained circumstances. Nathaniel did not subscribe to the theory that people could simply die of grief, especially when Mary's death had occurred so quickly after she had publicly declared an interest in investigating her husband's supposed accident.

Within nineteen short days after that earlier Nathaniel Barton's accidental death, both his home and business premises were up for disposal and his wife was dead. It was if he had never existed.

Nathaniel opened The Book again so that he could re-read the final passage. Once again he felt that unexplained tingle, and he was also conscious of becoming rather tired.

He rapidly flicked through the pages, but inadvertently went one page too far. Now, instead of that next page being blank, it was filled with a cursive script which from the very first word seemed of a different character to the earlier part of The Book.

Instead of a hotch potch of events and dates, this was now more of a diary. Incomplete, and sometimes ambiguous in meaning, but clearly narrating a life in a chronological order. Without considering how he could have missed this when he first turned that last page, Nathaniel read on voraciously, instinctively feeling that this would solve the mystery.

The Book was no longer a collection of random jottings. It told the tale of a lad in his early teens, whose parents had suddenly died within days of each other. Fortunately for the youth, his father had been a respected member of the Guild of Weavers, Fullers and Shearmen, and there were funds available to ensure he did not sink into penury.

Even better, the son's education became the responsibility of the Guild, and he was taken under the wing of a 'fencing master' who ensured his fighting prowess matched his growing facility with languages, mathematics and musical composition.

Just as Nathaniel was beginning to admire the development of this prodigy, he learnt that this too was a Nathaniel Barton who could now, with stunning originality, be christened Nathaniel #2.

But at the very point that he was beginning to warm to the youth, the story took a more unpleasant turn.

Chapter 16

Faith had had, by her standards, an idle weekend. First, the obligatory phone calls back home. She may be on the up as a young academic but she still needed the patient reassuring voice of her mother to keep her grounded. She'd also carried out a few domestic chores – washing, making a shopping list for when she next went into town, paying off her credit card account.

Then she'd hung out a while on campus. She'd realised that ever since she had arrived, she'd thrown herself into her project and hadn't really taken time to enjoy her surroundings or even meet new people. Exeter University was fortunate to be spread across a beautifully landscaped site on the hills overlooking the city, and Faith took some time out to explore the grounds in the spring sun. Mature trees alternated with younger, more modern planting. Every now and again, a small pond or larger expanse of water reflected the April sky. Faith spotted what she was sure was an Egyptian egret preening itself among the reeds.

She also checked out some of the bars and cafeterias dotted around. Most undergraduates were away during the Easter vacation, but there were plenty of older students like Faith around, and she had no problem joining a group on a terrace outside one of the newer coffee shops.

After the usual exchange of names and reasons for being there, Faith thought she would see if anyone else had had a similar experience to hers at the Phoenix.

Opinion was strongly divided. One blond jock, Mikey, found the reggae poet pretentious, while his friend Josh (same tan, same mop of hair, same sweatshirt) thought he was 'really something'.

All the females there shared Faith's view. Perhaps there was something about that deep languorous voice that pressed the right hormonal buttons.

What everyone was agreed on, though, was that although Natty had been around 'for ever', no one knew much about him or his background. However, one of the group, Alice, had apparently had a couple of casual conversations with the poet in the past and she offered to introduce Faith next time he performed.

So, as Faith readied herself that Monday morning for her first foray into espionage, she was able to console herself with the thought that Exeter was just full of mysteries. Wherever she turned, there was something inexplicable or just plain odd.

She reflected that it was her urge to find answers to questions that had inspired her to pursue historical research in the first place. So a little quiet poking around to find out what Mr Nathaniel Barton was up to in the Institution was no big deal. An introduction, a slice of humble pie, a few innocent questions, job done. She could not have been more wrong.

With a forecast of a dry day, Faith decided she would walk down into Exeter. She smiled as her route took her through an area called Pennsylvania, something to tell her ma next time they spoke, she thought. Then, having walked down a long steep hill, she found herself having to climb another steep incline before arriving at the end of the High Street. She wondered whether a cooling drink might be justified, but readily persuaded herself this was just a ploy to put off confronting the subject of her investigation. So she walked on until once again she arrived at the Cathedral Close.

She was buzzed in to the Institution, but no-one came out to greet her today. She peered through the glass panel in the door of the Librarian's Office to see a distinctly pallid Lionel Simpkins leafing through a journal in a desultory fashion.

Left to her own devices, Faith pushed through the double doors into the Major Library and was delighted to see that, apart from a slumbering form in a corner, she was alone with Nathaniel Barton. This should not take too long.

As she approached Nathaniel, she could see that he was intently reading an old leather-bound book, his lips moving silently. He paused from time to time to jot things down on a small black notepad. It would appear that all she had to do was politely ask what he was looking at, and then report straight back to Marcus.

Nathaniel did not look up as she arrived next to him, and it was then Faith saw the strangest thing. The page that Nathaniel was apparently devouring, lips silently moving, appeared to be completely blank.

When a discreet cough did not work, Faith gently tapped Nathaniel on the shoulder. He started, catapulting notepad and pens on to the floor.

'So sorry,' said Faith sweetly, 'My turn to surprise you, I think.'

Emerging from under the table clutching his pens and book, Nathaniel resembled a hedgehog awaking after its winter snooze.

'Goodness me,' said Nathaniel, 'I was miles, maybe years, away.'

'Must be good. Can I have a look see?'

Almost proudly, Nathaniel held The Book open before her, and Faith's first impression was confirmed. The pages were plainly and absolutely blank.

Misinterpreting her look of surprise, Nathaniel happily babbled on.

'As you can see, it's a fascinating story. This is a young man, born and brought up in eighteenth century Exeter, and he's being trained as some sort of international assassin. James Bond has nothing on him. Already he's bumped off King Gustav of Sweden and here, look, it seems he's being bundled off to France to knock off one of the leaders of the Revolution, only I thought that Marat was killed by a mad Frenchwoman. Anyway, the weird thing is, he's got my name: Nathaniel

Barton. Sorry, yes, should have introduced myself, Nathaniel Barton, that's me, sorry.'

Faith resisted the temptation to admit that she already knew who he was.

'Faith Codrington. I'm carrying out research for my doctorate; I'm originally from Exeter in Canada, which is a happy coincidence.'

Nathaniel tapped the side of his nose in a knowing way. 'Coincidence is the compliment that intelligence pays to chance.'

'I've not heard that before. Is anything *really* coincidence?'

'Well, I can give you a few coincidences to analyse if you like, from this very book. Let me just pop it back on the shelf and I will take you out for that cup of tea I promised you.'

With a remarkable burst of speed, Nathaniel closed The Book, picked it up and shot into the Minor Library, returning to scoop up his notebook and pens before Faith could react.

How irritating, Faith thought. Now I don't know what that book is or where it's shelved. Still, I should be able to winkle it out of him while we're having tea.

'Everyone who comes to Exeter should go to Mol's,' pronounced Nathaniel as they left the Institution.

'Well, we sassy young Canadian girls don't miss a trick,' said Faith with a smile, 'I've been there twice already and I've only been in Exeter just over a week!'

'So let me take you somewhere new.'

Faith, fearing a long trek, was delighted when Nathaniel indicated an outside table for two just a few steps further on.

'MC Cafe,' he announced, 'Nothing, praise be, to do with the unfortunately ubiquitous McDonalds, but one of the many outlets run by Exeter's star chef, Michael Caines.'

Faith smiled politely and took her seat. She had to admit to herself that she had always thought Michael

Caines was only an English actor, though a prolific and talented one. She'd never realised he cooked as well.

A waitress promptly took their order, and Faith, none too subtly, asked Nathaniel to expand on The Book and coincidences. Being a sleuth had its moments, but it was starting to become boring. She really wanted to get some answers and then to get out of there.

'Before I start on The Book, let me give you another coincidence. You share a surname, Codrington, with my ex-wife's second husband, Tristram.'

'Well, I think I can...,' started Faith, but then paused when she saw the look of horror on Nathaniel's face. It appeared, though, that this was not at what she was saying but at what he could see over her left shoulder.

'God, *she* mustn't see me,' muttered Nathaniel, and before Faith could ask why, he was up and away, disappearing down a narrow alley just as a pot of tea for two arrived.

Turning to discover what hideous apparition accounted for Nathaniel's hasty departure, Faith turned to see a pale slim woman in a formal suit approaching. Mid fifties, perhaps, but still with a good figure.

'I see tea's arrived, and we appear to have an empty seat. Do you mind if I join you?'

In for a penny, in for a dollar, thought Faith. I'll do what any self respecting private eye would do.

'Of course not. My name's Faith.'

'How do you do? My name's Sophie. I think we should talk about Nathaniel, don't you?'

Chapter 17

When he reached the High Street, Nathaniel paused for breath and looked behind him. No sign of Sophie, also known as CK's snitch-in-chief. The question was, had she seen him? It was one thing to convalesce gracefully in the calm setting of the Institution. Nathaniel felt confident (in his stronger moments) that this was perfectly defensible.

But taking tea, brazenly and in broad daylight with an attractive, no, a *beautiful*, young woman half his age? What would Sophie think?

Well, *that* was a rhetorical question if ever there was one. Not only would Sophie place the worst possible interpretation upon it, she would then broadcast that opinion as fact to anyone who cared to listen. It would be bad enough if he had been seen in as compromising a position at the weekend. On a day when by rights he should have been at home nursing a sore head, well, he could safely predict CK's reaction to *that* little titbit. Goodbye, bonus.

It was a morose Nathaniel that trudged wearily up the inevitable Exeter hill back to his home. In a way, what most depressed him was that he felt he had been on the verge of a really exciting discovery in The Book, but he could hardly go back to the Institution this afternoon with Sophie's antennae all aquiver.

Still, as he unlocked his front door, he reflected it need not be an afternoon entirely wasted. He had his notes, and he might be able to do some useful background research using his laptop. He booted the machine up on his dining room table while, unconsciously mimicking his daily work routine, he plugged the kettle in for a cup of tea.

The act of making the tea reminded him of his ungracious departure from the cafe, and he resolved to look out for Faith and make yet another apology. That's if she didn't, as she was entitled to, cross the road to avoid him.

Mug in hand, he sat down in front of his laptop and decided he would start with a little fact checking. He had been encouraged by the fact that the Flying Post, which he could assume was a reasonably objective source in matters of this sort, had both confirmed the existence of Nathaniel #1 and also provided a rational explanation for the abrupt ending of his contribution to The Book. He reckoned a bit of intelligent googling would similarly support some of the other content in The Book as well as giving him some useful context.

Before typing in his first search terms, it occurred to him that this was the first genuine moment of excitement, adventure even, in his pedestrian life for many a long year. Whatever the reason behind that impulsive dash to the Institution a few short days ago, the decision was more than vindicated by the thrill of this investigation.

Right then. He recalled reading how Nathaniel #2, having lost his father when he was only 14, was taken on by the Guild's fencing master and given a fairly wide-ranging education. Checking his notes, he saw that in addition to Latin, Nathaniel #2 had acquired a proficiency in French and, oddly as it had seemed to Nathaniel at first, Swedish. At the age of 15, he'd been apprenticed as a clerk to the Exeter Bank. So, determined Nathaniel, what would be his first search?

What information on the Exeter Bank could be gleaned from the ever-helpful internet?

A great deal, as it happened. The Exeter Bank was one of a clutch of businesses founded in Exeter in a twenty-five year period at the end of the eighteenth century: the Exeter Bank itself in 1769, the Devonshire in 1770, then the City, the General and finally, in 1793, the Western Bank. What these businesses all seemed to have in common was that they were founded by wealthy (obviously) wool traders, who were almost all immigrants by origin and nonconformist by religion.

This made sense, thought Nathaniel.

From what little he remembered from those interminable school trips along the Exeter Woollen Trail, clipboard and printed questionnaire in hand, this was the period when the Devon wool trade itself was in decline. Those who had made their profits on the backs of sheep now needed other outlets for investment and other sources of income. Exeter, with its port at Topsham to the south and, as long as the canal functioned, extra capacity at Exeter Quays, was a key route into the southwest of England for a wide range of imports as well as being the natural outlet for Devon's justly famous agricultural produce. So there were opportunities for families such as the Duntzes and Barings, German migrants both, and Nathaniel was intrigued to see the name of Kennaway as one of the founders of the Western Bank.

The Baltic trade in particular was long established. This, Nathaniel realised must have been the reason for Nathaniel #2 to acquire a grasp of Swedish.

So, now to Sweden. What he'd been reading when he had been interrupted by that young woman with an uncanny knack of turning up at inappropriate moments was that Nathaniel #2 was despatched to Stockholm in the February of 1792 with a mission to assassinate King Gustav III. The republican in Nathaniel wryly noted that only the upper classes were 'assassinated'. Ordinary folk were simply murdered.

Without fully comprehending the detail of eighteenth century economics, Nathaniel understood that Gustav's ambitions for Sweden were at odds with the interests of Exeter merchants as represented by the Guild. It was not just that the Swedish king was eager to send troops to oppose the French revolutionaries whose activities had opened up opportunities for keen eyed English businessmen. He was also looking to take control of the profitable shipping interests in the Baltic where Devon, and presumably Guild, investments were prominent.

Nathaniel #2 took up with a clique of disaffected and impoverished Swedish nobles and convinced them that they would be well rewarded if Gustav were to be eliminated.

The ideal opportunity presented itself at a masked ball in the Opera House. While everyone else was suitably disguised, the king, either through arrogance or congenital stupidity, was easily identifiable because of the shining Silver Star of the Order of the Seraphim that he wore proudly on his chest. Backing him into a corner, the conspirators were, despite some fumbling, able to let off a single shot that blew a large hole in Gustav's back.

In the ensuing confusion, Nathaniel #2 had been able to slip away. In fact, he was safely back in Exeter before the king finally expired of his wounds on 29 March.

Nathaniel began to scroll through the results of his first online search. As he dipped in and out of the various items he'd retrieved, he was able to confirm his own handwritten notes from earlier in the day. He stood up from his chair and paced slowly up and down the room, partly to relieve a nagging pain in the small of his back but also to reflect on something he had put off considering.

He clearly recalled that, when he first looked at the commonplace book, the pages after Nathaniel #1's final entry had been blank.

But when he had completely read those initial entries, he had been able to see an account of Nathaniel #2's life and times.

He could get no further than a conclusion that this was indeed odd, but he was in no position to resolve the matter until he had the actual commonplace book back in his hands.

Nathaniel returned to his laptop and decided to check the facts of Nathaniel #2's next commission.

While it had not been explicitly stated, Nathaniel had got the distinct impression that the Guild had a distinctly ambivalent attitude towards the French Revolution. They were generally encouraged by the chaos generated by the activities of the revolutionaries, but were less comfortable with the more extreme direction being taken by some of the more radical politicians, stimulated in particular by the writings of the fiery journalist, Jean-Paul Marat.

The device used in Sweden, where Nathaniel #2 had seized on existing opponents of his target to carry out the actual killing, seemed to be one worth using again.

Within a few weeks of arriving in France, he had identified a disaffected opponent of the revolution, Charlotte Corday, as his ideal cat's paw. A pretty brooch, a couple of discreet suppers, and free conveyance in his cabriolet to the Hotel Providence in Paris were enough to secure her support. Nathaniel #2 was simply able to hand her the fatal kitchen knife and then slip away quietly.

The story of Charlotte Corday's assassination of Marat was well known. It was immortalised in iconic paintings and had formed part of Nathaniel's history syllabus at Exeter Cathedral School. But confronted by the realisation that it was a Nathaniel Barton that had masterminded that particular murder, he had to place his notebook down, stand up, and walk around the room once more.

What was this monster, this namesake of his, perhaps an ancestor, who had ruthlessly murdered and then allowed others to take the blame and pay the ultimate price? Jacob Johan Anckarstrom had been tortured and executed for allegedly killing King Gustav III and Charlotte Corday had famously gone to the guillotine.

But Nathaniel #2 had simply returned to his humble clerk's post in the Exeter Bank with no-one, apart from, he assumed, the Guild of Weavers, Fullers and Shearmen, being any the wiser.

Suddenly Nathaniel had lost the appetite for any further research. He closed down the laptop and went for an early supper at his local pub.

Had he realised it, that would be his last meal at the Rusty Bike.

‘Kennaway collared me at the Club last night.’

‘Not another contribution to his blasted shark charity, I hope?’

‘No, it’s our friend Barton again. Years of being the perfect employee – solid, reliable, cheap – and now he’s all over the place.’

‘Anything to do with that accident at the Institution?’

‘Not directly. Signed off work for a week, of course...’

'That's the way of it these days.'

'...but now he's been spotted going taking tea with a young filly. Well enough to do that, it seems, but can’t manage the final few yards to the office, apparently.’

‘But what’s it to do with us, with The Guild?’

‘Marcus thinks...’

‘Oh, Marcus thinks*, does he?’*

‘Marcus thinks Mr B may have uncovered something he shouldn’t.’

‘Not very likely, is it?’

‘Worth checking out though. And Marcus made a little joke.’

‘Now I know *you’re wandering. Marcus with a sense of humour?’*

‘Yes – he said we’ll just have to rely on faith...’

Tuesday 9 April 2013

Chapter 18

Faith had had another restless night.

Little Faith was beginning to think that Exeter, Devon, was not suiting her half as much as Exeter, Ontario. Then Big Faith gave her a slap and told her not to be blaming Exeter, Devon, for her troubled thoughts.

What was really disconcerting her was this business with Marcus and having to act the spy, contrary to her own nature. Faith liked to think of herself as frank and open. With her, what you saw was pretty much what you got. Mind you, she reflected with a smile, she had played her part pretty well yesterday afternoon when that embodiment of bitchiness and bile had joined her for tea.

Faith was a great believer in always telling the truth whenever you could. As a historian, she also believed that we only ever know part of the truth. So when, after a few initial pleasantries about the weather and Faith's reasons for being in Exeter, Sophie had asked how it was that Faith just happened to be taking tea with a local solicitor who was supposed to be off ill from work, she was able to reply with a good conscience.

'He, literally, bumped into me. I wasn't looking where I was going, I guess, and he seemed a little preoccupied, under the weather even. So he offered to buy me a cup of tea, like a proper English gentleman, I would say.'

So far, so true, even if the sequence of events had been somewhat shortened. And when Sophie sweetly enquired again about the topic of their conversation, Faith could continue her account with a deceptive honesty.

'To tell you the truth, we'd only just ordered tea when he dashed off. You must have seen him? I can't say I know why. I don't think it was anything I'd said.'

That was the cue Sophie had been waiting for. With a range of verbal virtuosity Faith would not have thought her capable of, she entered into a monologue which detailed all the perceived faults and inadequacies in the hapless Nathaniel. From his pathetically slow progress up the career ladder, through his calamitous marriage and loss of custody of his son, his appalling dress sense, his non-existent manners, his *total* lack of charisma, his celibacy, his lack of humour, and last but not least, his current malingering and mendacity.

'And to cap it all,' continued Sophie with barely a pause for breath, 'I had to take a call for him this morning from a *very* important client in Exmouth who was wondering when Nathaniel would be making a visit. Yet the little slug told me last week that he was on his way there. What would CK think?'

As Faith sat at her kitchen table on Tuesday morning eating her granola, she thought it would not be long before CK – presumably the boss man – learnt of his junior partner's missed appointment and other misdemeanours, real or imagined.

Faith was, in general, prepared to give people the benefit of the doubt, but even on first acquaintance she had come to the rapid conclusion that Sophie was one very nasty piece of work.

Stripped of hyperbole and gratuitous rudeness, Sophie's portrait was of an inoffensive, hard working man. Disappointed in married life, parenthood and career, he had nevertheless plugged away through the years.

Faith was no expert on English legal firms, but she reckoned that Nathaniel must at the very least be one extremely competent lawyer to have stayed the course at what Sophie had *assured* her was one of the longest established and most highly regarded practices in the south west, if not the country.

And then there was Marcus.

Why was *he* so interested in what this inoffensive milquetoast was reading in his spare time? Faith had been brought up to approach every new acquaintance with an open and fair mind, and to always seek to see the best of them.

Frankly, if Marcus, unpleasant piece of work that *he* was, and Sophie (boy, would *they* make a perfect couple!) both had it in for Nathaniel Barton, Faith felt herself increasingly inclined to take the middle-aged lawyer's side.

Washing up her breakfast bowl and spoon, Faith recalled with a wry smile how she had got herself into this situation in the first place. She was in Exeter to get sight of unpublished papers of the Guild of Weavers, Fullers and Shearmen. It appeared that Marcus effectively controlled access to those papers and it was unclear what, if any, influence Sir Professor Stephen Duntze MBE (for all his titles) had over the 'officer of the Guild'. If she couldn't come up with something soon, her trip halfway round the world would end up as a waste of time, and her future academic career would be in severe trouble, if not ruined.

Next steps then. She needed to find Nathaniel again, and soon. She now knew where he worked, but she also knew he would not be back at his desk before next week. Heavy hints dropped by Sophie even indicated that this might not be taken for granted. She had no other contact details for him, no home address, no phone number.

Her only hope would be the Institution, though she had been intending to spend the day in the university library. Still, with a couple of files and her ipad, she would be almost as productive in the Institution. And, given that Nathaniel was prepared to take a risk with his job to spend time there, he would be bound to turn up sooner or later. It was now 10 o'clock. She'd better get a move on.

Just under an hour later, she was pressing the now familiar brass bell to be admitted to the tired lobby and creaking doors that led to the Major Library. Her luck was in. Nathaniel was in the same chair she had seen him last, and again the library seemed empty of any other human presence, if one discounted the gently snoring mound in the corner.

When she saw his face, Faith pulled up short and inadvertently put her hand to her mouth in shock. Nathaniel's skin had taken on a damp grey sheen, his eyes were bloodshot, and his brow furrowed. He seemed totally oblivious to her presence, and even when Faith got within touching distance and murmured 'Nathaniel? Mr Barton?' he showed no signs of recognising that she was in the room.

She had to look down at whatever was absorbing him. He was gripping the nondescript brown volume she had seen him looking at on her last visit.

He scanned it rapidly, muttering obscurely to himself, and she saw with a strange feeling of dread that, as before, the pages he appeared to be reading were completely blank.

Chapter 19

Nathaniel had spent a restless Monday night. He had fretted about Sophie and the growing certainty that she *had* spotted him in the close, apparently enjoying himself when he was supposed to be languishing on a bed of sickness.

And, he confessed to himself, it wasn't just an appearance of enjoyment. He had taken genuine pleasure in the all too brief time he'd spent with Faith, half his age and two inches taller. But what was this when weighed in the balance against the consequences of their brief encounter?

Assuming Sophie had not simultaneously lost her sight and her vicious tendency to gossip, Nathaniel's presence at the MC Cafe would now be the talk of Kennaway & Partners. It would therefore be only a matter of time before it came to CK's attention, and Nathaniel could already map out the sequence of events.

A summons to the senior partner's office immediately on his return next Monday. A short interrogation with one inevitable outcome. Nathaniel would be pronounced a slacker, a liability, a waste of good office space. The verdict was predictable. Less so would be the sentence. A stiff dressing down, for sure. A smaller annual bonus, or maybe even none at all. He might escape with a written warning on his file, or it could end in dismissal.

Nathaniel knew he was a damn good conveyancer but the legal profession, along with much of the UK economy, was currently taking a few body blows. There were plenty of other lawyers out there who would leap at the possibility of a job at Kennaway's, though there might be reservations about the size of the package.

Worried as he was about his career, Nathaniel had been in even more turmoil about his experience of reading The Book. The initial notes of the first Nathaniel Barton had been charming if sometimes a little discursive. Nathaniel had warmed to the man and learned some interesting snippets about life in eighteenth century Exeter along the way.

But reading the life of Nathaniel #2 had been an altogether more unpleasant experience.

Whatever allowances you made for the premature and tragic death of his parents and his unorthodox education, the fellow was a nasty piece of work however you looked at him.

In a perverse way, Nathaniel could sympathise with someone who killed for love and even for financial gain; but to, as it were, kill to order, coldly and without remorse, and then to allow others to be accused, tortured and executed – that was loathsome.

It was around three that morning that Nathaniel experienced the real insight that had driven petty concerns about his future career right out of his head. The Book had revealed to him the existence of two Nathaniel Bartons in Exeter, father and son, spanning the end of the eighteenth century and the beginning of the nineteenth. And here *he* was, in 2013, in a line of three consecutive Nathaniel Bartons – four if you included his estranged son. It was inconceivable that the two Nathaniels in The Book were not his direct ancestors.

Which made him the descendant of a cold blooded murderer.

A pale dawn had broken before Nathaniel finally fell into a heavy dreamless sleep. An hour later he awoke, tangled in sweat soaked sheets and with a sense of panic at missing his alarm. Remembering that he was still signed off work for the rest of week (perhaps the rest of the year, he thought ruefully) he awkwardly clambered out of bed and tried to ginger himself up with a cool shower.

A cup of tea later (no time for anything else!), he was back at the Institution just as Lionel Simpkins was unlocking the door. The librarian seemed to have aged ten years since Nathaniel had first met him a few short days before. He nevertheless flashed his yellow teeth in a reasonable facsimile of a smile and wished Nathaniel a good morning.

'I haven't really opened up properly yet, old fellow, but do go in and make yourself at home. It's not often we get such conspicuous displays of enthusiasm here.'

Bending to unlock his office, Simpkins allowed Nathaniel to lever his way through the double doors into the Major Library. Turning on the lights, Nathaniel was quietly relieved to see the corner armchair was empty. Whoever the perennial occupant was whenever Nathaniel had been there before, he, or she, seemed at least to have a home to go to.

Nathaniel set out his notepad and pens on the map table next to his usual chair, and retrieved The Book from its shelf in the Minor Library. It was still just before 9 o'clock.

Whether it was to reassure himself that he had in fact read of the vile behaviour of his eighteenth century forebear or whether he wished to look for some redeeming feature in the narrative, Nathaniel had determined on his walk down into the city that he would start again at the beginning of the story of Nathaniel #2.

He soon found himself being immersed in the history it told in a way that was totally unlike the mundane reading of a regular text. When Nathaniel later tried to describe the experience to himself, it most reminded him of that long hot summer (he must have been ten or eleven) when he was introduced to Arthur Ransome. That series of books about the Swallows and Amazons, children of around his own age messing about in boats in an impossibly idyllic pre-war England, had totally absorbed him. He had read them all in sequence from cover to cover, and once he'd finished, he'd started at the beginning again. Never had six weeks flown by so quickly, and never until now had he had that sensation of being totally inside the book he was reading.

So when the Swedish conspirators drank impossible quantities of akvavit and laughed about how they would dispose of their autocratic monarch, Nathaniel was in the room with them, smelling the mixture of tobacco, sweat and breaking wind. And Nathaniel almost found himself looking away in embarrassment as Nathaniel #2 charmed a coquettish Charlotte in his broken French with a mixture of empty flattery and thoughtful praise for her political writings.

The story now took another unexpected turn. Following the narrative beyond the point at which he'd been interrupted by Faith, Nathaniel found himself plunged into domestic English issues. An efficient and effective Tory politician, Spencer Perceval, had recently become Prime Minister.

Though Nathaniel could not follow the political and economic arguments in detail, Perceval had clearly managed to annoy the Guild, or at least those wealthy members who were beginning to invest in a Europe largely under the sway of Napoleon. It seemed that Perceval was both able and willing to prosecute a war against the little Corsican when a peace settlement would have better protected the interests (and income) of the Guild.

Nathaniel #2 was duly dispatched to London. His language skills might no longer be required, but his ability to strike at a target through an intermediary was put to use once more.

John Bellingham was a British businessman who had been imprisoned for some years in Russia on, he claimed, a trumped up charge. Returning home and subsequently finding his fortune had evaporated in his absence, he chose to blame the British government rather than his own lack of caution in certain dealings in St Petersburg. Over the course of a couple of good suppers in Rules Restaurant washed down with rather too much fine claret, Nathaniel #2 had persuaded an already angry Bellingham to strike a blow for justice and liberty at the very heart of the new administration.

Armed with a pair of pistols thoughtfully supplied by Nathaniel #2 and an ironclad belief in his own cause, Bellingham had been able to accost Perceval in the lobby of the Houses of Parliament and to shoot him cleanly through the heart. He had then resumed his bench seat against the wall and waited calmly for an agitated Member of Parliament to point him out to the Palace of Westminster police.

Once again, Nathaniel #2 was able to return to Exeter and a grateful Guild with no trace of suspicion attaching to him.

Before Nathaniel could read further, he became dimly aware of a firm hand shaking his shoulder.

'Nathaniel? Mr Barton!! Are you OK? Look at me, look at me.'

Chapter 20

Faith was genuinely worried. It had seemed to take Nathaniel an absolute age to emerge from his torpor. Although the grip on the dusty tome in his hands never slackened, it was with irritating slowness that he turned his face up towards hers. Faith was reminded of an elderly pet tortoise being tempted by a limp lettuce leaf when it really wasn't that hungry, but it had still felt obliged to entertain his eight year old owner one more time.

'Mr Barton, I think your medic was right. You really should be at home convalescing.'

'How, how do you know about that? Oh God, Sophie told you. She *did* see me, oh no no no.'

For a shocked moment, Faith thought the older man was about to burst into tears; instead, he firmly closed his book, pinched the brow of his nose and looked up at her with a mute appeal for – what?

She sat down next to him and surprised herself by taking his left hand between hers as she spoke.

Looking straight into his sad eyes, she said: 'I don't know you and you don't know me, but what I *do* know is that there is something crazy going on here. The other thing I know is that – pardon my Canadian French – you look like shit. I am going to suggest that you put that book away now, and let me take you home for some rest.'

Contrary to her expectation, Nathaniel nodded vigorously, looked like he regretted the sudden movement, and then meekly carried The Book back to cabinet M IV. Resisting the temptation to take him by the hand, Faith led the way out of the Institution into the close.

As luck would have it, a taxi had just dropped new guests outside the Royal Clarence. Bundling Nathaniel into the back seat, Faith realised she did not even know

Nathaniel's address. As the cab driver delicately executed a three point turn, Faith was able at a second attempt to extract this key information from her still befuddled companion.

Fifteen minutes later, Faith found herself on the pavement in front of a small terraced house. She cajoled Nathaniel into locating a house key somewhere in his jacket, let them both in through a purple front door, and led her still slightly dazed companion through to a sofa in the front room.

She sought out the kitchen and located the makings of a pot of tea, always the first recourse when trying to revive a Brit, she thought. Taking two mugs back through to where Nathaniel sat, she found him sitting more upright and wiping his face with a rather grubby handkerchief.

'Looking a bit more *compos mentis*, I see,' remarked Faith brightly.

'Sorry, don't know quite what came over me there. So sweet of you to rescue me.'

'No trouble. Do you feel like telling me what's going on here?'

Faith sat on an armchair across the room from Nathaniel while he talked her through the sequence of events that began on that fateful Thursday a mere twelve days before. What had started as a very human account of an eighteenth century Nathaniel Barton had continued with the shocking revelation that his son, another Nathaniel Barton, was an assassin in the pay of a malevolent Guild.

As Nathaniel spoke in a quiet monotone, Faith was beginning to understand more about the Guild than she had ever learnt from her academic research. Clearly there was some unpleasant business here. It may have been three centuries ago, but the benevolent charity of today would hardly want any of this unsavoury history known to the world, even now.

This left Faith in something of a quandary. As a historian, her natural prejudice was to search out the truth and to reveal it, however unpleasant the consequences.

And as a human being, she was beginning to feel a great deal of sympathy for the sad, lonely, tired man in front of her who was now sat in a silent reverie gazing at a spot on the wall above Faith's head.

So how was she going to square the circle? Tell Marcus what Nathaniel had uncovered, only for him to bury the secrets ever deeper? Or say to him that she could discover nothing and lose out on access to those Guild papers that were essential to her doctoral thesis?

When in doubt, she thought, let food provide the answer.

'Nathaniel, did you have breakfast yet?'

He shook his head mutely.

'Right then, let me fix you – us – something for lunch. What have you got in the kitchen?'

Nathaniel shrugged disinterestedly, but refusing to be deterred, Faith went on a mission of exploration. An under-stocked fridge and even emptier cupboards revealed little. But Faith had been brought up in the back room of a Bob's Jerk Shed and Bistro, and she knew how to improvise.

Into a boiling pan of salted water she threw a couple of handfuls of dried penne. While the pasta cooked through, she softened some chopped onion in another pan with olive oil and dried basil. Some tired rashers of bacon were snipped with scissors into small squares and added to the pan along with an egg of indeterminate age and two spoonfuls of yogurt. She had at first turned up her nose at the packet of ground Parmesan, but it would do, and in it went too.

When the pasta was al dente, it was quickly drained and added to the pan. A quick stir, a sprinkle of the parsley that sat morosely on the window sill, a twist of black pepper, et voilà – pasta carbonara for two!

Calling Nathaniel into the kitchen, she spooned the steaming pasta onto large white plates and dug some cutlery out of a drawer. Faith, as ever, wolfed her food down and Nathaniel was now clearly showing signs of coming to, whether as a result of the tasty dish before him or simply because he was feeding off Faith's incessant energy.

When the plates had been cleared, Faith suggested they return to the front room. It was time to talk.

Where earlier Nathaniel had been the one with a story to tell, it was now Faith's turn to bring Nathaniel up to speed. She told him about her reasons for being in Exeter, her doctoral thesis and the embarrassing conversation with Sophie. Nathaniel was expressionless, apart from a wry smile and a comment at the name Duntze.

'Good grief, it was the same family that employed Nathaniel #2 in their bank. Small world.'

Relieved that Nathaniel now seemed to be back in the land of the living, Faith continued.

'So the way I see it is this.

I came to Exeter to carry out some rather dry research into the way the Exeter Guild of Weavers, Fullers and Shearmen were able to survive to the present day. Along with other guilds across the country, they were threatened by Charles II with the loss of their powers and privileges. Luckily, though not for the king, he died while they survived. Not just survived, but prospered.

Now that's an interesting story in itself. And if I had the access I have been promised to the Guild papers of the time, I'm sure I could come up with a nice account of their concerns, their debates, their relief at being spared the axe. But to do that, I'll have to spill the beans to Marcus. I'd have to tell him what you've been uncovering, and from what little I know of the guy, I'm not sure we would like the consequences.'

Nathaniel nodded slowly. 'I'm sure you're right.'

'Frankly, and I know I'm being selfish here, the far bigger story is what you're uncovering. Your story of the two Nathaniel Bartons is going to be far more useful for advancing my career than some dry old minutes of Guild committee meetings.'

Though Faith's reasoning was sound at the time, neither she nor Nathaniel could know how wildly optimistic that conclusion was.

'So, what I shall do,' she concluded, 'is that I shall tell Mr Officer of the Guild Marcus he can spin. I'm not doing his dirty work for him. If you'll have me, I'm going to work with you and your ancestors and let's blow the cover on this sanctimonious Guild and their history.'

She looked across to Nathaniel for assent but saw his eyes drooping and the grey pallor beginning to creep across his face once more.

'Ah, I see the patient is going into another decline. Let's get you somewhere you can lie down and get some rest. Then we can meet up again at the Institution tomorrow?'

Nathaniel rose unsteadily to his feet and nodded a meek assent. He allowed Faith to take his arm, and she led him up the stairs into a large white bedroom at the front of the house.

Two sash windows draped in white muslin looked out on to the street. A photo of a small boy with curly blond hair sat on an otherwise empty mantelpiece above a small Victorian fireplace. She assumed it must be Nathaniel's estranged son.

Not *quite* sure what she was doing alone in a bedroom with a man she hardly knew, Faith motioned Nathaniel to sit on the bed while she removed his shoes and socks. He unbuttoned his shirt absentmindedly, swung his legs on to the bed, and rested his head upon the pillow.

Faith watched him, almost tenderly, as he closed his eyes and his breathing slowed. When she was sure he was dead to the world, she slipped quietly down the stairs and let herself out of the front door.

It was when she was walking back towards the University campus that she remembered the most curious aspect of Nathaniel's book. It was that the pages he had been so avidly reading were, to her eyes at least, totally blank.

'Have I heard right, that poor Simpkins has turned up his toes?'

'Afraid so. I understand Marcus was there at the time.'

'What did he do, exactly?'

'I don't believe he did anything. He was just, well, Marcus.'

A pause for reflection.

'Yes, I can see how that could kill a man.'

'The quack said it was a heart attack. Off colour for a while, apparently.'

'Good innings though. Died in harness, as it were.'

'We're none the wiser, though, are we?'

'Well as Marcus remarked, we still have faith. More port?'

Wednesday 10 April 2013

Chapter 21

When Nathaniel woke at 6am on Wednesday morning after fourteen hours of a deep if troubled sleep, he struggled to remember how it was he found himself lying almost fully clothed on top of his bed. As the events of the previous day came to mind, he experienced a sequence of emotions.

A shiver at the revelations of his morning's stint with The Book; embarrassment at his rescue by a far from distressed damsel; and an unaccustomed feeling of pleasure at having been cared for by another human being for the first time in many years.

While the kettle boiled for tea, he placed the detritus from the previous day's surprisingly delicious meal into the dishwasher and popped a slice of bread into the toaster. As the day was a little on the cool side, he slipped on the jacket he had worn on the previous Friday. By the time he'd locked his purple front door behind him, he was feeling considerably more cheerful and he strode off for his assignation at the Institution with a genuine spring in his step.

When he arrived, he found Faith and her ipad sat next to his usual place at the map table. To his surprise, she stood, bent forward slightly and lightly kissed him on both cheeks.

'Let me just tell you what I've found out so far. First, the three assassinations you tell me Nathaniel #2 was responsible for? Well, they all happened at the times, dates and places you say, and yes, in each case, someone else was fingered for the crime. I've also checked back in the local paper about your Nathaniel #1, and it confirms he died when you say he did.'

Nathaniel didn't mention that he had already checked the newspaper and the published details of the first two assassinations. It was wonderfully reassuring, though, that this new found friend confirmed the reality of what The Book had told him. He had been beginning to doubt his own sanity.

'But there's one thing that is *so* bugging me – and I need your help to sort it out. Can you please be a dear and go get your book.'

With a small smile, Nathaniel retraced his familiar route to the Minor Library to recover The Book. It had been a while since anyone had called him 'dear'.

'Now,' said Faith, 'Open this for me at the beginning.'

Together they read the opening dedication which had first captured Nathaniel's attention. Faith could now see how he had become ensnared, sucked into a narrative which, even as someone who was not a Nathaniel Barton, she found strangely seductive.

As they read the pages together, Nathaniel slowly turned the pages.

'This is great source material,' murmured Faith, 'you can really understand the man's mindset, what was important to him, what the world felt like back then...'

Nathaniel turned the page on Nathaniel #1's last entry, and continued reading.

'Stop!' hissed Faith, then quickly looked around in embarrassment. They were still alone in the lofty room, much to her relief.

'Faith, what's the problem?'

'You're still reading, right?'

'Of course – this is where the story of Nathaniel #2 starts.'

'But there's nothing there...'

'Don't be ridiculous, look for yourself.'

Nathaniel thrust The Book in front of Faith, both of them now looking confused and slightly hurt.

'Nathaniel – *you* might be seeing something, but I'm not. How can I prove it to you?'

Inspired, she picked up her ipad and used its built in camera to snap the blank pages. 'There, see.'

She scrolled rapidly through the camera roll, but her final shot was simply a blaze of light.

'Is it working?' asked Nathaniel.

Faith fired off a couple of shots of the library, and showed him that they displayed perfectly. Trying to photograph The Book again produced the same result; it looked as if someone was shining a bright torch directly into the lens.

'Doesn't prove things one way or the other, does it?' said Nathaniel, 'Hang on a tick, I've just remembered something.'

He reached into his top jacket pocket and pulled out the index card that he'd inadvertently taken away with him the previous week. Silently, they read it together.

'*Common Place Book of Nathaniel Barton Esq.' {fol. 128pp Leather bound (Florence?) No later than 1767? Manuscript, largely blank, ref. M IV 1}.*

'See,' said Faith triumphantly, 'largely blank! Told you.'

Instinctively, Nathaniel slipped the card back in his pocket and, for a brief while, neither of them knew what to say. It was Nathaniel who was the first to break the silence.

'Let me just run this thought by you. It's the only way I can make sense of what we know. I'm a Nathaniel Barton, living in Exeter, as was my father, and his father before him. It's too much of a coincidence to say that the two Nathaniel Bartons of Exeter in The Book are not related. So we have a chain of Nathaniel Bartons over the centuries, connected by blood and history.'

'With you so far,' muttered Faith.

'For no obvious reason, I'm shaken out of my mundane routine and I find myself joining this Institution. I stumble across a book that would hold no significance for anyone else and it tells me my family history, a history that is becoming increasingly unpleasant.'

'And that's where I lose it,' interjected Faith. 'How can you read it but I can't?'

Nathaniel shrugged. 'I don't know, and to be honest that's as far as I can go myself. I couldn't make this sort of stuff up; and I don't *think* I'm losing my mind.

You say the pages are blank, yet to me they are full. So maybe there's some sort of psychic or spiritual connection, though I'm not a religious man as such. I'm not sure I want to speculate any further for now but what I think we *must* do is to get what information we can out of this book while we can.'

'And,' said Faith with an uncharacteristically serious face, 'I think it's time for me to fess up. It's not just a happy coincidence that we met. You know that I'm studying in Exeter and that my interest is in certain historical documents stored in this very library. But to get access to them, I had been, er, asked...'

Faith looked away in embarrassment. Now that she was about to spell out the request made to her by Marcus, she was struck by how sordid her behaviour could seem.

Nathaniel placed a hand on her arm. 'No, go on, I'm intrigued.'

'Well, you must understand that being here, in a prestigious university with a chance to get my hands on some unique historical material, it just means so much to me. It's what I've spent my whole life working towards, and I don't know what I would do if I couldn't complete the work.'

They were interrupted by the arrival of two elderly women in matching cardigans who headed straight for the armchairs in the far corner of the room, pausing only to pick a couple of bound volumes of *Country Life* magazine from the adjacent shelves.

Leaning closer, Faith continued in a conspiratorial whisper.

'The thing is that a very heavy hint was dropped by a most unpleasant man called Marcus that I would not actually get to see the papers I needed unless I carried out a small task for him.'

'Which was?'

'It didn't seem a big deal at the time. I just had to discover what it was that a Mr Nathaniel Barton had found in the Institution and to report back.'

Nathaniel stayed silent for a moment and then asked in a much colder voice, 'So what will you do now that you have seen what Mr Nathaniel Barton has found in the Institution?'

'Don't get huffy. I'm on your side. This book of yours is pure dynamite and I can see why the Guild would want it covered up. But that's exactly why we need to keep this out of the clutches of Mr Marcus and his cronies. Trouble is, as a student member, I'm not allowed to take any books out of the Institution.'

'And I've got to wait until the Committee approves my membership before *I* can borrow anything either. But hang on a tick, I've just thought of something.'

Nathaniel's boyhood reading had not been confined to Swallows and Amazons. He also recalled devouring Edgar Allen Poe's short detective stories. In *The Purloined Letter*, the detective hero, C. Auguste Dupin, was asked to find the eponymous document which contained compromising material and had apparently been hidden in a Parisian apartment. Successive thorough searches by the police had failed to find the document, but Dupin was able to produce it immediately from where it sat – in a letter rack in full view on a mantelpiece.

'Where better to hide a book than in a library?' mused Nathaniel. He patted the top pocket of his jacket. 'As long as I hold on to this index card, Marcus has no way of locating it.'

'I like your thinking, Batman.'

'So I shall put The Book back where it belongs (for now) – top row left, bookcase M.1' Nathaniel slipped into the Minor Library, and then rejoined Faith in the lobby.

'If you don't mind, I'd like to check with Simpkins when my membership will be confirmed. I'm not convinced it's safe to leave The Book here indefinitely.'

The glass panel in the door to Simpkins' office was obscured by a dark green blind, so Nathaniel knocked before entering.

Instead of the cheerful old librarian, he saw behind the desk covered with heaps of papers and index cards the bespectacled female who he had met on his first brief visit to the Institution. Behind her glasses, her eyes were red and she had clearly been crying not long before.

'Ahem,' coughed Nathaniel in an attempt at discretion, 'is Lionel Simpkins around?'

At this innocent enquiry, she gave vent to a high pitched wail and the noise brought Faith into the room. Concerned, she went straight to the woman's side and, employing the arcane skill that Nathaniel had observed in all females of his acquaintance, she produced a handful of paper tissues from thin air.

Between sobs, the occupant of Lionel Simpkins' chair was able to stammer out 'Poor Lionel – he's d...dead. Heart attack yesterday afternoon. An officer of the Guild was with him, but could do nothing. Thanks be to the Lord, it was quick.'

Faith and Nathaniel exchanged glances. Was it coincidence that 'an officer of the Guild' was on hand at the crucial moment? But now was not the time to interrogate a plainly distressed woman. Leaving the tissues in her plump hand, Faith gently disengaged herself, Nathaniel mumbled a few sympathetic words and they left.

Chapter 22

Once outside in the close, Faith had to ask.

'So is this one of your famous coincidences?'

'What do you mean?'

Faith began counting off the points on the fingers of her left hand.

'First, you find your blessed book. Second, the man from the Guild asks me to find out what this book is. Third, a man from the Guild is with Simpkins, asking what? Fourth, Simpkins dies.'

'Well, he did seem to be rather unwell lately.'

'World of difference between being rather unwell and being extremely dead, wouldn't you say? I can see Marcus...'

'If it *was* Marcus...'

'...putting the frighteners on poor old Lionel.'

Faith and Nathaniel walked back in silence to Nathaniel's house. Once inside, Faith thought it was time to take the initiative.

'Right!' she said, 'plan of action required. We need to move this along, and I have a bad feeling about the Institution. What I need you to do is to restock your fridge and larder. I need to go back to my digs and sort out a few things. I'd like to come back round here tomorrow morning, say ten?'

Nathaniel was slightly out of his depth. He was used to picking up a few basics from the corner shop which he supplemented with pub meals and takeaways. Faith sounded as if she wanted to stock up for a siege.

'Good grief, man, do you need a wife!'

Faith carried out a quick review of the kitchen and handed Nathaniel a list.

'Not too complicated for you, I hope; I just have a feeling that this may take us more than a day.'

Without quite knowing why, Faith bent and kissed Nathaniel briefly on the cheek before leaving through the purple front door. She realised she could turn right and head up the street to Hoopern Valley. From here, she could see the University campus in the fitful April sunshine. Though she still had to walk down one side of the valley and then up the other to reach her apartment, she welcomed the opportunity to reflect on what she and Nathaniel had learnt.

Sherlock Homes had once remarked, 'When you have eliminated the impossible, whatever remains, however improbable, must be the truth.'

Faith ran through the salient facts in her head.

1) The Book existed

2) The jottings of a Nathaniel Barton from the end of the eighteenth century could be read by both Faith and Nathaniel

3) Nathaniel alone claimed to be able to read pages that appeared blank to Faith but which related events that could be externally verified (though not with the particular slant given by The Book)

4) The Book could not be photographed, at least by an ipad. In Faith's world, that was all the proof needed that something very strange was going on

'Shoot,' thought Faith, 'This is straight out of Alice in Wonderland or Harry Potter.'

Without entirely conceding the supernatural explanation, Faith had concluded that she and Nathaniel needed to properly test the hypothesis that, for whatever reason, he was able to extract a narrative from The Book that was not accessible to others. A couple of days should do it. Hence the need to get some food in, and also the reason why Faith was going to pick up an overnight bag.

Given what Nathaniel had intimated about the links between the Institution and the Guild, she was unsure that the Major Library was the best place for them to pursue the investigation. That was why she had resolved to smuggle The Book out of the Institution first thing tomorrow. She hadn't told Nathaniel of her plan as she instinctively felt his inherently compliant nature would have led him to raise objections. She believed, however, that confronted with a fait accompli (or a Faith accompli!) he would be able to accept it without complaint.

She arrived back at her university flat, pleased that despite walking briskly she had not broken into a sweat. As she turned the key in her door, she felt a distinct chill. Then opening it, she saw on the mat another black and white postcard of the Institution. On the back was inscribed:

LIBRARY III post meridiem M

The cheek of the man! Why did he think she should be at his beck and call? Still, after this initial angry reaction, she did concede silently to herself that he was indeed perfectly entitled to get a periodic update on the task he had commissioned her to do.

Mind you, he would be getting precious little real information from her. She'd heard enough from Nathaniel to know that, potentially, The Book contained more exciting research material than she could possibly hope to find in the Guild's official papers.

She made a mental note to talk to Duntze later in the week about a change in strategy for her thesis, assuming of course that he was not in the pocket of the Guild. Would have to be a damn large pocket, thought Faith with a smile.

As she pondered on her next steps, she was moving around her apartment, stuffing items into her backpack. Change of underwear and top (she anticipated having to stay over for one night, if not two); her ipad and charger;

a notebook and pencils (ever reliable); a paperback in case she had some time to kill.

Ten to three – time to meet the friendly Marcus.

No sign of him on arrival, so Faith slumped down on one of the colourful beanbags and considered what she might feel able to say.

Before she could properly gather her thoughts, he was there. He had somehow just glided into her field of vision. He gazed down on her and she felt strangely vulnerable.

Marcus raised an eyebrow. Faith gulped.

'Um, nothing to report so far, I'm afraid.' Faith knew that, even to herself, she sounded unconvincing.

In a voice like a spider's web, Marcus slowly enumerated:

'Monday 8 April, Devon & Exeter Institution, Major Library;

Monday 8 April, MC Cafe, briefly;

Tuesday 9 April, Nathaniel Barton's home;

Wednesday 10 April, Major Library, Devon & Exeter Institution.

Need I go on? In all this time you have...'nothing to report'?'

'Well, Mr Barton is being quite elusive...'

'Faith Codrington, I am reluctantly forming a view that it is *you* who is being quite elusive. I am not sure why this is, but I will find out, in time. You disappoint me, and I think you will be disappointing Sir Professor Stephen Duntze MBE.'

Before Faith could reply, Marcus had gone, with the same smooth and silent motion.

When Faith had been just eight years old, she had seen on a gleaming white plate in her mother's kitchen a perfect, shimmering passion fruit cheesecake. She had cautiously tested it with a small pudgy finger, then fashioned a chunk with two hands. She had never tasted anything more delicious.

She had then realised that, possibly, the cheesecake was not actually meant for her. Slowly at first, and then more frantically, she had tried to mould the damaged cake back into a complete circle. But the harder she had tried, the more it resembled one of the sand pies she made with her little bucket on the family's occasional visits to the banks of the St Lawrence.

The door had creaked behind her, and she had sensed, rather than seen, her mother's grim expression. That had been one true humiliation, and that was the feeling she now experienced.

For a brief moment, she felt that she should run after Marcus, to grab his hand, to plead with him, to say sorry, and to tell him what Nathaniel was reading (even if it was in his own head). She wanted to offer herself to Marcus, to abase herself, to do *anything* to avoid his disapproval.

Fortunately, for her and for Nathaniel, the moment had passed, and she was left with a feeling of nausea and inadequacy.

She rose to her feet unsteadily, and headed back towards her accommodation. As she walked, she felt the old resolve flood back into her veins. What malevolent influence Marcus could exercise over her seemed to evaporate once he was no longer around. She was Faith Codrington. Her ancestors had been slaves, but they and their descendants were strong and true. They worked hard, they were honest, and they were kind.

She would do the right thing and she would see this through.

Thursday 11 April 2013

Chapter 23

Clutching her backpack, Faith arrived at the Institution's front door at nine o'clock sharp on Thursday morning. As she bent to press the bell, she saw a small card that had been sellotaped to the inside of the glass panel:

LIBRARY CLOSED FOR RE-INDEXING

Faith recognised the handwriting and, unusually for her, was frozen in indecision. Luckily, at that moment, the door opened and Dolores Nunan burst out. She headed straight past Faith, placed her tweed-clad posterior on the low wall running round the cathedral lawns and pulled a crumpled packet of cigarettes out of her capacious handbag.

Faith caught the unmistakable scent of an unfiltered Gauloise wafting towards her and Dolores, spotting her wrinkled nose, offered a brief apology.

'Awfully sorry, dear. Relic of Paris '68, I'm afraid. '

Faith, who generally thought she was able to sum people up after a first meeting, struggled to reconcile this dowdy tweed-clad figure with that of a sixties radical, and gave up.

'Yes, I know. I don't look like your typical Marxist hippy, do I? Still, *tempora mutantur* and all that.'

'Why is the Institution closed?'

'Ha! No interest in closing for a day in memory of poor old Lionel – he was with me in Paris, by the way – but once the University or the Guild or some other bloody bureaucrat decides it's time to attack the indexing system, then it's sod the members and the volunteers, and put up the shutters *sine die*.'

Unnoticed by Faith, her new friend Alice from Uni had also come out into the close. She produced a cigarette and looked to Dolores for a light.

'Alice, hi, what brings you here?'

'Surprised you're not involved already, Faith. They've rounded up a load of us post grads to digitise the card index. Honestly, you should muck in, it's top dollar for *very* little intellectual effort.'

As it was obviously the only way Faith was going to get in the building in the foreseeable future, she chatted companionably to Alice and Dolores until they'd had their nicotine fix, and then accompanied them back through the wide white door.

In the Major Library, it was a hive of activity. Around the map table, a dozen or so young people sat, each with an ipad or tablet and one or two of the card index drawers. Methodically, they were digitally scanning each card in turn. It looked tedious work, regardless of the hourly rate, and Faith certainly had no intention of applying herself to the task.

With an assumed air of indifference, she wandered through to the unoccupied Minor Library, retrieved The Book from the top shelf, and slipped it into her backpack. Walking back through the Major Library, she remarked in as casual a manner as she could muster, 'Sorry, Alice, not for me. I've got a piece of work to tie up for old Duntze tomorrow.'

Alice, who had the misfortune to share a supervisor with Faith, responded 'No worries. Oh, by the way, your favourite performance poet is on at the Phoenix next Monday. Fancy meeting up in the bar at eight?'

'Sure thing.'

As she found herself back out in the close, Faith realised how absorbed she had become in this book which was even now burning a hole in her backpack. A change of mood after next weekend might be just what she needed. Hopefully, by then it (whatever *it* was) would all be over.

She walked back through the city centre, up the impossibly steep lane beside the forbidding prison wall, and rang Nathaniel's front doorbell. As if he'd been standing in the hall awaiting her arrival, Nathaniel opened the door promptly and with a cheerful smile. Faith had no choice but to smile back, and when she found a jug of freshly brewed coffee and a plate of tempting white chocolate chip cookies, she subsided into a chair at Nathaniel's dining table with unfeigned pleasure.

'I bought all the things on your list,' Nathaniel said with some pride, 'and a few other bits I thought we might like.'

Faith rather liked the 'we', and it was clear Nathaniel was positively blooming in this new quasi-domestic situation.

'Ta-dah!' Faith produced The Book with a flourish.

Immediately the mood of relaxed cheerfulness evaporated.

'My God, Faith! Where did you get that?'

'Well, you don't need Hercule Poirot's little grey cells to work *that* one out. What's really interesting is that the Institution appears to be under some sort of lockdown while the index system is being furiously scanned by a troupe of overpaid post grad students.'

'You know why that is, don't you?'

Faith, who had spent the walk up to Nathaniel's house idly trying to imagine Lionel Simpkins and Dolores Nunan as a couple of sixties revolutionaries, looked back at him blankly.

'Once everything's in a computer readable database, they'll be able to pull out anything that mentions me or the Guild or ...'

'Hang on, Nathaniel – I thought you still had the index card?'

Nathaniel's first reaction was one of relief, but then a look of horror spread across his face.

'What's up now?'

'I know what you're saying but, Faith, when you took The Book off the shelf – did you put a pink slip in its place?'

'What pink slip? What do you mean?'

Nathaniel explained: 'It's a form they use to show that a member has legitimately taken a book. Now there's just a gap on a shelf that shows that someone has taken a book they shouldn't.'

Faith put her hand to her mouth.

'So how long before they work out what's gone and that we've got it – and before they come after it?'

Nathaniel looked thoughtful.

'My brother David was, shall we say, on the grey side of the law when it came to some of his accounting practices. He was eventually exposed, but he'd held the wolves at bay for years by keeping a double set of books. One was for the auditors and one for himself. We might do something along the same lines. Just give me ten minutes.'

Faith concentrated on her coffee and cookies. She rather liked this new, more purposeful Nathaniel. Yes, he still looked a little as if he'd been dragged through the proverbial hedge backwards and it would improve his appearance if he learned how to tuck a shirt in *all* the way around his trousers. But he was certainly showing more spark than that bumbling little idiot that had a habit of bumping into her. Five minutes on his laptop were followed by a couple of brief incisive phone calls.

'Right,' said Nathaniel, 'what had you planned for this weekend?'

When Faith looked back blankly, Nathaniel continued: 'Well, you'll need to refresh that backpack by Friday afternoon. We're off to Salisbury.'

Despite Faith's enquiring left eyebrow, Nathaniel indicated that before then they should be getting back to the matter in hand, namely reading the next pages in The Book. Faith powered up her ipad to take notes and

Nathaniel opened up at what was, to Faith's eyes, yet another blank page.

'OK,' said Faith, 'I'll need you to tell me what you're reading because I promise you I can't see a blessed thing. And I just need the salient points. My typing is not that fast.'

Nathaniel was now reading the history of Nathaniel Barton #3, born within the first year of Nathaniel #2's marriage to Elizabeth Jeffery. Following a pattern that was becoming familiar, this Nathaniel too was apprenticed to the Exeter Bank and his education was delivered through the Guild.

The purpose of this coaching became clear in September 1830 when Nathaniel #3 was dispatched to execute a coup which would both end the career of a notable Member of Parliament, William Huskisson, and deliver a blow to the reputation of the then Prime Minister, the Duke of Wellington. Huskisson's death is best remembered as the first in the world resulting from a railway accident but what fewer people know is the detail of what actually happened.

While their train was halted at a station, Huskisson walked along the track to shake hands with the Duke, a political opponent with whom he sought to be reconciled. He was struck by a train on the adjacent line and he died later the same day in hospital. The Duke's government fell shortly thereafter, and the Guild's diverse financial interests were once again protected.

What was not recorded by history, but what was spelt out in chilling detail by The Book, was that it was one Nathaniel Barton who accompanied the MP on his final journey, who suggested the informal meeting with the Iron Duke, and who escorted him down the dangerous and ultimately fatal track.

The same Nathaniel Barton – Nathaniel #3 – escaped both injury and recognition. He later travelled back to Exeter by stagecoach to the acclaim of the Guild.

Nathaniel #3 had a further important commission to carry out, though whether this was for reasons of policy or for personal revenge was not clear. John (formerly Johann) Baring of Bremen had become apprenticed to a Guild member in 1717, prospered and then settled permanently in Exeter as one of its wealthier residents. A son, Francis, became a trader and financier in London, and Barings was soon one of the capital's leading merchant banks.

However, they were soon overtaken by the more aggressive and expansionist N.M. Rothschild & Sons which almost brought Barings to its knees in the early nineteenth century. The Guild's response was to dispatch Nathaniel #3 to the wedding in Frankfurt of Nathan Meyer Rothschild's eldest son. The Book did not go into details, but it was no coincidence that the older Rothschild was reported as dying speedily of a 'stomach abscess' before the celebrations were concluded. And yet again, a Nathaniel Barton was able to melt away with no evidence to link him to a capital crime.

Faith was conscious that, once again, Nathaniel seemed to be slipping into something resembling a catatonic state. She closed down her ipad, took hold of Nathaniel's wrists, and slowly but firmly prised his grip from The Book.

It took him a good few minutes, a glass of water and a reassuring hug from Faith for him to recover his good spirits.

'There's a bit of a pattern here,' he said ruefully. 'I'm really beginning to dislike being a Nathaniel Barton. One bad apple after another.'

'Don't be silly,' said Faith with a smile. 'These guys are dead and gone. You can't really be sure that they're related to you, can you? Anyhow, the Nathaniel Barton of Exeter 2013 is no scheming assassin, is he?'

Nathaniel had to reluctantly agree, and the two of them lunched simply on soup and rolls.

Without any great enthusiasm, but knowing this was a job that had to be done, they returned to The Book for a longer afternoon session that covered the lives of Nathaniel #4 (1823 -1881) and Nathaniel #5 (1848 - 1908).

The tale of Nathaniel #4 began with a rare failure. As Nathaniel read on, he realised what a partial view he had had of the reign of Queen Victoria, a view shared, it has to be said, by the majority of his contemporaries. From the perspective of the early twenty-first century, Victoria tends to be preserved in aspic as a serene mother of her people, dressed in a widow's black and appreciated by all. What has been forgotten is the number of individual attempts to assassinate the young queen while Albert was alive, followed by the widespread public hostility when she retreated into widowhood and appeared to utterly abandon her people for almost a decade.

It appeared that the Guild at that time sided with public sentiment and may indeed have been behind more than one of the many plots to kill Victoria. None of these seem to have involved a Barton. What The Book did actually document was the attempt to assassinate the young son of Victoria, Prince Alfred, Duke of Edinburgh and second in line to the throne. He had been taking a tour of the Empire, working to strengthen the bonds with the old country and to boost the popularity of the monarchy. While attending an event on a Sydney beach, Alfred was shot in the back by Henry James O'Farrell who had recently been discharged from a mental hospital. Nathaniel #4 had engaged the poor man's sympathies by claiming he could, by this act of valour, gain membership of the Fenian Brotherhood, an Irish Republican movement that O'Farrell had long admired. The would-be assassin was secured by an angry crowd, arrested, tried and hanged. Alfred recovered speedily and completed his tour to much acclaim while Nathaniel #4 quietly returned to Europe.

Nathaniel #4 did however go on to claim a spectacular victim in the form of Czar Alexander II. Ingratiating himself with the revolutionary group 'Narodnaya Volya' (The People's Will), Nathaniel #4 had adopted the proven tactic of encouraging others to take the lead. However, he made the mistake of being on hand to witness for himself the assassination on 13 March 1881. The first bomb missed its target, and the Czar went to inspect the damage. Nathaniel was swept along in the crowd of onlookers who foolishly trailed in his wake. When the second bomb was thrown, the explosion fatally wounded not only the Czar and the young revolutionary who had hurled it but also Nathaniel himself. He would not be the last Nathaniel Barton to die alongside his victim.

Nathaniel #5 continued what was now a family tradition. Through the second half of the nineteenth century, he was much assisted by the explosive growth of anarchist movements across Europe, and most notably in the Italian peninsula.

In quick succession, the Guild's scheming secured the murders of the French President (1894), the Spanish Prime Minister (1897), and Empress Elizabeth of Austria (1898) – all attributed to 'Italian anarchists' but all stage managed by one Nathaniel Barton.

For the assassination of the Italian King Umberto in 1900, Nathaniel #5 had plotted with an émigré weaver in the United States, Gaetano Bresci. With a shearman's attention to removing loose threads, he also arranged for Bresci himself to be killed while in jail. By the standards of the Guild, it appeared that this Nathaniel was the most successful of the Bartons so far.

Faith had to prompt the tiring Nathaniel from time to time to speak up so that she could continue to log the details of the apparently blank pages he was reading to her. He was visibly wearying. So that once he had reached the wedding of Nathaniel #6, one year after his father's death, Faith judged it was time to call a halt.

'Nathaniel, my dear, you look utterly drained. Why don't you go and have a shower, change into something a bit more relaxing and I'll fix us some supper?'

'No, I can't, I really can't, not part way through one of the lives.'

Nathaniel had just read through Nathaniel #6's role in the assassination of the US President McKinley. The services of an unpronounceable Polish-American anarchist had been procured by Nathaniel #6 with the usual mix of deceit and gold. And after one failed attempt in September 1901, Leon Czolgosz hit his target on the following day. The President who had done so much to thwart the Guild's business activities by his hard line protectionism took eight long days to die.

So Nathaniel, clearly tiring now and starting to slur his words, continued to read out loud the last few sentences on the page.

'Jean Jaures is not well known this side of the Channel, but M tells me he is an influential socialist and anti-militarist. If he has his way, France will negotiate with Germany to avoid any armed conflict. If need be, radical trade unionists in both countries will sabotage the war that we expect to break out in the next few years. M and the rest of the Guild know what profits can be secured for the wise investor when countries are at war.'

Faith looked up from her ipad.

'My god – could this Jaures fellow have stopped World War I?'

Nathaniel appeared not to hear her. Gripped by The Book just as fiercely as his hands gripped its cover, he read on. A week before Jaures was due to attend an international conference aimed at securing peace, a rabidly nationalist student shot him twice in the head. A week later, war broke out. Europe never fully recovered from its after effects, but the Guild's balance sheet had never looked better.

Only when Nathaniel #6 had passed away peacefully in his own bed could Nathaniel be persuaded to gently place The Book on his dining room table. He nodded silently and rose stiffly from his chair. Faith carefully closed The Book, and moved to the kitchen as he shuffled up the stairs. The man was plainly exhausted.

Faith walked pensively into the kitchen and turned on the oven. She took a pack of chicken pieces out of the fridge, tossed them in oil and then rubbed them with a mix of spices before placing them on a foil covered metal tray. She wiped her hands and popped the tray in the oven.

She chopped some onions, garlic, celery and peppers and gently softened them before adding a tin of chopped tomatoes and a generous handful of fresh coriander. She checked the condition of the chicken, and then opened a bottle of Picpoul de Pinet which had been chilling for the past few hours.

After coarsely chopping some dates and spring onion tops, she put a couple of handfuls of cous cous into a stainless steel bowl, turned on the kettle and poured the wine into two large glasses that she had thoughtfully placed in the freezer fifteen minutes earlier.

Reckoning that Nathaniel would by now be washed and reasonably decent, she took the wine upstairs.

Friday 12 April 2013

Chapter 24

The following morning, Nathaniel was propped up on pillows in the middle of his bed, staring at the ceiling. He could sense another person in the room but hardly dared turn his head in case he was only imagining things. His mind appeared to have been playing too many tricks lately for him to be *absolutely* certain of anything.

What he *thought* he remembered was that after what had been a painfully hard slog through The Book, Faith had ordered him upstairs for a shower. He had executed that simple task, but hadn't got as far as properly drying himself. He had clambered absentmindedly onto the bed, a towel loosely around his rather too corpulent waist, when Faith came in the room with two glasses of chilled white wine.

Seeing at once her momentary embarrassment, Nathaniel said 'No, no – please don't go.' He patted the bed by his side. To his surprise, she smiled, sat down, and handed him a glass. They clinked rims, simultaneously said 'cheers', laughed and took their first sip of wine.

Then Faith put her glass carefully on the floor, placed a hand gently on either side of Nathaniel's startled face, and kissed him. A slow lingering kiss that lengthened and developed into something more. Without quite understanding how, Nathaniel had carefully placed his own glass on the bedside table, lost his towel, and found himself inexpertly fondling a Faith who was now down to her underwear.

A sudden cry of 'Fuck!' was followed by Faith leaping off the bed and disappearing through the bedroom door. Nathaniel, who by this time had managed to work out that that was exactly what they were going to do, felt rather deflated, both metaphorically and literally.

He had been relieved but not restored when Faith returned, minus her underwear, to reassure him that she had adjusted the oven setting for the chicken and that they would be able to eat later.

Later, much later, they did indeed eat. Nathaniel was propped up against the bed head, Faith sat cross-legged at his side and they finger picked from a large bowl of steaming couscous and spicy chicken. It was impossible to think of a tastier or more special meal. By the time they had emptied the bottle of Picpoul, licked each other's fingers and carefully put the bowl and glasses to one side, it had occurred to Nathaniel that he might be up to a second bout. As indeed he was.

With the morning sun now streaming through the white muslin decked windows, he finally had the courage to turn to face Faith. She was staring quietly at something that Nathaniel couldn't see. With impeccable timing, they both began to speak at the same time.

'Sorry, I didn't...'

'Sorry, I don't normally...'

Faith persevered. 'This is how I see history. It's not what happened – it's how we interpret it, what we do with our understanding. How does our behaviour change, how do *we* change? You know how politicians edit history to present the electorate with their particular view of what we should do next; it's the same with us. It's not about what we did, it's about what we are, and where we go from here.'

'Bit pretentious for first thing in the morning, don't you think?'

Faith's eyes blazed and she made as if to hit him; but then they both laughed, and kissed, briefly.

All business now, Faith stood up, stretched in front of the window and then turned back to Nathaniel.

'Right, Mr Barton. Let me shower first, and then I'll fix us both breakfast. Then we need to crack on. By my reckoning, the next Nathaniel Barton you will read about will be number seven. I don't suppose this is getting any easier for you.'

As Faith's pert bottom disappeared round the door, Nathaniel felt he had to agree. So far, the procession of Nathaniel Bartons – rather like the procession of kings in the fourth act of the Scottish play – was somehow unreal. They were just characters, literally, in a book. But with Nathaniel #6, they had moved into the twentieth century and, in all probability, the next *assassin du jour*, Nathaniel #7, would be his own grandfather.

Grandpa Barton was a flesh and blood figure he had known personally and come to love dearly before his unexpected death abroad. It was Grandpa Barton who had taught him to swim, who had taken him fishing for tiddlers in the tributaries of the Exe, who had shown him how to fly a kite on Haldon Hill during those long hot endless summers that only exist in the imaginations of sad middle-aged men. In many ways, he had been more of a father to Nathaniel than the rumbustious wheeler and dealer known as Johnny.

Now this hero of his childhood was to be transformed into Nathaniel #7. Would he be a quiet fixer and behind-the-scenes schemer like his predecessors? Or would he have more blood on his hands? Given what Nathaniel knew of his grandfather – his frequent mysterious trips abroad and his mercurial temperament – he rather feared the latter.

So it was with a heavy heart that he showered, dressed and proceeded downstairs in response to Faith's cheery cry of 'Breakfast!'

Chapter 25

Marcus was becoming irritable. This was not a pleasant experience for him. Patience was his strength, his forte, the rock on which he had built a life that seemed to him to be endless. Ye gods, he had spent most of his damned life waiting.

In his considerable experience, any problem could – would – be solved, given enough application and time. But well into the second day of his thorough assault on the Institution's indexing system, he still had nothing to show for it. A couple of references to innocuous Guild papers already open to the public, nothing to raise concern. No link to any of the long line of Nathaniel Bartons. So what had today's Nathaniel Barton been looking at?

The group of university students that started work yesterday had more than doubled in size when word had got round about the more than generous rates of pay being offered for what was little more than routine clerical work. Marcus noted that Faith Codrington was not one of their number, and wondered where she might be. Her lack of information (or indeed, cooperation) was beginning to perturb him.

Unable to stand still and watch the effort being expended to no apparent purpose, Marcus began to pace up and down. Then he stopped dead in his tracks. The obvious conclusion had just struck him. He could not see Faith Codrington in the room because she wasn't there. He could not find the index card he was looking for because it wasn't there. Nathaniel must have taken it with him. So if the index card, why not the book itself?

Marcus stared wildly around him. Here and there on the shelves of the Major Library there were occasional gaps where books had clearly once stood. In every such gap, a little pink slip fluttered. Marcus took the one nearest him and saw it contained, in an educated hand, a book title along with a name, address, and contact telephone number.

He turned towards the busy students ranged around the big map table. Slapping his hand firmly down on the leather covered surface, he said, simply and calmly, 'Stop!' His voice was at a normal conversational level but something in the way he spoke caused all the others in the room to immediately stop what they were doing and look towards him.

Quietly, caressingly, compellingly, Marcus continued in the same tone: 'Change of plan. Put the index drawers back and bring me all the pink slips you can find in both libraries. Now!'

No obvious urgency, no pleases, but the students leapt to it. Fortunately, there were not very great numbers of members borrowing books, and within minutes, Marcus had on the table before him between twenty and thirty pink slips which he was able to quickly scan.

Again, nothing. Marcus wrinkled his nose. What was he missing? From his recent keen observations of Nathaniel Barton, Marcus had assessed him as being extremely, if not obsessively, compliant. He was surely the last person in the world to take a book from the Institution without following the correct procedure. There was one roll of the dice left.

The students were now standing round in small groups, conversing in low murmurs and unsure as to what to do next. Marcus asked a question. On the answer to that question, the success of his enterprise wholly depended.

'Thank you for your efforts, yesterday and today. Something has occurred...but no matter. You may all leave now but rest assured, you will be paid for two full days. Before you go, I have one question: did any of you, when retrieving those pink slips, see a gap on a shelf with *no* slip in it?'

As heads shook in silent denial, Marcus felt bile rise in his throat. Then one of the group spoke up. 'Yes, in the Minor Library. I remember because it was a shelf out of my reach and I thought the paper must have somehow got out of my sight. I got the library steps to check, but there was nothing there. Let me show you.'

She moved to take Marcus' arm, thought better of it, and then led him proudly through to point out her discovery, or rather her non-discovery. Marcus noted the case number and impatiently shepherded the students out of the Major Library, through the lobby and out into the close. He then turned smartly back and went into the librarian's office.

A startled Dolores Nunan, sitting uncomfortably at Lionel Simpkins' old desk, looked up from a well thumbed copy of Tariq Ali's *1968 and After: Inside the Revolution.* When *was* this blasted man going to get out of her Institution, her life? Seeing the expression on Marcus' face, she thought better of actually voicing the sentiment, but asked sweetly 'Job done? Can we re-open now?'

Marcus elbowed his way past the not inconsiderable form of the Acting Librarian and stood in front of the high bookcases that covered the entire rear wall of the office. These contained the Acquisitions Books, listing in chronological order every book, journal, newspaper or other item acquired by the Institution since its foundation in 1813. No use whatsoever to Marcus if he did not know the year in which Nathaniel's book – whatever it was – had arrived.

'If you're looking for the Acquisitions Index, it's over there,' volunteered Dolores. Wiping her eyes with the back of her hand, she continued 'Lionel had made it his life's work. He realised that members might need to know more about the origin of a book than...'

Marcus had already barged past her again and tuned out the rest of her reminiscences. Finding the volume for Section M, Bookcase IV, he began to leaf avidly through pages covered in Simpkins' distinctive spidery handwriting. And there it was. This *had* to be the subject of Nathaniel Barton's keen interest, an interest so keen that he was acting wholly out of character even at the risk of losing his job.

'Commonplace Book of Nathaniel Barton Esq. Donated by Geoffrey Kennaway, June 1968.'

With no word of thanks to the hapless Dolores, Marcus walked out of the office and on into the close. He always preferred action to talk and now was the time for his team to act. As he marched across the uneven cobbles, he could feel the shield across his shoulders and his right hand on the hilt of his still sheathed sword.

This afternoon Mr Nathaniel Barton would be receiving a visit; then he would understand the consequences of crossing the Guild.

Chapter 26

Breakfast eaten and cleared away, the reading of The Book on that Friday morning was particularly taxing. In quieter moments on Thursday night, Nathaniel had spoken to Faith of the affection and regard he had had for the memory of his grandfather; there was every prospect that this morning's session would yield secrets he had no desire to hear. And that was how it had transpired.

Any illusions Nathaniel might have had about his grandfather were cruelly dispelled. The amiable white-haired old cove who after every visit had slipped him a florin (and later, for the last couple of years, 50p) put Nathaniel #2 in the shade when it came to murder. Nathaniel #7's legitimate business interests in Central America had provided a more than adequate cover for the 'removal' of the Bolshevik Leon Trotsky (though a drunken Ramon Mercader found himself fingered for that).

Back in Europe, in 1943, it was Nathaniel's beloved grandfather who had engineered the crash off the Spanish coast of the plane carrying the Polish war leader, General Wladyslaw Sikorski. While conspiracy theorists still speculated on the motives for eliminating the general just at the time when a blueprint for the post war future of Poland was being negotiated, no one appreciated that – as The Book told the story – the Guild's *real* target was the General's travelling companion, the Conservative MP, Colonel Victor Cazalet. A rising star in the Conservative party and guaranteed a leading role in a future government, he was clearly someone the Guild did not want to exercise any further influence.

In 1961, things were different. This time it *was* the star passenger who was the key target – Dag Hammarskjold, the Secretary General of the UN.

By now, Nathaniel was almost immune to the cavalcade of revelations; but the intricately planned assassination of John F Kennedy brought him up short. Despite himself, he had to concede the truth: 'Good heavens, Grandpa was bloody good at this!'

Faith just looked up from her ipad in bewilderment and shook her head slowly.

The death of the radical writer, Pablo Neruda, in a Chilean hospital provided a sad and fitting coda to Nathaniel #7's murderous career. Minutes after disabling the old poet's life support system, Nathaniel's grandfather himself had collapsed with a stroke in the hospital corridor and died two days later.

Nathaniel remembered that bleak September afternoon when he had been summoned from school to Exeter Airport. There, his grandfather's coffin had been gently lifted down from a private jet (whose he never knew) to be taken back to the family home in St Leonard's. It was the only time he had seen his father cry when sober.

Once again, Nathaniel found himself drained. Somehow the effort of reading those bafflingly blank pages seemed to suck the energy out of him. He put down The Book, and waited patiently while Faith made him a cup of tea.

To Nathaniel, the Guild seemed strangely indiscriminate in its actions. Sometimes the figures they 'removed' were of the left, sometimes of the right; sometimes they had no obvious political leanings at all.

As a historian, the deaths that most resonated with Faith were the high profile ones, the ones everyone had heard of but for which the official stories wildly diverged from the accounts in The Book.

For Nathaniel, over the decades of killings, it was the brief references to murders of the unknowns that touched him the deepest.

The motorbike accident that killed the Austrian customs official; the apparent heart attack of a

Malaysian bank clerk; the unexplained illness of the radiologist that led to a prominent US Senator receiving the wrong dose. Every one a death that rippled outwards, with beneficial consequences for the interests of the Guild but causing irreparable damage to innocent families.

Faith remembered that they needed to leave Exeter by one o'clock if they were to make Salisbury in good time. She had ladled a couple of extra spoonfuls of sugar into Nathaniel's tea in the hope that this would speed his recovery from what was clearly a stressful experience.

It seemed to do the trick. Within minutes of closing The Book, Nathaniel looked up into Faith's expectant face and smiled.

'Let's go.'

Chapter 27

'You did what?' shrieked Faith, making Nathaniel swerve briefly on to the hard shoulder of the A30 to Honiton.

'Well, naturally, when I first conceived the plan for us to go to Salisbury, I booked us separate rooms at the hotel. But after last night, I thought...'

Conscious of the five foot eleven of seething indignation on his left, Nathaniel couldn't persist with what even he could see was a fairly flimsy defence.

'First up,' said Faith through gritted teeth, 'Thursday night was Thursday night, not a commitment to a life of undying love. And second, the Honeymoon Suite? What sort of a sick joke is that?'

Nathaniel was about to explain that it was the only vacant room left at such short notice, but he could not deny she had right on her side, so remained mute. Faith, who had been brought up to believe that however right a woman is (and she almost invariably is) she should never kick a man who is down more than twice, did likewise.

In this state of mutually assured silence, the miles passed. Both the driver and the passenger in Nathaniel's rather elderly VW Golf were able to reflect on the events of Thursday night and Friday morning.

Faith reflected on her impromptu seduction of a man twice her age, a first for her in many ways. Though a devout Christian, Faith's mother had always been remarkably liberal about sexual matters. For objective evidence of this, Faith had to look no further than the implausibly short time between the wedding date of Bob and Celeste Codrington and the birth of their first and only child. For Celeste and for Faith too, sex was a natural part of life and a matter of celebration. Mr Right, love and marriage would come in due course, but meanwhile...

Still, the heavy petting of South Huron District High, a spontaneous loss of virginity in Toronto, the occasional liaison in New York, and some – in retrospect – scary adventures in Jamaica had not prepared her for Nathaniel. He was, frankly, dull and in no sense an obvious object of sexual desire (though he had shown her something with a mouthful of white wine and an ice cube that might bear repetition). But he was sweet and a little bit lovely, and he was certainly mixed up in something very peculiar. He had brought out a mothering instinct in Faith, though not one that Doctor Spock would have recognised.

For his part, Nathaniel had also been musing about the events of Thursday night, though from a very different perspective. Since the rather abrupt end to his marriage in 1992, Nathaniel's sex life had been largely moribund. In Exeter, he had lost himself in work; when on holiday, he had mastered the art of locating single women of a certain age who subscribed to the view that whatever happened in Vienna (or Paris, or Istanbul, or wherever) would stay there. But even these one or occasionally two or three night stands lost their allure over time, and Nathaniel had long since resigned himself to a life of celibacy.

Thursday night had been a revelation. Though it was Faith who had initiated, inspired, cajoled and led him through a heated and sometimes passionate night, he was confident he had played his part well, and had astounded himself at his own stamina, inventiveness and, yes, rediscovered sense of fun. He'd felt almost like a cheeky schoolboy when he'd changed the reservation at the Rose and Crown to a double room. Now, of course, he bitterly regretted it.

Nathaniel was the first to seek an end to the period of armed neutrality. He glanced across at Faith and saw a smile on her lips. Fortified by this, he tried again to mollify her.

'The Honeymoon Suite – well, I'm pretty certain it's exactly that – a suite. I'm sure you can have the bedroom, and I can bunk down on a sofa somewhere.'

'Hush,' said Faith who at this stage wasn't *quite* sure what tonight's sleeping arrangements would be. She wanted to change the subject, but was unwilling to review what they had learnt of Nathaniel's grandfather while he was negotiating the tricky bit of road passing Stonehenge.

'Tell me about this bookbinder, then,' said Faith brightly. 'Who is this Daniel Klein, and why not use someone nearer home?'

Faith had found the way to raise Nathaniel's spirits. He had been so pleased to have come up with what he called his 'cunning plan'. Both he and Faith had been upset at first by her error in stealing The Book without leaving a deliberately misleading pink slip behind. Whatever the vagaries of the Institution's indexing systems, they had agreed it was only a matter of time before the theft was discovered and suspicion fell on Nathaniel, if only because of the coincidence of the name.

Nathaniel, who on a daily basis was becoming both more ingenious and more spontaneous, had conceived the idea of having a duplicate copy of The Book made. Although he could read The Book and Faith couldn't, there was no evidence that other people might not share Nathaniel's preternatural ability. Even if this wasn't the case, the Guild would doubtless seek to recover it. And although the full circumstances of Lionel Simpkins' sudden death were far from clear, there was a distinct possibility that trying to hold on to The Book could prove fatal.

'It was a few years ago now, CK – my boss, Charles Kennaway – commissioned a slim volume to mark the practice's bicentennial.'

Nathaniel remembered it well. It was a rather self-congratulatory work with copious references to the Kennaway family and their relations and no mention of the poor souls whose lowly paid toil had actually made their fortunes for them.

He shook his head and continued,'...and of course it had to be the finest binding and ornamentation. I have to say that, although it was impossible to read the contents without throwing up, the craftsmanship of the book was second to none. Reuben Klein was the man then, and it's his son, Daniel, who runs the business now. Well, he said on the phone he's semi-retired, but he was intrigued by the commission. Anyway, I'd trawled the net for bookbinders nearer Exeter, and frankly there weren't any that seemed to come up to scratch.'

'If he's such a craftsman, how can he reproduce The Book over a couple of days?'

'He won't have to. Do you really think anyone has looked at The Book since it went on the Institution shelves? All we need is something that *looks* as if it's old Nathaniel's commonplace book.'

Faith nodded. She felt it was now time to be looking forward rather than to the past.

'And the place we're staying at this weekend?'

'The Rose and Crown? Thirteenth century coaching inn with, I hope, twenty first century plumbing. Fine view of Salisbury Cathedral across the water meadows, apparently, and only ten minutes walk from Klein's place. And if we weren't already in a world of more coincidences than you can shake a stick at, guess what? We have to walk up an Exeter Street to get there!'

Unsure quite what to make of this, Faith smiled sweetly and the pair lapsed into a more companionable silence for the remainder of their journey.

Chapter 28

At almost exactly the same time as Nathaniel and Faith were checking into the Rose and Crown Hotel in Salisbury, a white van bearing the logo and contact details of Sovereign Removals pulled up outside Nathaniel's little terraced house in Exeter.

The passenger on the front seat of the van got out and, using a bunch of keys attached to his belt, opened Nathaniel's front door on the second attempt and stepped inside. The driver went round to the back of the van and opened the double doors. Two other men, each with a large black holdall, stepped out, and the three of them went in through the front door. This was firmly closed, and at the same time the blind on the front window was drawn. The whole procedure had taken less than ninety seconds and had been totally unobserved.

Meanwhile, Faith was standing at the large double windows of the Honeymoon Suite gazing at a perfect facsimile of a Turner oil. Across the lush green water meadows there gleamed the impossibly thin and tall spire of Salisbury Cathedral.

Where Exeter's Cathedral was magnificent, Salisbury's was ethereal. Where Exeter had the bulk and build of a college athlete, Salisbury was Nijinsky and Nureyev. Exeter was built to impress the populace with the power of the church and God's representatives on earth; Salisbury simply pointed heavenwards.

When they had arrived at the Rose and Crown – clearly a building of some antiquity but surrounded by a small assembly of Victorian terraces and Edwardian villas – Faith had initially been disappointed. But now they were there, Faith realised that, in the words of her dearly loved father, she was like a pig in muck.

'I'm such a slut,' she thought. 'I'd go to bed with people a lot worse than Nathaniel Barton for a view like this.'

And the suite did indeed live up to its name. A small but comfortable sitting room with a view of the water meadows linked to a second generously sized room with a large open fireplace and a magnificently dressed half tester bed. Opening off the bedroom was a beautifully tiled bathroom with antique bath, well proportioned power shower and a wide range of perfumes and unguents.

Nathaniel, feeling a little hangdog and rather damp from the effort at bringing their cases up two flights of stairs, was astounded and then gratified when Faith turned from the bedroom window, gave him a huge hug, and kissed him on top of the head.

'No promises,' she said, 'but for now, you are officially forgiven.'

Although tempted to put that to the test immediately, Nathaniel was conscious of the time.

'Right – ten minutes to freshen up, I think, then we need to go and see Mr Klein.'

One minute was taken by Nathaniel randomly smoothing his hair with his hands; the other nine were taken by Faith who – with a series of deft movements and the aid of innumerable devices and materials removed from and then replaced in her handbag in quick succession – transformed the slightly crumpled traveller into an exemplar of elegance recently risen from a fragrant couch in her boudoir.

Hand in shy hand, the couple turned left out of the hotel and crossed the river over a narrow mediaeval bridge. All too soon, they found themselves on a busy roundabout, but soon they were once again in a quiet side street. On their left was the high blank wall of the Cathedral Close; on the right, a motley assemblage of shops and private houses. They followed Exeter Street for a little while (Faith had to concede that this was indeed a coincidence) and turned left through an ancient archway into North Walk, which formed one boundary of the Cathedral Close.

The ancient buildings around the close were less densely packed than their counterparts in Exeter and the charming scene was lit by a sun that had only just begun to contemplate setting. Whatever the dark tales they had uncovered in Exeter, this could not have looked less like a location for a murder.

If Nathaniel or Faith had known what horror the next few days would bring, they might have abandoned their mission then and there.

Still, as has often been remarked, the greatest gift humanity possesses is a total inability to know, to *absolutely* know, what will happen in the future. So Nathaniel and Faith, still holding hands like a courting couple, excitedly pointed at this ivy-clad building or that charming fruit blossom, chatting away merrily until they arrived outside the premises of R E Klein & Son, Bookbinders.

First impressions were not good. The building itself had certainly seen better days. Mortar was crumbling between the good Georgian bricks. The paintwork on the door and windows was cracked and peeling and, through a small window on the ground floor, they could dimly discern a poorly lit display of a couple of matching volumes of Dickens against a backdrop of dusty green baize.

Beside the door hung a long old fashioned bell pull. Nathaniel gave it a half hearted tug, and it came off in his hand. At the same moment, a small first floor window flew open and a voice cried down.

'Saw you perambulating up the road like a couple of turtle doves. Expecting you. Door's open. Come straight up.'

Nathaniel carefully laid the bell pull on the step as Faith pushed open the door and led the way upstairs.

The interior was very like the exterior. It had obviously been a fine place in better days, but it seemed that little or no money had been spent on upkeep in the past thirty years. The contrast with the room at the top of the stairs could not have been greater.

The dividing walls of the original house had all been removed to provide a single large room, with walls, floor and ceiling painted in a matt white. Along the rear of the room ran a long workbench with vices, clamps, racks for small tools, and a large magnifying glass mounted on a stand. Set in the ceiling above were a pair of large skylights. A large wicker basket in a corner held what looked like a selection of animal hides. On the walls at intervals were small shelves or brackets, each holding a small volume, some open to display the beautiful illustrations and script, others closed to show off the fine craftsmanship of the binding.

From his position at the window overlooking the close, someone who could be none other than Daniel Klein bounded across the room to greet them. He was both short and round. It seemed to Faith that he would have been as tall lying down as he was standing up. Flowing black curls framed a cheerful open face. The many creases and lines that ran across it seemed testament to a life of smiles rather than one of sorrow. Tufts of dark hair with aspirations to become a beard adorned his chin. He clasped Nathaniel's right hand in a firm grip.

'Welcome, welcome from the last of the House of Klein. Mr Barton, I presume?'

'Indeed, Mr Klein. What a fine room!'

'It is my world, Mr Barton, my world. And who, may I ask, is the *schwartze shikse*?

Assuming he must mean Faith, Nathaniel replied 'Faith Codrington, a f-friend. She is a history postgraduate and she has an interest in the volume I have for you.'

Shaking her hand vigorously, Klein led them both across to his worktable and pulled up stools for them to sit on.

'Ah yes, the book, the book – I am intrigued.'

Faith produced The Book from her bag and both she and Nathaniel were disappointed to see the expression on the bookbinder's face. He took The Book in both hands and it suddenly seemed so cheap and tawdry in that wonderful workshop.

Klein closed his eyes, and ran his chubby fingers over both covers and the spine. Opening his eyes, he then held The Book up at arm's length, and holding each cover he let it fall open. He then brought the covers together and slammed The Book on to the worktable's wooden surface. His mood was transformed. The sunlit blue sky was now replaced by the blackest of thunderclouds.

'Right. Sewn on a concertina with double flexible linen cords. Alum-tawed goat with a tight-back. Looks like cheap northern Italian work – eighteenth century, perhaps? This is the...hmm, 'book' you wish me to copy?'

Nathaniel, feeling rather small and ashamed, nodded mutely.

Klein leapt off his stool, shuffled to an ornate set of shelves and returned with two small volumes, apparently identical.

'Look at these,' he commanded brusquely.

Faith and Nathaniel placed the books side by side on the worktable. By modern standards, they were tiny – perhaps six inches by four and about an inch thick. The stitching was gold thread, the covers and spine were studded with what looked very like precious stones, and they were fastened closed with a gold buckle.

'Open them, open them,' chivvied Klein.

They unclasped the buckles and they each opened their book at the front page. It was as if the sun shone out of the pages. Glorious crimsons and buttery yellows and a deep cerulean blue glittered in the late afternoon light shining through the workshop windows.

'The Book of Hours of Duchesse Aveline du Mas de Flory, circa 1450,' Klein could not keep the sense of pride out of his voice. 'Faith has the facsimile that I made four years ago. You, Nathaniel, hold one of the original five produced. The only other one in private hands went for four and a half million euro at auction in Amsterdam last month. I defy even experts (which I know you are not) to spot the difference between them.'

Nathaniel and Faith had to agree. The binding, the paper, the illuminations and script – they could find no fault.

'And now you' – a plump finger wagged at Nathaniel – 'bring me' – the finger pointed back at himself – 'Daniel Klein, son of Reuben Klein, grandson of Isidore Klein, God rest their souls, bookbinders of Ulm since 1542 – you bring me *this*, this ...*dreck*!' What kind of *schmo* do you take me for?'

Nathaniel was struck dumb, but Faith, who had in her short time at NYU heard more than her fair share of Yiddish banter, turned on the rotund bookbinder. No-one was going to upset her Nathaniel!

'Listen up, you *schlemiel* – we didn't come all this way to watch some off-Broadway comic give a poor impression of Jackie Mason. *Schmendrick!*' Faith had no idea what this last word meant, but it was meant to be very rude the last time she heard it.

Klein looked at Faith with a new respect. He appeared to be about to launch into another stream of invective but instead smiled broadly and said: 'My mother would turn in her grave if she had one. My guests have been here for ten minutes already and I have offered them nothing. Tea?'

Faith nodded, and Klein scuttled off to a small kitchenette in the corner of the room. Faith smiled weakly at Nathaniel and they continued to leaf through the exquisite treasures in front of them. Klein was absolutely right. His reproduction could in no way be distinguished from the original. If this was truly his work, they need have no worries about the service they wanted him to perform provided, of course, he was happy to accept the commission.

Klein waddled across the room and placed before them two porcelain bowls of black tea and a small plate of almond biscuits.

'Apologies for my rudeness. Can we start again? I was always taught that before people got down to business they should first talk about their family. It is often the case that the parties are related, have some distant connection which might help to conclude the deal.'

He looked meaningfully at Faith. 'In *your* case, my dear, this may not be likely.'

Faith bridled, and responded 'In which case, *Mister* Klein, let me give you my family history, and then you can see if we have any bonds. I don't know much about my folks before the eighteen hundreds. They were forcibly taken somewhere they didn't want to be. But I do know that they were slaves on the Codrington Estate in Barbuda in the 1830s.'

There was a sharp intake of breath from Klein.

'With legal emancipation in the 1830s, slaves were meant to be free, though most of them lacked the gumption, or resources, to move on. I was lucky. Great times nine grandpa Codrington upped and out of there. He worked his passage to Mexico, then after various wanderings over the next hundred years, we fetched up in Canada.'

Faith smiled sweetly. 'Seems to me that my people have got more in common with your people than you might have thought?'

Klein sipped thoughtfully at his tea. 'You are right of course. Experience can often mean so much more than blood. People of my faith have suffered their share, more than their share, of enslavement and wandering. I have the advantage of you, however. The Torah that has been in my family's possession for over five hundred years has every detail of my father's father's father's father and many more begettings before that.'

To keep it brief, I am Daniel Ezekiel Klein, only son of Reuben Ephraim Klein, only son of Isidore Nathaniel Klein. Our craft of bookbinding has been passed from father to son and, until certain events of the last century, we resided in Ulm on the banks of the Danube.'

Nathaniel caught Faith's gaze; they both appreciated what those 'certain events' had meant for European Jews in the twentieth century.

'In truth, it was bookbinding that saved my father's life. He, with the rest of my family, was shipped – at the German government's expense, I might say – to the charming Polish resort of Treblinka, that paradise that was so attractive that so many entered and so few left. The camp commandant was ahead of his time. He had an absolute mania for recycling. Those of us that weren't turned into soap or potash or whose gold teeth were not melted down to fund the war effort could be flayed and our skins could be used for book binding. Of course, when my father's trade became known, he was taken out of the queue for the gas chamber and put to work. He told me that his first commission was the complete works of Goethe, but when he recognised the tattooed number of his mother on the next hide in his basket, he decided to stop remembering. He kept his life, but he lost his faith.'

There was a silence while all three sipped their tea.

'After the war, he was able to come to England. The Cathedral Chapter here were very kind, remarkably kind seeing that he did not share their faith, and the business they gave him enabled him to set up shop here in this very building.'

'And your faith?' enquired Faith quietly.

'Oh, I follow my father in that, as all things. Despite appearances and ' – a nod to Faith – 'occasional lapses into the mother tongue, I am not a practising Jew, only Jew-ish.' He cackled at his own joke.

'But Mr Barton, what of your family?'

During Klein's awful account of his family history, Nathaniel had decided to be totally open. He briefly narrated the story of his own dull life before recounting how he had come across The Book and then briefly summarising the tales of those other Nathaniel Bartons that had preceded him.

'And the weird thing is,' interjected Faith, 'only Nathaniel can read this stuff. Look, see for yourself.' She pushed The Book across to Klein who leafed through the first few pages of handwriting, found the blank pages, and had to agree. He handed The Book to Nathaniel, who then started to re-read the account of Nathaniel #2.

'He's not making this up, Mr Klein. That's just how I remember it the first time.'

Klein closed his eyes for a while; when he opened them again, they appeared to positively twinkle.

'*Now* I am interested. Tell me – why do want a copy made?'

Nathaniel gave himself a little shake, closed The Book, and with some difficulty explained.

'Long story short. This book – The Book – gives chapter and verse on nine generations of my family who in one way and another have served the interests of an organisation that still operates out of Exeter. This has involved theft, fraud, treachery and murder. I believe that this organisation wants to recover this book and will stop at nothing to do so. My scheme is to throw them off the scent by letting them take a copy, and we know that you will be able to create such a convincing copy.'

Klein nodded in acknowledgement.

'In the fullness of time, I, with the scholarship and support of Faith here, will expose them for the villains they are.'

Faith regarded Nathaniel with new found admiration. The pathetic pipsqueak she had first met two weeks before was, to all outward appearances, exactly the same man. But he now had a sense of purpose, a strength and a humanity that seemed to have lain dormant all his life. She was going to have to be careful not to fall in love with this new Nathaniel Barton.

Klein nodded, then rose from his stool.

'I am with you, Nathaniel, and with you, Faith. This commonplace Book' (he seemed to place an undue emphasis on the word 'common') 'will be back in your hands on Sunday afternoon with the copy you require.'

'Will that be enough time for you?' asked Faith.

'Frankly, my dear, I will not want this so-called book in my workshop a moment longer than necessary. And Nathaniel has already told me he does not need a true copy, just something that will mislead someone who has never seen this book before. I will, however, pay it the compliment that I do to all my commissions.'

'Which is?'

'You have seen how remarkably exact my facsimiles can be. Many of my family's creations were in fact copies of other works. It was only proper that we should ensure that one could always be distinguished from the other. There are quite a few impoverished aristocrats who have tried to sell off an alleged family treasure while secretly retaining the original. We made sure that all the major auction houses in Europe knew what to look for.'

'So how did you do that?'

The bookbinder reached up and plucked a long black hair from the crown of his head.

'On the back cover of every copy we make, a hair is woven in with the binding thread. You might say there is a little bit of Klein in everything we do.'

'Thank you so much for your help, Daniel.'

'I do not pretend to understand what you have become involved in, my boy, but will do all in my power to help.'

He treated both Faith and Nathaniel to more unnecessarily vigorous handshakes and conducted them back down the rickety stairs.

With a rueful gaze at the deceased bell pull, Klein wished them well for the weekend and promised to receive them again at four o'clock on Sunday.

Chapter 29

Faith and Nathaniel agreed that the drive from Exeter had been tiring, and that they would wait until the following day to properly explore the city of Salisbury. Nathaniel nevertheless appreciated that Faith was still new to England, and came from a country where a building dated 1830 constituted an ancient monument.

So he steered her towards the cathedral. Even late on a spring afternoon, the close was swarming with tourists from around the world. Here was a party of Germans being shepherded by their guide; there was a Sri Lankan couple with their slightly bemused eight year old son gazing up at the western facade. But for all the people swarming about the lawns, there was no sense of being crowded. Unlike Exeter, the buildings that made up Salisbury's Cathedral Close stood at a respectful distance from the magnificent building at their centre.

Taking Faith's elbow, Nathaniel steered her through the cathedral entrance but, instead of turning left into the inevitable cathedral shop, Nathaniel veered right into the cloisters. Faith was dumbstruck. In an instant, she was transported back to the fifteenth century. Lightly ornamented stone arches were endlessly repeated around a square of plain green grass. In the centre, a pair of sturdy oaks reached heavenwards. This was a scene that endless generations of contemplative souls might have seen and reflected upon.

Nathaniel and Faith found themselves alone in the cloisters. For a time that never seemed long enough but which stretched endlessly around and before them, they stood silently.

Faith could only wonder at the sudden turmoil that now engulfed her after what had seemed a simple decision to extend her academic career by carrying out some research in the namesake of her birthplace.

Nathaniel reflected upon the strange series of events that had led him from a mundane life in a quiet provincial backwater to a secret mission to uncover a sequence of assassinations. As he pondered, he gazed at random around the cloisters and noticed in the far corner a small collection of interesting sculptures.

He walked slowly over, pausing only to read an A4 sheet of paper sellotaped to the wall that announced that these were 'contemporary works addressing the age old question of evil.'

'How timely,' he thought.

The centrepiece was a grey and white marble column some two metres tall and about 200 centimetres round. Although at first glance classical in execution, on closer inspection the column comprised a series of naked male figures, in contorted positions and grimacing fiercely. It seemed more like a North American totem pole or a pillar from a Hindu temple. Carved simply on the front of the base – in clear Times Roman capitals – was the single word SINS, and round the other three sides what were clearly biblical references: Deuteronomy 5:9, Exodus 20:5, and Exodus 34: 6-7.

Nathaniel's religious education had been cursory to say the least and he had no idea what these verses would have been about. Suddenly Faith appeared at his side with her ubiquitous iphone. A few deft finger movements later, she read out what she had found.

'OK – first verse is '*for I, the Lord your God, am a jealous God, visiting the iniquity of the fathers on the children, and on the third and the fourth generation of those who hate Me*'.

Then again, Exodus: '*I, the Lord your God, am a jealous God, visiting the iniquity of the fathers on the children, on the third and the fourth generation of those who hate Me*'. Same words, just as nasty.

And again, '*yet He will by no means leave the guilty unpunished, visiting the iniquity of fathers on the children and on the grandchildren to the third and fourth generation*'.

'Wow!' said Faith, 'certainly making a point.'

Wow indeed, thought Nathaniel.

It seemed to him that this was a pretty fair representation of the Barton bloodline, with himself at the bottom of the pile bearing the weight of all those other Nathaniels before him.

At the top of the pillar was Nathaniel #1 – apparently the only innocent in the family – who died mysteriously in 1780. Below him, Nathaniel #2, the trained assassin with at least a king, a revolutionary and a prime minister in his resumé.

Nathaniel #3 had accounted for another Member of Parliament and a prominent banker, while his son had more of a mixed record. The botched attempt on Prince Albert in Sydney contrasted with the spectacular assassination of Czar Alexander II of Russia.

Beneath Nathaniel #4 was a hunched figure with a rather self-satisfied smirk. Nathaniel #5 had outdone his father in securing the deaths of a French president, a Spanish prime minister, an Austrian princess and an Italian king. No wonder he looked rather pleased with himself.

He squatted on the shoulders of yet another crouching villain whose face was hidden. His first victim had been an American president, neither the first nor the last to have died from an assassin's bullet. His second was the French socialist and pacifist, Jean Jaures. The death of one man, but one that might well have changed the timing of the First World War.

Then came a burly figure who could represent Nathaniel #7, his own grandfather. Over fifty years and across four continents, he had eliminated several of the twentieth century's more prominent figures.

Beneath him was another writhing form who could be taken for Johnny Barton, guilty of crimes as yet unread but which Nathaniel knew would surely be recorded in The Book.

And at the bottom of the pile, bearing on his weary shoulders the pillar of pure evil above? That had to be Nathaniel himself, who had done nothing to deserve that burden.

When he shared this rather gloomy thought with Faith, she punched him playfully on the arm.

'No way, José! Your bottom is so much nicer than that little fellow's.'

Nathaniel who never before had had his bottom mentioned, let alone remarked favourably upon, by a member of the opposite sex took Faith in his arms and kissed her.

Faith, being a well brought up Canadian with a sense of fair play, thought it only right to reciprocate enthusiastically.

Their embrace was interrupted by a small hand bell being rung vigorously by one of the Cathedral attendants. Clearly it was time to leave.

Without exchanging another word, Faith and Nathaniel walked back into the close, and turned left towards the Rose and Crown. Instead of traffic strewn streets, they found themselves walking across the water meadows back to their hotel.

'I suppose we *are* doing the right thing?' said Faith, almost to herself.

'I don't think there's anything else we *can* do,' replied Nathaniel. 'At least, I know I have to follow this through, for myself and, I suppose, for my son, wherever he might be. *You* don't have to be involved, though. It's hardly your fight.'

Faith thought for a while.

'I guess we both want the same things for different reasons. There's something hinky about that book of yours. You need to understand it because you are a Nathaniel Barton. I need to understand it because, although I'm just a country girl from Ontario via New York City, I am a historian, and the truth matters to me.'

She slipped her hand in his as they walked the last few yards towards their hotel.

'I honestly don't think I could do this without you, Faith.'

'Don't worry, hon, you won't have to.'

'Tickets for Lords came through today.'

'What do you reckon? Aussies up to scratch this time, d'you think?'

'Never underestimate the capacity of an English team to find a spanner in the works when overwhelming odds support them.'

'Speaking of spanners, what news of young Barton.'

'Sore point, I'm afraid. Marcus is playing his cards close, but I get the feeling he's floundering.'

'Not like Marcus.'

'Keep out of his way if I were you. All I know is that our Nathaniel has an 'item of interest' and Marcus can't find it. Won't rest until he has.'

'Has Marcus ever *rested?'*

'I shall frame that and hang it in the Institution, labelled 'Rhetorical Question'.'

'Very droll. Be a good chap and pass the humidor.'

Chapter 30

As they walked back through reception at the Rose and Crown, Nathaniel and Faith agreed upon a quiet hour or so in their rooms before going down to dinner on the terrace overlooking the Cathedral. But, shortly after returning to their suite, they were interrupted by a sharp knock on the door. Nathaniel opened it to see a figure dressed as if for a Gilbert & Sullivan operetta.

'Good evening sir,' said the liveried flunkey whom Nathaniel could only assume was an employee of the hotel. Without waiting for a response he pushed a gleaming silver trolley into room. As it rolled past, Nathaniel could see a bottle of Ruinart in a generously filled ice bucket and sundry silver trays of canapés.

'But I haven't ordered anything,' spluttered a flustered Nathaniel. Standing near the bed, Faith was furiously miming to him to shut the hell up. She knew a good bottle of bubbles when she saw it.

'Compliments of the management, sir. This is all part of the Honeymoon Suite package.'

Nathaniel now understood why it was he'd been asked to substantially increase the charge on his card when he had changed the hotel booking. He had sufficient presence of mind to slip a five pound note into the waiter's hand as he glided effortlessly back through the door.

'Well,' said Faith.

'Well,' said Nathaniel.

'I need a shower,' said Faith, 'If you could do the honours with the champagne?'

A few minutes later, Nathaniel, clutching two glasses, wandered into a steamy bathroom where he could see Faith's silhouette behind an opaque shower screen.

'Get your clothes off, and get in here,' shouted Faith. Nathaniel needed no further invitation.

Later, they lay on the king sized bed with an oval plate of delicious nibbles between them. Both of them were still naked and they were well into their second glass of Ruinart.

'This cannot be real,' said Nathaniel, draining his glass.

'What do you mean?' said Faith coquettishly, draining her glass too.

'All this – honeymoon suite, you, me, the Guild, Marcus, The Book – why, how?'

Faith fell serious. 'Was it bad yesterday, reading about your grandpa?'

Faith waited in silence while Nathaniel sat listlessly on the bed. He was clearly in no mood to talk, no mood to dress and go down for dinner, no mood to do anything. Faith drew deep on the well of patience that Codrington women had relied on for generations when dealing with menfolk with the blues. She gently took his empty glass from his hand and they both slid under the embroidered counterpane.

Neither of them knew how long they lay there, hand in hand, staring sightlessly at the ceiling while the Wiltshire sun faded and their room darkened.

Saturday 13 April 2013

Chapter 31

Their period of quiet introspection had not lasted long before they fell into a restful sleep. When they woke on Saturday morning, Faith and Nathaniel were both wonderfully refreshed. Neither of them had experienced the troublesome dreams from which they had both suffered recently. After skipping dinner the previous evening, they both went down for breakfast with healthy appetites.

Nathaniel was impressed to see Faith devour an English breakfast almost as large as his own. She had only passed on the fried bread and the black pudding, neither of which qualified as real foodstuffs in her eyes.

As they walked back through the hotel lobby, they were accosted by an eager receptionist.

'Telephone message came for you late last night. Didn't want to disturb you...'

The young woman rolled her eyes and gave that special look that hotel staff reserve for occupants of Honeymoon Suites. Irritated, Faith snatched the piece of paper from her hand, and started to read it as they got into the lift.

'It's Daniel Klein. He's not very specific, but he's asking if we can call in and see him as soon as possible.'

As they had planned on spending the day in Salisbury anyway, it was no great inconvenience to retrace their steps of the previous afternoon. The bell pull still lay on the step looking up accusingly at Nathaniel. Klein's door was on the latch and they went straight up.

'You got my message. Excellent, come on in, the kettle's on.'

Klein gestured them over to the workbench where leather bound boards were gripped between iron clamps.

Large sheets of yellowing parchment were ready for cutting into the correct sizes, and a mortar containing a glittering black paste awaited the pestle.

Gazing eagerly up at Nathaniel and Faith, he placed a plump finger alongside his nose.

'I have news, important news, some bad, I expect, but some that you may find good. That is the way with all news, I suppose.'

Before he could give them any more information, he was summoned by a shrill whistle from the corner of the room and he scuttled off to attend to their drinks.

Once they were all sat at the table in front of steaming bowls of black tea, Klein coughed portentously.

'When I was a young boy, I looked at my grandfather's name – Isidore Nathaniel – my father's name – Reuben Ephraim – and my own name – Daniel Ezekiel. Being the first of my family taught to speak English as his first language (and at a decent public school at that), it was obvious to me that my grandparent's name was *incline*, my father's *recline*, and my own, *decline*; so I feel a constitutional tendency to give you the bad news first.'

This weak play on words which had obviously been wheeled out many times before still had the power to make him chuckle to himself.

'Please, forgive my *narrishkeit*, my foolishness'

Faith asked: 'But have you no children yourself?'

'Afraid not, my dear, my proclivities are directed elsewhere. I remember that when my dear father learnt (I think within the space of a single week) that I had no intention of embracing either Judaism or heterosexuality, 'Only one letter difference between *goy* and *gay*' was the response.' Klein shook his head ruefully.

Nathaniel, who could see the opportunities for pleasant meanderings around Salisbury evaporating by the minute, felt compelled to butt in.

'Come on, Daniel, why are we here?'

'Yes, you're right. Time flies and we must fly with it. To start with, then, the bad news is that the copying work is not going to be as straightforward as I thought. I know you planned to leave on Sunday. But is there any chance you can stay over an extra night and pick it up from me Monday morning?'

'No!' came the simultaneous reply from Nathaniel and Faith. He knew he would have to be back at work promptly Monday morning to face whatever music Sophie and CK would even now be composing for him. And she had her next appointment with her supervisor which, if she read the runes correctly, might be something of a last chance saloon for her and her thesis.

Klein dismissed the response with a wave of his hand.

'*Nisht degeidet.* There's a courier I always use. He can have it with you Monday afternoon, I promise you.'

Nathaniel was strangely worried about being away from The Book for too long, but appreciated there was nothing he could do nothing about it.

'If that's what we have to do, so be it. But what's the good news?'

'Well, it's really the reason for the delay. The first thing I do when I'm working on this sort of project is to feel my way round the book. It's hard to explain, but what I do is that I have a blindfold I put on (I can't trust myself not to peek, you see), then I hold the book closely. I work my fingers round it, I sniff it; sometimes I find myself licking the leather.'

Faith wrinkled her nose in disgust, and avoided Nathaniel's gaze.

'With your book' – and Klein could not help but look slightly disapproving – 'it was clear that this was not a very high standard of workmanship. The spine was slightly askew, both covers had different numbers of stitches, and the back cover in particular seemed to have been taken apart and then, quite amateurishly, reassembled.'

'Next, I take very precise measurements of every dimension, *every* dimension. That's when I spotted it.'

'What?' demanded Faith, who, like Nathaniel, was feeling that these were going to be minutes of her life she would never get back.

Like a conjurer, Klein produced from within his capacious smock a small yellowing parchment tied with a faded green ribbon.

'This was concealed between the board of the back cover and the endpaper. As you can see, it's not very thick – octavo folded three times – but I'm surprised you didn't spot it yourselves.'

'What is it? What does it say?' enquired Nathaniel eagerly, the sights of Salisbury now quite forgotten.

'What kind of *klutz* do you take me for? The book – yes, you have given *that* to me freely to copy and, I assume, to read if I so wish. But this document? You did not know of it, you were not knowingly giving it to me and therefore it is private. Furthermore, it is very clearly addressed to you.'

'What?!' exclaimed Nathaniel, 'How can that be possible?'

'Perhaps not literally. This document is clearly very much older than you are. But, as you tell me this is a family possession, I think you have title to anything it contains.'

Klein passed the folded paper across. In a faded but still legible hand, there could clearly be seen the words: *To Nathaniel Barton.*

'So, I have done the right thing, no? And you can now understand. I must first repair the original book, then continue making the copy, and *then* damage the copy so it resembles the original. I promise you – both the original and my oh so plausible copy will be with you by Monday afternoon.'

By now, Nathaniel was more concerned to find out what was in the mysterious document than to spend another moment in the old bookbinder's company.

Misinterpreting the nervous glances, Klein sought to reassure him.

'Don't worry about the *gelt*. I have your deposit, and my price will not increase for the extra work. This book of yours intrigues me and I am happy to be on the side of the angels.

All Jews are not stereotypes. We can talk about money when you have received the original and copy and evaluated the work for yourself. Now, *mach shnel!*'

With profuse thanks and repeated handshakes and sincere apologies, Nathaniel and Faith were able to make their escape.

Nathaniel was all for sitting on a nearby bench to see what the document had to tell them. But Faith pointed out the gathering clouds above and suggested they would be better off back in their hotel room. They ran laughing into the hotel lobby as the heavy rain drops began to fall and, spurning the lift, continued running up the stairs. The reception staff exchanged amused glances. They had never seen a honeymoon couple *quite* like this one before.

Chapter 32

Once in their room, it was clear to both Nathaniel and Faith that the task of teasing open the mysterious letter was one that could not have been satisfactorily carried out on a park bench, whatever the weather. While the document did not appear to be particularly fragile – Nathaniel had encountered much worse when researching titles to old properties – this wasn't going to be simply like opening up today's *Sunday Telegraph*.

The dry green ribbon resisted careful attempts to untie it, but that was simply resolved with a pair of nail scissors. Nathaniel then laid the document on the dressing table and with the aid of tweezers and a couple of emery boards from Faith's bottomless handbag, he carefully unfolded it.

Faith peered over his shoulder. This was no magical book with invisible writing but a bona fide historical document – just the sort of original source material that was a historian's stock in trade.

The first shock was the date at the head of the page in a clear hand: 8th February 1685, almost a hundred years before Nathaniel Barton #1 had first written in his commonplace Book. Worse was to come.

'*My dear son, Nathaniel,*' the letter began, '*I have this day committed a deed so foul, so impious that I fear I shall be struck down by a vengeful God before I see you and your dear mother again. I am travelling back to Exeter from the Palace of Westminster. In time, the news will reach people there that the King is mortal ill and fain to die. I must confess that I am he who has brought him to this sorry state.*'

'Charles II,' murmured Faith, 'Look at the date – this Nathaniel is saying he murdered Charles II!'

Nathaniel had forgotten more history than he remembered. 'So how did he die?'

'It's well enough documented.' She picked up her ipad and turned to the ever helpful Wikipedia. She read out loud:

'Charles suffered a sudden apoplectic fit on the morning of 2 February 1685, and died aged 54 at 11:45 am four days later at Whitehall Palace. The suddenness of his illness and death led to suspicion of poison in the minds of many, including one of the royal doctors; however, more modern medical analysis has held that the symptoms of his final illness are similar to those of uraemia (a clinical syndrome due to kidney dysfunction).'

'As a method of murder, poisoning at the time was not uncommon,' commented Faith, 'but the symptoms for most poisons were well known and would have been readily diagnosed. Unless,' she paused for thought, 'it was a poison that had not been used before. Hang on a minute...'

Faith's eager fingers danced across the surface of her tablet for a few more minutes. Then she looked up with a broad grin and punched the air with a cowboy yell that she had last used as a teenage cheerleader.

'What is it?' asked Nathaniel.

'OK. I *know* as a historian one should never assume, but let's just suppose that the Nathaniel Barton of 1685 is one of your murderous ancestors...' Nathaniel winced.

'And let's suppose,' she continued, 'that as well as being <u>in</u> the Guild of Weavers, Fullers and Shearmen, he actually *was* a weaver or a fuller or a shearman.'

'Oh,' said Nathaniel, 'I think the weaver is the only one with a job I can understand.'

'That's a pity, because I have a hunch that this Nathaniel Barton was a fuller – do you know why?'

'Well, what *I* can tell *you* from my own research (ahem) is that our Nathaniel #1 – the chap who made the first entries in The Book – rented a fulling mill. So it may well have been a family tradition...'

Nathaniel felt a little pleased at having out-researched the postgraduate researcher; but she quickly trumped his ace.

'Quite possibly, but I don't expect a twenty-first century pen pusher like you to know what a fuller, otherwise known as a tucker or walker, actually did.'

Nathaniel assumed an appropriately blank expression. He thought he had better sit patiently through the course of the lecture he could see heading towards him.

'Right then. Weavers you know. They took the wool and wove it into lengths of cloth. Shearmen are also fairly self explanatory. Those guys worked on the finished cloth with what were in effect giant pairs of scissors, which they used to snip off any little knots or tangles that ruined the smooth finish.

Fullers or tuckers (hence Tuckers Hall where the Guild is based) did the mucky bit in between. The lengths of cloth were soaked in fuller's liquor, a rather unsavoury mix of urine, water and fuller's earth (clay to you and me) to clean out all impurities. The cloth was then bashed until the fibres matted together. In Exeter, as in many other places, there were water-driven mills powering giant wooden mallets to do most of the donkey work. Then the cloth is washed and stretched out on frames to dry and recover its shape. Simple, eh?'

'But what's the connection with poison?'

'Urine. Let me explain. Back in the seventeenth century, there was little to choose between alchemy and chemistry. Alchemists had a passion for discovering ways of producing gold, and in 1669 a German named Brand thought (heaven knows why) urine could be a good starting point. First, he let most of it evaporate and then boiled down the rest until he got a paste. He didn't have gold, but in some ways something even better. The thirteenth element, phosphorous.'

'How do you know all this stuff?'

'Not me, I'm afraid, my old buddy Wikipedia again. Anyway, while there are lots of exciting uses for phosphorous, it is extremely toxic and, in 1685, it was virtually unknown. Don't want to boast, Mr B, but I wouldn't be surprised if your ancestor wasn't able to rustle up this stuff and slip old Charley boy a lethal dose.'

Almost simultaneously, they both realised that they had no need of speculation. On the dressing table was a letter that could settle the matter. As one, they moved over and both sat, shoulders touching, on the richly upholstered bench.

It was not an easy matter to decipher the manuscript, but their combined skills were up to the task, and after less than thirty minutes, the sequence of events was clear to them both. It was Faith who spelt it out.

'This is precisely what I came to Exeter to research! Charles II was clamping down on guilds all across the country. He saw them, as I do, as self-serving cartels that protected the influence and interests of the tradesmen rather than the consumer and ordinary citizen. But where, if I can presume, Charles II and I disagree is that I would have liked to see a more open marketplace for goods and employment. Charles' plan was to take the privileges and profits of the guilds for himself as an autocratic monarch.

With the Exeter Guild, he so very nearly succeeded. The legal processes had begun, the Guild was required to respond before the case went to Court, and they called an assembly, or Hall, to discuss how they should proceed. The minutes of that assembly are public and brief. In essence, all they agreed to do was to call a second Hall, though time was running out.

The minutes of that second Hall were unpublished, though I believe they still exist.'

'And I know you don't like assumptions,' ventured Nathaniel, 'but might we not infer that this second Hall came up with a rather drastic proposal? Get rid of the King, the legal process collapses, and the Guild survives?'

'Well, here we have a Nathaniel Barton (and we now know a bit of the family history!) who confesses to experimenting with phosphorous and smuggling in the poison in a bowl of hot chocolate heavily laced with brandy. Not my cup of tea, I have to say.'

'Nor Charles' neither.'

'And that's where we came in, with your blessed commonplace book. During some legal task or other, your Nathaniel #1 must have somehow discovered this document in the Guild's records, recognised its significance, and hidden it inside The Book.'

Nathaniel continued the thought: 'And when the loss was discovered and the document could not be found, Nathaniel #1 goes out on an uncharacteristic drinking spree and ends up in the River Exe.'

Nathaniel had fallen silent. This imagined scenario seemed like a cruel foreshadowing of the death of his own father.

Sensing his sudden loss of good spirits, Faith made a show of looking at her watch.

'Well bless me! Time flies when you're enjoying yourself. Why don't we go down for an early supper and then we can make a prompt start in the morning? We don't have to hang around for Klein any longer, and we both have an important day on Monday.'

With a heavy heart, Nathaniel agreed. Whether it was gloom at finding yet another homicidal Nathaniel Barton in his family tree or the depressing prospect of a confrontation with CK to come, he wasn't sure.

Faith likewise was not looking forward to her next supervision with Duntze; nor was she sure how she should handle Marcus at their next meeting. Now she was so firmly in Nathaniel's camp, it would be impossible to pretend that she was also spying on him.

But there was nothing to be gained by introspection, so they were soon tucking in to the Rose and Crown's roast supper with all the trimmings.

For Nathaniel, life would not get happier than this again.

Sunday 14 April 2013

Chapter 33

They had gone to bed early and had the time to make love without urgency. Breakfast was served in their room and they were packed and ready to leave by nine o'clock.

There was one last surprise for the couple. As Faith was checking every drawer, cupboard and cavity in the suite to ensure that nothing from their small weekend bags had been left behind, Nathaniel wandered rather aimlessly round the room.

Standing by the huge oak beamed fireplace which incongruously framed a three bar electric fire, Nathaniel gazed back at Faith. When she did not (as he had furtively hoped) gaze back with some semblance of affection, he turned his attention to the gnarled mantelpiece. He ran his fingers over the blackened and pitted surface of the wood, and then froze in a mixture of surprise and horror. Carved deep in the fireplace surround, in letters no more than an inch high, were the characters **NB1685**.

This could surely be no coincidence. This was, after all, a coaching inn that had been standing in the outskirts of Salisbury for eight hundred years. It was a natural stopover on the long journey between Exeter and London. He called Faith over to show her his remarkable discovery.

'It has to be a Nathaniel Barton, don't you think…?'

'And 1685, of course, the year he travelled from Exeter to London.'

'And back again. Was this his way of ensuring that, after he'd regretted his murderous act, he literally left his mark?'

Neither Nathaniel nor Faith felt they could voice the thought '…in case something happened to him.' They stared in silence at the six characters, laboriously carved by the same man who had painfully written his confession on the document safely packed in a holdall behind them.

There was an increasing sense of a story unfolding, of a purpose to this gradual ensnaring of the modern Nathaniel with the tangled skein of his forefathers' lives. Nathaniel tenderly touched the carved initials and felt, or imagined he felt, a mild tingling up his arm. It reminded him of the vicious shock that had propelled him from the library steps a mere nine days earlier.

Faith sensed his disquiet and tenderly took his hand. They stared out of the hotel window to a past they were now beginning to understand and a future they could only guess at. The journey back to Exeter on Sunday was, if anything, rather more silent than the drive to Salisbury on Friday, though for very different reasons.

Nathaniel was strangely bereft. Since finding The Book, this was the longest period he had been away from it, and they would not be reunited for another twenty four hours.

Faith for her part was formulating her new approach to Professor Duntze. She had concluded that, as far as Marcus and the Guild were concerned, she had burnt her boats. She was prepared not only to make that clear to her supervisor but also to reveal the insidious role played by Marcus. Then, of course, she would play her trump card: irrefutable evidence that Charles the Second, by the Grace of God, King of England, Scotland, France and Ireland and Defender of the Faith, had been murdered at the bidding of Exeter's Guild of Weavers, Fullers and Shearmen.

She had no doubt that Duntze would demand to be cited as co-author of the articles she would have to write. But that would be a small price to pay for the immense kudos she would gain. There were not that many dramatic historical discoveries these days, and certainly none as potentially explosive as this.

Though silent, the drive to Exeter was companionable enough, and Faith readily accepted Nathaniel's invitation to his house for a cup of tea before returning to her university rooms.

The first surprise came when Nathaniel went to insert his key in the front door and found that it swung open easily. The floorboard in the hall that had been loose for so many years had been ripped up to reveal a gaping hole. The hall carpet had been roughly torn up, and as Nathaniel and Faith moved silently through the building, they saw little but devastation. In the kitchen, food from the fridge and freezer had been emptied onto the floor where it was mixed indiscriminately with broken crockery.

In the front room, cushions were slashed, books pulled roughly from shelves, pictures torn off the walls. Before Faith could mount the stairs, Nathaniel took control. He led her back outside, took her overnight bag out of the car, and reached for his mobile.

'Are you calling the police?' asked Faith

'No point,' said Nathaniel bitterly, 'We both know who did this. They're looking for The Book, and thank heavens they couldn't find it. I'm calling you a taxi; I need to be on my own here, to clear up, and you've got tomorrow to prepare for.'

Faith protested – she *must* be able to help. Nathaniel contrived to be both downcast and determined, and she had to admit defeat.

Once Faith had been driven safely away, Nathaniel returned to his shattered home. He picked up an apparently undamaged dining chair and sat on it to collect his thoughts. It seemed he was now well and truly in the sights of the Guild, but he could perhaps take some perverse comfort from the fact that the search had been so very thorough. It would surely not make sense for the vandals to return in the near future.

He turned towards the under stairs cupboard where he kept his cleaning materials and a few large sacks for garden rubbish. He smiled ruefully when he realised that the cupboard had been subject to the same assault as the rest of his house and the broom, dustpan, brush and rubbish bags were rather obligingly scattered across the floor within easy reach. Rolling up his sleeves, he began the depressing task of restoring order.

Meanwhile, Faith was unlocking her own front door. Her short journey back to the university campus had passed in a blur of self-recrimination, fear and doubt. All of this evaporated the instant she saw that her own small flat had suffered the same treatment as Nathaniel's terraced house. She could take no more. She subsided against the wall and hugged herself as the sobs started to rack her body.

'Faith, hon, what's up?' Her neighbour and fellow post grad Alice was walking and then running up the corridor towards her. Faith could not speak; she struggled to her feet, and wailing, threw her arms around her bewildered friend.

It was thirty minutes, two cups of sweet tea and a warm shower later before Faith could snuggle down on Alice's sofa in a borrowed dressing gown. She felt unable to give Alice a complete history of her chance meeting with Nathaniel, their blossoming affair, or the tortuous history of The Book and the succeeding generations of Bartons. But she was able to hint at a new man in her life and could be open about the double break-ins and the vandalism, though denying any idea of who or what was behind them.

'No two ways about it, girl. You are staying with me tonight, and tomorrow we'll sort that flat out for you. Are you sure you don't want to call the police in?'

Faith shook her head as tears welled up again.

Alice fell back on her tried and tested solution to most problems – a chilled bottle of wine and a plate of toasted cheese. For as long as her DVD of *Love, Actually* played, the two young women were able to lose themselves in a cloud of alcohol, romantic comedy and excess calories.

As the closing credits rolled, Alice looked across to the sofa to see an exhausted Faith was curled in a ball and snoring gently. She covered her friend with a duvet and dimmed the lights.

She suspected there was more to Faith's distress than a break-in or two, but she was prepared to give her friend the space and time to come to terms with whatever it was. She gently closed the living room door behind her, and soon Alice too was deep in a dreamless sleep.

Monday 15 April 2013

Chapter 34

For Nathaniel, Sunday evening had proved to be an ordeal that he preferred to forget. He had concentrated on attacking his kitchen, bathroom and bedroom. Some basic order had been restored, but there were plenty of sacks in his back yard filled with spoiled foodstuffs and soft furnishings damaged beyond repair.

Fortunately, although much of his clothing had been unaccountably torn and slashed, he was able to locate an undamaged shirt and suit for work. Outwardly he looked the typical office worker prepared for the week ahead. Inwardly, he had a heavy heart and a mind wearied by a series of unprecedented events.

As every weekday (before his unscheduled week's absence), he arrived at the office at 8:45, walked in through the front door of number fourteen and nodded a silent greeting to Sophie. Much to his surprise, she acknowledged his greeting with a warm smile and a cheerful 'Good morning, Mr Barton!'

Something was wrong. He set off up the four flights of uneven coarsely carpeted stairs without pause; and, as every weekday, he paused on the third landing. He then strode up the last flight and turned the highly polished knob on his office door.

Something *was* wrong. The door was locked, and of course Sophie had known it. He had no alternative but to go back down to the ground floor to ask what was going on.

Sophie was finding it hard to conceal her enjoyment at her colleague's discomfort.

'Oh yes, Mr Barton, I should have said. Mr Kennaway would like to see you in his office at your earliest convenience.'

Naturally, CK's office was in prime position on the ground floor with a fine view of Southernhay. Nathaniel tapped nervously on the door and, in response to the bellowed 'Come!' shuffled nervously in.

'Barton, yes, yes. Take a seat. It's that time of year, isn't it? Performance review, bonuses, promotion where appropriate.'

For a brief mad moment, Nathaniel thought that – contrary to his fears – this was going to be good news after all. But that moment soon ended.

'However, the senior partners have concluded that, like everyone else at this difficult time, Kennaway & Partners have to engage in a little belt tightening. We cannot carry dead weight, yes, dead weight, Barton. A person who just takes a week off when it suits him, who sends in a sick note but is well enough to flaunt himself with a floozy not a hundred yards from his office. Not a Kennaway's kind of chap, not at all.'

CK continued, but Nathaniel could no longer distinguish the words. This was appalling. It would have been bad enough to have received a written warning, but dismissal? Just like that?

He briefly regretted not having specialised in employment law, but he already felt that, whatever rights he might have, whatever statutes CK was currently driving a coach and horses through, no wronged employee would succeed against the might of Kennaway & Partners.

'I'll be asking young Tetley to accompany you to your office while you remove any personal effects, and you will be paid to the end of the month. Two words: gross misconduct. I don't think I need say any more?'

Twenty minutes later, Nathaniel was outside in Cathedral Close, clutching a black rubbish bag which held the few sad mementoes of his many years at Kennaway's. Ahead of him was the tempting facade of the Well House. It would be all too easy to drown his feelings (such as they were) in alcohol. But on his right was the front door of the Institution; remembering the solace he had once found in Duke Humfrey's Library, he pushed the brass bell. His spirits were lifting as the door opened, and as he stepped into the lobby, he could feel a smile forming on his lips. But not for long.

Acting Librarian Dolores Nunan came out of her office like a greyhound out of a trap.

'Mr Barton, a word if you please.'

'Oh yes, my membership. Has it come through?'

'Quite the reverse, I'm afraid. You've been blackballed.'

'But, but, but...'

'I know, extraordinary thing, I had to check, and this hasn't happened since 1983. That was a Barton too.'

With a flash of inspiration, Nathaniel realised: 'That must have been my father.'

'Good heavens! Perhaps someone has it in for your family. Sorry and all that, but I have to ask you to leave.'

No job, no hobby, a house in ruins. It would not be enough to sit in the Well House sipping pints of bitter. Nathaniel set off for the nearest supermarket, bought two bottles of own label whisky and trudged mournfully back to the place he still called home.

Chapter 35

Faith woke on an unfamiliar sofa with a trace of a hangover and a feeling of immense sorrow. Slowly, painfully, she stretched then sat upright. As she recalled the sequence of events from Sunday night, tears began to well in her eyes. Her flat, Nathaniel's house, what was going on here? She rose unsteadily to her feet as an irritatingly fresh looking Alice came into the room with two mugs of cappuccino in one hand and a plate of muffins in the other.

'Sit down again, girl, caffeine, sugar and carbs are what you need right now. There's no rush – Josh, Zara and Penny have been tidying up your room. It wasn't as bad as it looked, though I'd still call the police if I were you. I'm not happy thinking there's some random nutter on campus.'

Faith remained quiet. If it had just been her flat, she could have agreed with Alice's analysis. But it was too much of a coincidence that Nathaniel's house had suffered the same treatment. The principal object of the unsubtle search must be The Book. The secondary object was, to Faith's mind, achieved in spades – the delivery of a clear message to her and Nathaniel. The vandals who had violated both her flat and his home must have come from the Guild.

She suddenly had the awful thought that things might have been a lot worse if either of them had actually been in when the Guild came calling. This had been ruthless behaviour by people who had no regard for the niceties, and probably didn't care if the police were involved or not. Faith suspected that they had been a law to themselves for a very long time.

A shrill ring came from Faith's handbag. Alice handed it over and Faith fished out her iphone. It was an alert for her supervision, due in thirty minutes.

'Shoot! Sorry, Alice, Duntze calls. Can I catch you later?'

'No probs. You take care now.'

Faith walked the short distance down the corridor to her own door. There was no trace of a forced entry – had the intruder had a key? She slipped quickly into her flat, left her holdall on the living room floor and half ran into the bathroom to freshen up.

Changing her weekend blouse for a crisper white shirt, she thought herself fortunate that she didn't have to worry about presenting any prepared work to her supervisor. Frankly, she hadn't got any. No, this session would be about the remarkable change of direction that her project was about to take. Would the portly professor believe her? Or would he think she'd totally flipped?

All she could do was to give it her best shot. As she picked up her handbag, she heard her phone go again. She pulled it out impatiently, thinking this was only the final alert for her appointment (these phones were so damned bossy), but instead the screen was displaying Nathaniel's home number.

Faith's nervous 'Hi!' was met with silence. Straining her ears, she thought she could just make out some rather heavy breathing. Before she could end the call, she heard the sound of a throat being cleared, rather noisily and somewhat painfully.

'Are you there, Faith?' His words were slow and slightly slurred.

'Yes, yes, I'm fine, just on my way to see my tutor.'

It was clear to Faith that Nathaniel could only speak clearly by concentrating very hard on each word.

'Look. I've had a couple of bits of bad news and I need to sort a few things out.'

Faith wasn't sure if he meant in his own mind or in his house.

Nathaniel continued: 'I don't know if you were thinking of coming round tonight but please could you leave it till tomorrow. I could do with a bit of time...'

Faith felt both hurt and affectionate at the same time. There was a part of her that resented his assumption that she would be going to see him after work as a matter of course. And there was a part of her that just wanted to hold him close until he felt better. But she was on a mission and she had no time to debate her finer feelings. So she quickly agreed and ended the call.

Now she was on the point of being late. She half walked, half ran across the campus to the building where Professor Sir Stephen Duntze MBE held court. Fortunately, whether because of his eminence or his bulk, the professor's rooms were on the ground floor and Faith arrived in the reception area with two minutes to spare.

The same secretary was in place behind her desk but, instead of displaying an air of sophisticated authority, she now looked positively cowed. Without looking Faith in the eye, she waved vaguely at the professor's door, and said, 'You can go in straight away.'

Ahead of Faith was the carved wooden desk and the back of the professor's chair. As it slowly swivelled towards her, Faith was shocked to see, instead of the massive frame and jowled features of her supervisor, the grey and saturnine features of the man she knew only as Marcus.

'Miss Codrington. Please sit.' The light, almost feminine tone of his voice contrasted unpleasantly with the thin smile on his lips and the burning intensity of his gaze.

'Miss Codrington. Professor Duntze is unable to be with you at this time, but that is of no consequence. Your stay at this establishment is to be terminated.'

As Faith struggled to understand the meaning of what was being said, short bony fingers pushed an envelope across the green leather desk top towards her.

'Here is an open air ticket to New York. Exeter to Amsterdam, and then an onward connection to JFK. It is valid for thirty days.'

On the way to her supervision, Faith had hastily composed a speech in which she summarised her startling revelations about the activities of the Guild and proposed that the focus of her thesis must now change. But none of that made sense now. Her academic career was collapsing around her.

'Why, when... Oh gosh. What will the professor be telling NYU?'

'That rather depends on you, Miss Codrington. An unexpected lack of source material, the indisposition of the professor, his recommendation that a talented student such as yourself should be given the option of a different research project. This would be the reward for your silence.'

The alternative remained unspoken, but Faith knew, as she knew that Marcus knew, that any attempt by her to behave otherwise would destroy her academic career before it had even started. Embarrassed by the speed of her admission of defeat, Faith mumbled 'Of course' and reached across the desk for the envelope.

Marcus' cold hand gripped hers. At the shock of it, Faith almost fainted.

'Miss Codrington. I will ask you this once only. Do you have in your possession anything which rightfully belongs to another?'

Faith was able for the first time in that mercifully brief encounter to return his gaze, with interest.

'No, Mr Marcus, I do not. Now let me go.'

With an exquisite slowness, Marcus disengaged his grip. Faith hastily stuffed the envelope in her handbag, got up from her chair and left without any further word. As she closed the door behind her, she thought she heard a long, slow, sibilant hiss.

She almost sleepwalked back to her rooms. As she opened the front door, she heard a scraping sound in the living room and tried to stifle a gasp. Had the intruder returned?

'Come on in, hon' Alice cried out cheerfully, 'I bought you some flowers'

When she saw her friend's expression, Alice ran to her and hugged her close.

'I'm so sorry, I didn't mean to scare you.'

Faith could hold back no more. Her body shook and tears poured from her eyes. Alice manoeuvred her carefully on to the sofa, but the sobbing continued. The events of the past few days – falling for Nathaniel, the history of the Bartons, the violation of their homes, and finally her abrupt dismissal from the University – they just overwhelmed her, and it was some time before Alice's tender attentions could slow her breathing and calm her down.

Faith was sufficiently in control of her emotions to give Alice only an edited account of her non-existent supervision. The story was simply that Duntze was taken ill, so it made sense for her to go back to New York to seek another project closer to home. And as for her other adventures, it made no sense to share those. She was still mindful of the need to get her academic career back on track. After some further conversation about the bad luck of it all, Alice stood to leave.

'Look, I'll understand if you say no, but I think you could do with a complete change of mood. That poet guy you liked? He's down at the Phoenix again tonight. Why don't I come round about 8 o'clock and we can share a taxi there? We can grab something to eat as well and you can say goodbye to Exeter in style, eh?'

Faith nodded silently. She had nothing else to do. No thesis to work on; and Nathaniel had been clear he didn't want to see her tonight. In fact, she wasn't sure if he deserved another visit from her again.

First things first. She could check that she could get a flight tomorrow morning (no point in delay), pack her cases this afternoon, and then do her best to relax. If that poet had the same effect on her as before, she would be able to face the world a heck of a lot better.

Chapter 36

With a disproportionate sense of loss, Nathaniel dropped the first of his empty whisky bottles into the bin. While he felt intellectually that the thirty degree proof spirit should have affected him in some way, he believed he was still perfectly in control of himself. That, he conceded, was the problem. He really needed the alcohol to render him totally insensible. Events had spiralled completely out of control, his emotions were totally scrambled, and he just needed to be in a place where he could feel nothing, understand nothing and be completely nothing.

As he started to wrestle with the unspeakable complexities of undoing the screw top on the second bottle, there was a loud banging on his front door. Almost guiltily, he stuffed the whisky down the side of an armchair and headed into the hall.

Sober, he might have worried that the mysterious individuals who had taken his home apart were returning for a second assault. Half cut as he was, he operated on autopilot. Opening his front door with a weak smile on his face, he saw a leather clad motorbike courier with a clipboard and a small parcel wrapped in brown paper and string.

'Parcel for Mr Barton!'

Nathaniel signed the proffered form absentmindedly and it was only when he got back to his living room that it dawned on him that the package held the two copies of The Book, or rather The Book itself along with Daniel Klein's facsimile.

Right. This needed sobriety and focus. Nathaniel walked purposefully into kitchen, switched on the coffee machine and took a pair of scissors out of a drawer. Despite a little loss of coordination, he soon had the parcel open and there were two apparently identical copies of The Book on the counter in front of him. The only distinguishing feature was that one was tied shut with a red ribbon, the other with green. For Nathaniel's benefit, there was a handwritten note which explained the difference in Klein's inimitable style.

'My dear boy, profound apologies for the delay. I hope you think the end result is worth it. I don't expect a schlemiel such as yourself to appreciate the difference between the master and the expertly rendered copy. So the green ribbon denotes the original, the red signifies the rather fine duplicate.'

Nathaniel had no real need for colour coding. Simply touching the volume with the green ribbon gave him the confirmation he needed, though the thrill was now more muted. Whether this was through familiarity, too little energy, or too much alcohol, Nathaniel was uncertain.

But he had to concede that the two volumes would indeed be indistinguishable to any other reader. Klein had carried out his commission perfectly.

Loosening the red ribbon, Nathaniel read once again that earlier Nathaniel's touching dedication of December 1767. Flicking onward through the pages, he came to the point at which the entries finished. From that page forward, blank sheet followed blank sheet, and Nathaniel experienced a momentary sense of disorientation.

Rapidly undoing the green ribbon, Nathaniel read through the same opening passages in the original. But unlike the first volume, he found the tale of Nathaniel #2 following on seamlessly. He at least needed no ribbons to distinguish the original from the fake, but he took care to rebind the red ribboned volume for Faith's benefit.

Thinking of Faith, he felt profoundly sad. What had happened there? A young woman half his age and from half a world away had somehow swept him off his feet, knocked him for six, and turned him inside out. What had *she* been thinking of? And all this in the context of this cursed, wonderful, damned book.

Which reminded him. He had read at length and painfully the account of his grandfather. He still needed to read the history of his father, and he was sure that that would prove no easier.

Dusk was beginning to fall. He drew the blind and secured the whisky bottle. Pouring out half a mug of hot black coffee, he topped it up with the supermarket scotch, drew up a kitchen chair, and settled down for the next dark chapter in the history of the Bartons.

Of course it would be difficult to top the murderous exploits of his grandfather. Even so, Nathaniel had to concede that Johnnie Barton, as he had perversely preferred to be known, had been more than capable of living up to family tradition.

As with generations of Nathaniel Bartons before him, young Johnnie had been tutored privately by the Guild. This gave Nathaniel pause for thought. If The Book was to be taken literally, *every* young Barton boy had been educated by 'the fencing master.' This had to be some sort of hereditary office, mused Nathaniel, as clearly no one person could have been alive for the best part of four centuries. It did make some sort of sense. Just as one Nathaniel Barton succeeded another, so could the role of tutor, physical trainer and mentor have been passed from father to son.

Parking that thought for now, Nathaniel, with a sense of foreboding and some embarrassment, followed the brief account of his father's life and exploits. Conscripted into the Army, young Johnnie had rapidly demonstrated both his technical prowess with weaponry and his linguistic abilities. In the uncertain waters of the post war Middle East, Captain Barton became an aide de camp to King Abdullah of Jordan in 1951. From that privileged position, Johnnie learnt of the tripartite negotiations between Jordan, Lebanon and the new state of Israel. This threatened to bring stability to a region where, so the Guild apparently reasoned, chaos and uncertainty would better serve their interests.

Johnnie accordingly followed the tried and tested route of persuading a local terrorist cell to carry out the actual deed. He then melted away once the King's death was confirmed.

Nathaniel of course was yet to be born, but he did remember the occasional evening when his father had invited the teenage Nathaniel into the room he rather grandly called 'the study' for a watered down brandy and a 'proper man to man chat.' As Nathaniel remembered them, these tended to be increasingly incoherent monologues rather than real conversations. But he tolerated them for the buzz of the illicit brandies, which became less diluted as the evening wore on. Needless to say, on these occasions his mother invariably retired to bed with some unmentionable female condition.

During these sessions in the study, Nathaniel could recall little of the actual content of his father's reminiscences. They were all distinguished only by their vagueness, though anyone listening would surely have come away with the sense that Johnnie Barton had singlehandedly secured the British interest in the Levant.

With The Book open in front of him, Nathaniel could at last appreciate that his father had made a contribution, however small, towards the establishment of perpetually warring factions in the world's most unstable region. He could hardly see it, though, as a cause for pride.

Reading on, he for the first time learnt of the reason for his father's hasty departure from Exeter in 1980. Nathaniel himself had been newly married and working to establish himself in Kennaway's, but he recalled that trip as representing a major turning point in his parents' lives. It was after his father's return from that unexplained absence that his mother had set out upon the path of alcohol and socialising that had reduced her to the pathetic shadow she was today.

And of course his father's fortunes had never been the same. The business had declined in his absence and collapsed on his return. He became increasingly embittered and dependent upon drink, and it had all ended badly on that fateful Christmas thirty odd years before.

That must have been when Johnnie had been blackballed from the Institution (one family tradition at least that he had managed to live up to). That was when, Nathaniel deduced, Johnnie's appeals to the Guild for support were rejected. And those appeals must have led to his cold body being fished out of an even colder River Exe.

It was clear to Nathaniel that this could no longer be seen as a case of suicide but, like that mysterious drowning of the eighteenth century Nathaniel Barton, as a cold blooded murder.

A few paragraphs later, The Book itself confirmed his deduction. Shockingly, it even named the killer. It was Marcus, the same 'fencing master' who had tutored the young Johnnie and set him on the trajectory that led to him being washed up on a lonely river bank.

To Nathaniel, his once comfortable home, stripped of many of its furnishings, pictures and books, was now very cold. He now realised that the next Nathaniel Barton he would read about would be himself. He topped up his coffee cup again from the whisky bottle, took a deep breath, and turned the page.

Chapter 37

A sharp knock on Faith's door pulled her out of her reverie.

Restored by Alice's kind attentions and perhaps too much Pinot Grigio, she had slowly but methodically stripped her rooms and packed her bags for the flight home. A few minutes on line had confirmed her seat on a flight from Exeter to Amsterdam tomorrow afternoon and then a connection to New York. The Guild hadn't stinted on the price of her ticket and she was beginning to look forward to being pampered on the flight back. The twists and turns of the past few days had left her drained. She needed to get away, from the Guild, from The Book, even from Nathaniel.

She had begun the week with a sense of excitement and purpose. Even the lugubrious Duntze had failed to quench her enthusiasm. The unexpected but delightful nights spent with Nathaniel, the mystery of The Book with its hidden messages and accounts of long gone intrigues, the dash to Salisbury and back, the brutal assault on their homes – it all seemed like a bad movie that should have happened to someone else. She longed for the familiarity of her Tribeca loft, her posse of friends and the edgy New York night life.

She also needed to put an ocean between herself and Marcus. Just the thought of him made her shudder.

Her one regret, she already knew, would be parting from Nathaniel. She could not begin to understand her feelings for him right now, but there was something in his innocence, his boyish excitement at the discovery of his ancestry. However tempered by the grim reality of their family history, that had touched her. She resolved to call on him on Tuesday and say her goodbyes to him properly.

At the knock on her door, Faith glanced at her watch. Yes, Alice was right on time. Draining the last of her wine, Faith checked her makeup and hair in the mirror, took a deep breath, and opened her front door.

'Wow, girl, you're saying goodbye to Exeter in style!'

'You've scrubbed up pretty well yourself, Alice. Shall we go?'

Arm in arm, they walked out of the building to a waiting cab. Sat in the back, looking even more goofy than usual, were the inseparable Josh and Mikey.

Faith raised an enquiring eyebrow.

'Look,' said Alice, 'I had to tell the boys this was your last night, and they both wanted to say cheerio. Hope you don't mind?'

'Of course not, it'll be fun. I'll really miss you guys and your wonderful country.'

The cab dropped the foursome at the end of Gandy Street and they picked their way over the cobbles and up the short climb to the Phoenix.

'My treat,' said Faith, and she headed for the bar with an order for two pints of San Miguel and a Cosmo. The same barman who had served her on her previous visit greeted her with a broad smile and reached for the Mayfair vodka.

'The usual?'

As Faith nodded, a tear came to her eye. She *would* miss this quirky city with its back alleys, churches, rich history and friendly people. Although, she hoped, this would be just one short chapter in her long and eventful life, she felt it would be one she would treasure forever.

On this, her final evening in Exeter, she had no idea that these hopes would be dashed within less than twenty four hours.

She rejoined her friends with the tray of drinks and they chatted inconsequentially while they waited for the hour the poet would start his performance. Faith was grateful that Alice had given the two boys the 'official' reason for her unexpected departure and they were able to pass the time without any searching questions.

Suddenly, like a school of fish swerving en masse at the arrival of a shark, everyone in the bar stood up and moved towards the studio theatre. Faith, Alice, Josh and Mikey went with the flow, and soon found themselves seats a couple of rows back from the stage.

Although Faith now knew what to expect, it was still a thrill. The darkened stage, the swelling bass rhythms, then the insidious snaking swirling words, weaving a path through emotions and feelings she only half realised she had.

As before, the end of the performance took her by surprise. It was as if someone had suddenly turned on all the lights in a darkened room or thrown a bucket of cold water over her. She felt both bereft and complete, wanting more but feeling satisfied.

Alice broke her mood. 'Look, we were thinking of going on down to the quay – you know, a couple more drinks and then dancing the night away?'

'Actually...'

'Sure, sure, we know you've got your flight tomorrow.'

Standing awkwardly between the close packed rows of seats, Faith and Alice hugged, and she waved half heartedly at the two guys who were clearly eager to leave without the embarrassment of showing any emotion.

'I'll email y'all from New York, promise.'

Faith sat down again. She looked around to find that not only was the stage empty but also the auditorium. She sipped at the last of her drink and wondered how she would get back to her flat.

'Excuse me?'

Startled, Faith looked up to see the poet in front of her.

'Didn't I see you at the last event?'

Faith nodded silently. It seemed strange to hear the guy talking with a standard English accent, with no trace of the strong Jamaican patois of his performances.

'I love your work. I know this sounds crass, but where did you learn to speak like that?'

'I've always heard people speaking *like that*, as long as I can remember. My step father, Tristram Codrington, had a holiday home in Barbuda. Most people confuse that with Barbados – they're both in the West Indies and...what's the matter?'

Faith had dropped her empty glass and put her hands to her mouth, in horror or surprise – she wasn't sure. This had to be a coincidence too far.

'Codrington. Did you say Codrington?'

'Sure, that's my name, though my birth name was B...'

'Barton. I know. I know your father.'

Now it was the poet's turn to be amazed. He sat down next to Faith and shook his head slowly.

'This is too, too bizarre.'

'It gets better,' said Faith. 'My name's Codrington too, as it happens.'

'Stop there,' said Natty, 'I think alcohol is called for at this point.'

They found themselves a quiet corner in the bar, which had emptied rapidly as the Monday night action switched to another part of town.

The barman, bravely concealing his disappointment at seeing Faith hook up with the poet, smartly brought over two Mayfair martinis and a bowl of pistachios.

They clinked glasses and Faith could hold back no longer.

'So, your stage name, Natty B – you *are* a Nathaniel Barton, then, like your father?'

'Well, I am legally Natty Codrington – ever since my mom married Tristram, but the Natty B thing is acknowledging my roots. But what do you mean – *a* Nathaniel Barton?'

'There are generations of you, one Nathaniel Barton after another, and they're all kill..'

Faith suddenly put her hand over mouth. It had been shocking enough for her to discover this hereditary guild of assassins in a quiet corner of England. She couldn't really break it to one of the family over a drink in a city centre bar. Natty saved her with a question of his own.

'And how come your name is the same as my late stepfather's? I hardly think you're related.'

'Don't be dense. There are plenty of slave owners who exercised their full 'rights' over their female properties. As it happens, my ancestors were slaves on the Codrington estate on Barbuda, which I guess is the place your step-daddy still owned, and where you went for your summer holidays and learnt to do your blacked-up minstrel act.'

From Natty's wounded expression, Faith realised she had gone too far. She reached out a hand to touch his.

'I'm sorry – that was rude. I really do appreciate your work, honestly.'

'Actually, the poetry is not what I'm proudest of. Would you like to come back and look at my paintings?'

Accepting the offer of a truce, Faith finished her drink, and she and Natty started the walk down to the quayside where Natty had his studio. As they strolled together down the dark back streets of old Exeter, Faith started to give Natty the bare bones of his family's history, from the murderer of Charles II down to his grandfather, drunken Johnnie, the last of the line of assassins.

Before Faith realised it, they had arrived at the quay. Old warehouses had been converted to nightclubs and even this early in the evening they and the local pubs were packed with young men and women embarking on who knew what adventures.

Natty led her past the crowded tables and small groups of revellers to an older building set a little back from the waterside. Eight stories high and built in the local red sandstone, it too had apparently been a warehouse of sorts, once. Projecting beams held rusting pulleys and hatches, and loading bays were dotted at random around the crumbling frontage. But the building had clearly been restored quite recently; Natty swiped an access card across the front of a steel and glass doorway and took Faith through into an elegant dimly lit lobby. Another swipe of the card gave them access to a lift which bore them silently to the top floor.

Faith was reminded of Klein's bookbinding studio but this was both more expensively fitted out and on a much larger scale. Bright Persian rugs were scattered on a white wooden floor. A large hammock piled with silken cushions hung across the far end of the room. Faith could see it was the perfect vantage point for the 80 inch plasma screen above the open fireplace.

Natty went over to a large bright red refrigerator and brought out a bottle of Wray & Nephew rum and a couple of chilled shot glasses.

'Grab a seat. I need you to go back over what you were telling me on the way down. My head's still spinning and I just can't take it all in.'

'Never seen Marcus in a fouler mood.'

'Too true. I had to hide in the Gents just now when I heard him stomping down the stairs.'

'Barton business?'

'Of course. He's snipping off all the loose threads but still...'

'He won't want any awkward questions at the next Hall.'

'Who do you know who would ask Marcus an awkward question?'

There was a period of solemn reflection.

'Last chappie to do that ended up in the river, as I recall.'

'Quite.'

Chapter 38

It was some time before Nathaniel could properly absorb what he had just read. Naturally, he had known that The Book's account of his own life would be free from the murderous intrigues of his forebears. But uneventful as his life in Exeter had been, he was frankly disappointed that he had only merited two short paragraphs. It was the second of these that had rendered him both dumb and motionless. He read through it again.

'*On the morning of Tuesday 16 April 2013, the body of Nathaniel Barton was discovered by his son and his son's future wife, Faith Codrington. He had died from a single thrust of a blade to his heart; no motive for his murder could be found.*'

Nathaniel had been assiduously topping up his coffee mug with scotch, and he now took a further long draught straight from the bottle. For all the apparently fanciful stories that The Book contained, Nathaniel had never doubted their authenticity; and everything that Faith had so doggedly checked seemed to tally with known facts. So it was hard for him now to disbelieve the truth of this particular statement. However well he felt right now (apart from the inevitable effects of the scotch), if The Book was accurate, he would not live to see the next morning.

In a sober state, Nathaniel would surely have been more anxious about his, apparently, impending death. But the combination of too much (far too much) alcohol and the weariness he felt after the helter-skelter sequence of recent events meant that he was now beyond caring. He found the circumstances following his death far more intriguing.

First, the appearance of a son he had not seen for nearly thirty years. How could that happen? Surely the boy – no, the young man – did not even know where he lived. And why would this long lost son turn up now, just when the race was, as it were, almost run?

And, even more improbably, how had his son and Faith met? And how was it that they would marry?

Nathaniel had no illusions about his own relationship with Faith. Though there was genuine affection on both sides, it couldn't be said to be much more than an extended one night stand. Both thrillingly unexpected and unexpectedly thrilling, there had never been any real possibility of the liaison developing any further.

To be honest, the thought of the two young people getting together was really rather lovely...then it hit Nathaniel that, according to The Book, he himself wouldn't be there to witness the outcome. He drained his coffee mug, turned to the whisky bottle again and registered the sad fact that it was now empty. That rather reflected his own feelings.

He looked at his watch and saw that it was already well past ten. He still had things to do. He needed to ready himself for his last night on this earth and, above all, he needed to secure the future of The Book.

He walked glumly up to his bedroom, and laid both copies of The Book on his pillow. Quickly undressing, he placed his dirty clothes neatly in the laundry basket and had a final shower. Drying off, he ran his hand over his jaw line, but reflected that there was little point in shaving.

He returned to the bedroom and looked for the final time at the silver-framed photograph on the mantelpiece. To him, his son would always be that curly headed toddler with the bright eyes, the broad smile, the chubby cheeks and an innocent optimism for a future that Nathaniel could never know.

Fuddled as he was by the whisky, he had conceived of one final plan, a way to secure The Book's future and to protect it, Nathaniel hoped, from those who would seek to take it from him.

Five minutes later, he climbed slowly into bed and lay on his back, The Book clasped in his hands on his chest. Nathaniel now knew his own future at least and he was reconciled to it. In the soft glow of the street lamp outside, still, beneath the white bedcover, Nathaniel in repose resembled a carved mediaeval tomb, though that of a scholar rather than a knight. That may have been his thought too, for as he drifted off to sleep, he could be seen to be smiling a small, private smile.

He did not hear the squeak of his front door opening, or the quiet tread of boots on his stairs.

Chapter 39

However many times Marcus had been present at the ending of a human life, it always struck him as a fresh thought that a corpse invariably looked lighter, smaller, more insubstantial than the living being of a moment before. Slight as an *animula vagula blandula* might be – the 'roving amiable little soul' of Emperor Hadrian's poem – its departure for Hades somehow diminished the flesh it had once inhabited.

One short upward thrust, through the bedclothes and into Nathaniel's heart.

As Marcus had twisted and withdrawn the blade, Nathaniel's eyes had opened. Dead, they looked directly into Marcus' equally lifeless eyes. Marcus had shuddered and then wiped the short sword clean on the corner of the duvet. He picked up the small brown book from Nathaniel's limp hands. Strangely disconcerted by Nathaniel's unseeing gaze, Marcus covered the dead man's face with the bedclothes. His eyes flickered over the strange word scribbled on the wall above the bed.

If he had known what it meant, a number of lives would have been spared.

Turning towards the glow of the street lamp outside, Marcus gazed curiously at The Book, his scar flickering like a lightning bolt. He could not be sure why it was that this inoffensive item could be seen as a threat to the Guild. But what he knew with an iron certainty was that his mission was to protect the Guild's interests at all times, whatever was needed, for as long as necessary.

In the Guild's service, Marcus had been involved in countless deaths over numberless years, but it was only in very few cases that he himself had dealt the lethal blow or supplied the poisonous draught or held the struggling head beneath the rushing water.

Remarkably, five of his victims had been Bartons. Marcus felt sure there would be no more.

Tuesday 16 April 2013

Chapter 40

The first thing that Faith saw when she opened her eyes on what was to be her last morning in Exeter was the bright yellow beak of a seagull, clearly silhouetted against a blue sky on the other side (thankfully) of a large skylight. In a momentary panic, she tried to sit up but felt the bed beneath her heave and shake. Beside her was the snoring form of her new friend of the night before, and she realised that they were both in the hammock.

My, was she relieved to see that they were both fully clothed! She tried sitting up again, but the combination of the hammock's unfamiliar motion and the throbbing of her head persuaded her that, for now at least, horizontal was the preferred option.

Her movement had woken Natty, who smiled broadly at her. With an ease that obviously derived from years of practice, he lightly stepped down from the hammock and began walking across the loft floor.

'Coffee? Juice? Breakfast?'

Faith was still struggling with the aftermath of a large gin martini and half a bottle of white rum, so Natty took the decision for her. Once she had rather inelegantly exited the hammock, visited the bathroom and applied cold water to various parts of herself, Faith was presented with a bowl of milky coffee and two slices of wholemeal toast with honey.

The impromptu breakfast was consumed in a friendly silence as both reflected on the conversations of the night before, a night that had lasted well until dawn had begun to break.

Faith had been exhausted with the constant repetition of the revelations in The Book. It seemed that Natty needed to have the stories of the various Nathaniel

Bartons repeated over and over again before he could believe them. He had been touched by Faith's account of the way that she had first met and then become more closely involved with his natural father. For her part, Faith had surprised herself by the way in which she could speak so openly to a young man she had only met for the first time a few hours before. She recognised in him, though, many of the traits she had found most engaging in Nathaniel – a frankness, a quiet but resilient optimism, and a gentleness that spoke directly to her heart.

It was only when Faith was thoroughly talked out that Natty had led her to the far end of his loft to show her some of his canvasses. They were uniformly blue squares – views, in fact, through the same skylight Faith was now looking through – but each had different patterns of white clouds. Some proud and fluffy cumulus, others frail wisps that could scarcely be seen, but all of them conveying a sense of calm and quiet beauty. Exactly what Faith needed after a long night of emotion and tension.

Over the coming months and years, Faith was to conjure up images of those sky paintings whenever she needed to gather her thoughts, to find a point of peace in the turmoil around her.

Coffee drunk and the last few drops of honey mopped up with a crust, Faith now felt she could speak without causing irreparable harm to her cerebral cortex.

'That was so good, thank you. Now, I need to be at the airport by half past one. That doesn't give me very long...'

'Must you go? I feel we have so much more to talk about.'

As well as telling and re-telling the tales from The Book, Faith had also told Natty of her own background, of her abortive research project, of her encounters with Marcus, of the trip to Salisbury and the burglaries.

'Natty, you know why I have to leave. There is nothing for me here now.'

Natty looked so crestfallen that Faith wanted to hug him. But she recognised that that could be the first step on a *very* slippery slope. She meant what she said. She *had* to leave Exeter, and soon.

'Can you do me a favour? I need a cab to go back to Uni to pick up my bags, and then I need to go and say a quick farewell to Nathaniel.'

'I can do better than that. Let me drive you myself. I feel it's about time I met my dad again after such a long time. We've got a heck of a lot of catching up to do. I'd really like to see this magic book you told me about. *And* we can organise you a cab from his house to the airport easily enough.'

Faith readily agreed. She had to admit that anything that postponed saying her farewells to Natty would be a good idea. And it also occurred to her that reuniting Natty with his father should take everyone's minds off her impending departure for the States.

She was beginning to have second thoughts about leaving Exeter. From the moment that Marcus had handed her the plane tickets, all the fight had drained out of her. All the energy that Nathaniel and The Book (and the letter) had generated just seemed to flicker out. Little Faith had taken over and she was slinking home with her tail well and truly between her legs.

Last night, telling Natty of what she and his father had found, Big Faith was threatening a comeback. Why *should* she just throw in the towel and be bullied into missing out on the greatest historical scoop of all time?

As she reflected, Natty put the breakfast dishes into the sink, picked a bunch of keys from a hook by the door and led her to the lift. He took Faith through the rear door of the building into a large garage carved out of the cliffs towering over the old quayside.

It was as they both climbed into a vintage Alfa Romeo Giulietta that Faith appreciated that, for all his casual attitude and even more casual clothing, Natty Barton was one very rich young man.

'This *your* car?' Faith enquired casually.

'It's the only one I keep at the studio.'

'Hm. Your paintings must sell well then.'

'I get a good price for them when I can be bothered, but to be honest I quite like holding on to them. I am still working to get them right. I still don't believe I have properly captured the light.

And the answer to the question you are very sweetly not asking me is that I inherited an obscene amount of my money from my stepfather. He and my mother couldn't have children together so I was the only son he had. It lets me live as I want. I know I'm very fortunate.'

Damn, thought Faith. Good looking, artistic, modest *and* rich. What a time for her to leave!

By now, they had arrived on the university campus and Faith was able to direct Natty to her hall of residence. She was rather relieved that there were no signs of life in the corridors. Clearly her friends had also indulged rather heavily on the previous evening, if indeed they'd come back to their own flats.

Faith returned to the car with her two cases and cabin bag, and she gave Natty directions for the drive to his father's unassuming terrace.

Both Natty and Faith had their own fears about meeting Nathaniel. Neither knew quite what to say. As they stood nervously on the pavement, Natty made the decision for them both.

'Look, Faith, you should go first, to say your goodbyes. You don't need me there, frankly. Just give me a shout when it's my turn, and then you can slip away. My dad and I will have plenty of chance to catch up after you've got your cab.'

Faith reached up to press the bell but, just as on that earlier day when she and Nathaniel had returned from Salisbury, the unlocked door swung open.

'I don't like the look of this, Natty. Please come in with me.'

Faith reached out and took his hand, and nervously the two of them edged their way into the narrow hall and through into the living room. Although the furnishings were sparse and the bookshelves were almost bare, at least there were no signs of further damage or violence.

'Nathaniel? Nathaniel!'

Almost on tiptoe and still holding hands, they peered into the kitchen and checked the small courtyard garden. Returning through the living room, Natty noticed the empty whisky bottle on the dining table.

'That explains it. The old bastard's still sleeping it off!'

With the tension lifted, they practically skipped up the stairs. Faith then held back. It felt somehow indecent for her to be accompanying Natty into the bedroom where she and his father had first made love. And there was also a rather unpleasant smell.

Natty had gone ahead. The sun was streaming in through the two sash windows; Nathaniel was apparently sleeping peacefully with the duvet over his head. Natty reached across to shake his father's shoulder, then recoiled in horror.

'Faith! He's not breathing. My god, is he dead?'

Faith came into the room and peered past Natty's shoulder. At the same time, they both saw the gash in the duvet and the dried bloodstains.

Faith tried to suppress a sob. Natty's first thought was that whoever had killed his father might still be around – after all, the front door was still ajar. He ran out to search the building, leaving Faith alone with her lover of a few short days, so quickly snatched from her.

She stood stock still, incapable of movement at first. At the same time, her mind was racing. Just a few short days ago, she had been a new arrival in Exeter, no cares in the world but bubbling with excitement at the prospect of some honest to goodness original research.

Then she had been caught up in an inexplicable tale of an unreadable book, a centuries old conspiracy and an all too brief affair with an unfathomable, inoffensive, lovely man.

A man who was now snatched from her by some unknown agent of that dark conspiracy. It was too much to process, let alone understand. Finally, she could move.

'No goodbyes then, Nathaniel. Just this, my dear.'

She kissed the end of her forefinger and placed it gently on his forehead.

It was then that she noticed the word written in black felt marker pen on the wall above the bed:

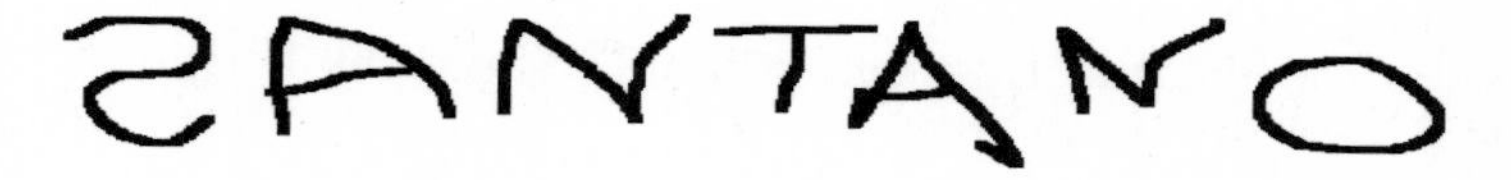

Chapter 41

Faith could keep the emotion back no more and burst into tears as Natty came back into the room. Natty held her close and, though his embrace was firm, Faith could feel that he too was sobbing silently.

Several minutes passed before they could bring themselves to establish beyond doubt what both of them now knew. Pulling back the sheet, the sightless eyes confirmed the awful truth.

Nathaniel's hands were cold and stiff. One of them held a scrap of brown paper, and glancing on the floor, Faith spotted a larger sheet of the same material.

'Look, he must have been holding The Book, and someone's taken it!'

She felt the loss of The Book almost as keenly as that of Nathaniel. Although last night she had been ready to draw a line under her Exeter experiences and move on, she now felt that this was still a personal fight, this was still a story that involved Faith Codrington, and she could not – should not, would not – just let it go.

As she looked up at Natty, she saw a half smile on his face.

'What's so funny?'

'The writing on the wall. You won't know what it means.'

'Isn't it Spanish or Italian or something?'

'Four year old English, I'm afraid. I was just a kid, old enough to know about Father Christmas but not old enough to keep quiet and accept the presents. There was no way I wanted a smelly bearded old man creeping into my bedroom in the middle of the night. So I'd piled stuff in front of the door to keep him out. To make sure, I'd hung this poster outside the window. 'Santa. No!', though I couldn't quite work out how to write S. I remember my dad – Nathaniel – telephoning on Boxing Day, and my mother told him the whole story. I was so embarrassed.'

Natty shook his head ruefully.

'Bless him for remembering the story after all these years. You know, I was so paranoid I'd even stuffed books in the fireplace to stop Santa getting in down the chimney. What an idiot!'

'What a genius!'

Faith half ran, half stumbled to the bedroom fireplace and reached up the chimney. With a cry of delight, she produced a small leather bound volume, somewhat the worse for wear, but to her eyes recognisably The Book that had started her and Nathaniel on their nightmare journey.

But was this The Book, or Daniel Klein's brilliant facsimile? There was one way to find out.

'Natty, help me here. Please take this book from me, now.'

With a look of puzzlement, Natty reached out, grasped the spine firmly, and found himself flung backwards across the room.

Faith gasped. Perhaps that had been a stupid idea. She ran to Natty's side and cradled him in her arms. As she muttered incoherent words of endearment, she looked down to see him gazing up at her with a worryingly goofy expression.

'What the hell was that?' he asked.

'That, my dear, proves that your legal name may be Codrington but you are a true Barton by blood and that this is the true Book. Whoever came here last night (and I have my suspicions) will have gone off with the copy.'

At the same time, it occurred to them both that they were currently in a very compromising position. In a bedroom with a corpse and holding something very valuable that, possibly, the murderer would return to track down.

Slowly, painfully, they climbed to their feet. Natty went over to the bed and touched his father's hand.

'Sorry I never really knew you, dad. I promise you I will look after The Book, for you and for my children.'

As he walked away with head bowed, Faith went over and kissed Nathaniel's forehead. The silent words of comfort that she spoke to herself were for the Nathaniel she had known and for the Natty she hoped she would get to know better.

'Come on, Natty, I think we need to get out of here.'

'Wait and think about this a moment. My dad has been murdered here. The police need to be told, but do we want to be the people found here when they arrive? And haven't we left rather a lot of fingerprints around the building?

I don't want to do this on my own, Faith. Please can we look after The Book together.'

Faith's head was saying no, but her heart was screaming yes. Before she could respond properly, Natty continued.

'I'm used to taking off at a moment's notice, so I can pick up a few things from the studio in minutes. I should be able to get a ticket to Amsterdam with you, and then we can work out where we go from there.'

'Not back to New York?'

'If this Guild is half the organisation you say it is, they'll be able to track you down at any of your known hangouts. We need somewhere they won't look, and I think I have a good idea as to where that might be.'

Natty and Faith carefully retraced their steps back to the front door, wiping with their handkerchiefs any surface they remembered touching. They climbed back into the Alfa.

As they pulled away, a curtain in the house opposite twitched.

Chapter 42

On the short drive back to his quayside flat, Natty was silent, and Faith could sense he was trying to think through what they should do next. Clearly getting out of Exeter was still top of the agenda, but what then?

They arrived back in the car park and Natty turned off the ignition. He looked Faith in the eye. 'I have a plan, but you will need to trust me.'

Faith concluded she had no choice but to place herself in the hands of her new friend. Too many people were dying, and Faith was determined not to join them.

'First thing is, as long as you – we – may be under observation, we should appear to be unconnected. So first thing you should do is take your bags down the quay to the Prospect Inn and call for a cab to take you from there to the airport.

I need to grab a few things from here, sort out my ticket, and make my own way to the airport. Whatever you do, don't recognise me, don't acknowledge me, don't talk to me. Clear?'

Faith nodded, a little taken aback by Natty's new stern tone. He continued: 'In Amsterdam, you should have picked up your bags and got into the main airport concourse by four. I suggest your first job is to dump your luggage in a locker and get some food inside you. Then do the normal hanging around in transit stuff, duty free, fashion shops, grab a magazine. At about half past four, I'll call your mobile. Write the number down for me. Take no notice of what I actually say, but try to look surprised. You must not say anything. When I ring off, you'll collect your cases, follow the signs to where the shuttle buses pick up, and take the one to the Radisson Blu. I'll meet you there.'

Solemnly Faith wrote her phone number on the back of Natty's wrist.

'And my number's on this card. But *please* don't call me or anyone else unless you absolutely have to. These first steps are the hardest for us. They might not know about me and let's keep it that way as long as possible. But they know where you're heading, so it will be fairly easy for them to keep tabs on you. Our first job will be to shake them off.'

Faith didn't need to ask the identity of 'them'.

Natty lifted the bags from the car and held the car park door open so she could make her way out on to the quay. Faith's warm feeling towards her knight in shining armour dimmed somewhat as she contemplated dragging two 50lb suitcases over cobbles towards the Prospect Inn. She realised it would save precious time if she called the cab firm before she started her short but tiring journey, and it was as well she did. She and her taxi arrived at the inn almost simultaneously. By the time cases had been loaded, city centre traffic had been negotiated and luggage had been checked in, she didn't have long to wait before her flight was called.

Ignoring Natty's earlier injunctions, she looked around to see if she could spot his distinctive blond dreadlocks, but he was nowhere to be seen. She began to worry that he might have been unable to get a ticket, or that his cab was delayed.

Then she thought she saw him, almost at the back of the queue for security. But was it him? The dreadlocks were gone, replaced by an unflattering crew cut. He wore rimless glasses, had a small blond goatee, and a large strawberry birthmark covering one side of his neck.

This gave Faith pause for thought. She had been searching for Natty, she had to admit, to gain some reassurance that there was someone looking out for her at the start of what promised to be a nightmarish journey. The fact that he had gone to such lengths in such a short space of time to disguise his appearance was an indication of the seriousness of the threat facing them.

The flight itself had no surprises and they touched down in under two hours and on time. Out of the corner of her eye, Faith saw Natty take down a rucksack from an overhead locker. And as he didn't materialise at the baggage carousel, she deduced he must be travelling light.

She willingly surrendered her own heavy cases to the left luggage lockers. Most of the stuff in them she had never worn, as her stay in Exeter had been so much shorter than planned. Right now, she wasn't sure if she'd need any of that luggage again. In truth, she had no real idea what Natty had in mind, where they would be going, what they would be doing...

Her spirits slumped and she sat on a bench, her head in her hands. Could she really go through with this? Yes, there was The Book, but was that *her* problem? Natty, presumably, had it in his rucksack now. It was surely his legacy, his issue.

But then she reminded herself of her own lifelong commitment to transparency, to truth and to history. And there were crimes going on here, people were being killed, and it seemed the Guild were getting away with it, as they had done for centuries. Tears began to well up in her eyes at the memory of Nathaniel, her sweet, inoffensive Nathaniel lying cold and stiff and alone in his little terraced home.

'Buck up, girl,' she said to herself. Realising that she hadn't eaten for seven hours, she decided to address her brief burst of self pity with some solid Dutch cooking.

Forty minutes later, she was on a red banquette in the Vlaamse Frites with the remains of a Burger Royale before her. Most of the mountain of fries doused in mayo had disappeared, but she was struggling with the burger. Time to wander through the shops and prepare for her 'surprise' phone call.

'Is that it?'

'I know – not much to look at, though it's cost a couple of lives.'

'That we know of.'

'Half a dozen pages of scribble that only make sense if you know the story already. Where's the danger in that?'

'Nevertheless, the fire's the best place for it, I reckon.'

The logs threw off sparks as the book hit them and fell open. The flames swiftly caught the dry pages and the smoke mingled with the smell of cigars and Stinking Bishop.

'Got Marcus' dander up, though. He doesn't often attend to business personally.'

'Something about the Bartons, I fancy. Thank heavens there are no more of them.'

'I'll drink to that.'

'Cheers!'

Chapter 43

After her over large but much appreciated late lunch, it had occurred to Faith that she ought to phone her mother. Heck, her parents didn't even know her stay in England had been summarily cut short. Without thinking of any transatlantic time difference, she dialled the first stored number in her phone.

'Faith, honey, don't you know better than to call during breakfast service. I only answered 'cause I knew this would have to be something pretty important.'

'Well, Ma, it's kind of hard to explain right now, but you see, I've had to leave Exeter...'

There was a loud crash and a shriek from Celeste Codrington that would have shattered a less experienced eardrum than Faith's.

'What are you telling me, baby? Have you done failed that course in the first two weeks?'

Faith knew she couldn't spend time explaining how postgraduate study didn't really work like that.

'No, ma, I'm still your golden girl. It's very complicated and I'm sure things will turn out fine, but for now I just have to have some time to myself for a while.'

For the next five minutes, Faith's mother ran through every possibility that a mother's imagination could conjure up, from shoplifting handbags through sleeping with a lecturer to falling pregnant. Faith had to repeatedly deny each increasingly ludicrous suggestion.

Eventually her mother ran out of ideas and Faith was able to interject more than one or two words of denial.

'Trust me, ma. I've stumbled across something that is incredibly important, but I need to, er, go to Europe to do some further research. So I'll be off radar for a while. But please don't worry – I'll call you as soon as things are sorted.'

'I know you, Faith, and you sure ain't telling me everything. But you're not a little bitty girl any more and yes, I do trust you. Just don't do anything to shame your ma and pa. Or yourself.'

Faith thought she heard a catch in her mother's voice as she said she had to get back to her customers; and Faith herself had to wipe away a tear as the line went dead. But now she had better get on with carrying out Natty's instructions.

She had been admiring some exquisite Italian slingbacks when she heard her phone vibrating in her handbag.

'The package is ready, bitch. Get it NOW, or you know what happens next...'

It was certainly Natty's voice, or at least the Caribbean patois version, but not the sort of call she had expected. Faith had no problem with looking startled.

Shaking her head briefly, she collected her cases from the lockers and went to find the shuttle bus. Twenty minutes later, she was being dropped off at the underground car park at the Radisson Blu hotel. As the other passengers made for the elevator to reception, Faith looked around in the half gloom. Out of the shadows, a hunched figure in a hoody emerged and tapped her on the shoulder.

'Sorry about the charade,' whispered Natty. 'We can talk now. I've taken out the CCTV camera.'

Natty led Faith across to a sleek limousine completely out of character with his scruffy clothing. The huge boot swallowed Faith's luggage with room to spare, and as they settled into their comfortable leather seats, Faith felt that for the first time that day she was safe.

Natty was about to remind her how wrong she was.

'Please give me your phone.' Faith complied meekly.

'Now, are there any numbers on here you need to have?'

'Only my mother's, and I know that by heart.'

'Good.'

Natty took Faith's phone, stepped out the car, and wedged it under the nearside rear wheel. Firing up the engine, he reversed over the device, then sped off towards the car park exit.

'We need to be untraceable. I've bought us a couple of pay-as-you-go throwaways which we can use for now. Paid for in cash and they're impossible to pin on us.'

Faith swallowed, and asked: 'So what now?'

'The end game is a family home in Tuscany but we need to make sure we can't be traced. I'm taking us to a hotel in Leiden tonight – that's to the west. Tomorrow we head south.'

Faith remained quiet as the car carried them to an anonymous hotel on the outskirts of Leiden. She was impressed to see Natty chatting easily in Dutch with the concierge, and even more impressed that he had booked two single rooms. What intrigued her further was that he paid in cash.

Wednesday 17 April 2013

Chapter 44

The next morning they had a simple breakfast of cold meats, hard boiled eggs and toast. For the first time Faith was able to have a good look at the radically transformed Natty in daylight.

'Whatever happened to the locks?'

'Let me tell you while we drive. We've plenty of time ahead of us.'

Once on the A12 into Germany, Natty turned to Faith and smiled.

'The first thing you need to know is that I used to be your typical upper class spoilt brat. Although Nathaniel had a decent wage, once my mom hooked up with Tristram, money was no object. I was at a public school (private as you'd call it on the other side of the pond) and we were trained in Imperviousness, Basic Arrogance, and Extreme Self Confidence.

Oxford University gave me more of the same, and at 21 I not only had no idea as to what my career would be but I also knew I didn't need a career.

So, obviously, drug dealing was the way to go. The best quality snow and blow, retailed to old school and uni chums at an obscenely embarrassing mark up. For two years I wheeled, dealed, reeled and concealed. I didn't really need the money, but I sure appreciated the thrill.

The key to success was having a choice of identities. At one time, the young Nathaniel Codrington had half a dozen passports, twice as many bank accounts and a different driving licence for every month of the year.

When I grew up and grew my locks, I put all of that behind me, but for some reason, I held on to some of the gear, packed in a little black bag.'

'Why?' asked Faith, intrigued at these new revelations.

Natty was silent for a few moments.

'Not sure. Might have been nostalgia, might have been paranoia. Whatever, it's pretty useful now.'

'So where does the extravagant birthmark come in?'

'That's easy. When you're living a secret life (or lives) the whole point is not being noticed, or rather, not being remembered. With a so-called deformity like this (thanks to stage makeup), people look away in embarrassment and all they remember is the birthmark. Everything else is out the window. Wash it off, and no one knows who you are.'

By now, the Mercedes had whisked them across the Dutch border and they were in Germany.

'So who are you now?' enquired Faith.

'Well, it was Alan Burn who flew from Exeter to Amsterdam and who paid for the car and the hotel. But with you I'd like to be just Natty.'

'Works for me! Now, enlighten me on where all this cloak and dagger stuff is leading us.'

'Our starting point should be that a Guild that has been operating for 500 years across most of Western civilisation wouldn't find it difficult to keep tabs on a couple of ordinary travellers, particularly in a world of internet and global connectivity.'

'Fair enough.'

'So, the little charade at the airport and the subterranean switch at the hotel might – just might – throw them off the scent for a while. Remember, they don't know about Nathaniel Codrington *or* Alan Burn, so they'll still be wondering what you are up to.'

'The phone call about the package should have them scratching their heads for a while...'

'Indeed so. I'm assuming that, somehow, they will find a way to listen to the conversation. That's why I used a payphone at the airport. The other thing is we'll keep switching our method of transport and we'll pay for everything in cash.'

Natty noticed Faith's raised eyebrow and added: 'Believe me. Money is not a problem. We'll never live long enough to spend what is in my trust fund, let alone my less than legal profits from a misspent youth.'

Faith smiled. She rather liked the sound of that 'we'.

'Drawing a veil over that, what's the plan from here?'

'First leg is the dreariest. Nine hours of soulless autobahn to Kitzbühl in Austria which is where I (or rather, Alan Burn) will be returning this lush vehicle to Mr Hertz.

Next leg is a scenic train ride to Venice via Innsbruck, then a short flight to Pisa.'

Faith, who had been bowled over by the trip from New York to Exeter, was reeling at the prospect of this whistle stop tour round European cities that until now had only been names in holiday brochures. Natty pulled over calmly to let a red BMW pass him at a cool 200 kilometres per hour.

'We finish up at a family villa in Tuscany, if you're agreeable...' Faith rolled her eyes '...and we hole up there while you pull together the historical revelation of the century.'

'Sounds good to me,' said Faith, 'd'you mind if I have a bit of shut eye.'

The next hours sped past in a bit of a blur. Just south of Cologne, they pulled into a rest stop for a full tank of fuel, two huge chicken sandwiches and a six pack of Diet Coke. There were many questions rattling around in Faith's head but she thought that she might get clarity on one issue at least.

'Alan Burn. Where did he come from?'

'The simple answer is that he was a poor young lad who died at three months old. I used his birth certificate to build my alternative identity during my drug dealing days.

But the real reason? Burn is not a terribly common name. *Burns*, like the poet, is *very* widespread, but Burn singular is not. It was my mother's maiden name. As she was an only child and the name looked likely to die out with her, I rather felt it would be good to preserve it.'

Faith nodded in agreement. Names were so important – Codrington, Barton or Burn.

They rejoined the autobahn and by six, they were pulling into the forecourt of the Krallerhof Hotel.

As they were shown to their first floor suite, Faith was reminded of her brief stay in Salisbury with Nathaniel. Who could have predicted that four tumultuous days later she would be in this prestigious ski resort?

'I took the liberty of booking you a massage in the hotel spa, Faith. Gives me time to drop off the car, make some calls and pick up a couple of things in town.'

Faith was happy to acquiesce. Their suite had two separate bedrooms as well as a large sitting room and a balcony overlooking the snow capped mountains on the other side of the valley. She claimed the larger room with the more impressive view, and spent some time transferring the contents of her cases to the capacious wardrobes. When she'd finished, it then occurred to her that she had no idea how long they would be staying. Indeed, would she need any of the things in that wardrobe again? She shrugged, and went down to the spa in the hope that some pampering could untie the knot in her stomach.

Thursday 18 April 2013

Chapter 45

As Sophie sat at her desk in the entrance hall of Kennaway & Partners, she surprised herself by considering how much she was missing the daily cut and thrust with Nathaniel Barton. Since his departure on sick leave followed by his summary dismissal three days ago, the atmosphere in the building seemed to be considerably more subdued.

Colleagues appeared less inclined to recognise that she was there as they passed her desk. Worse still, the steady stream of gossip which she was accustomed to receive, judiciously edit and then re-circulate had dried up entirely. Did no-one trust her with secrets any more?

Even CK himself was avoiding her gaze as he came to and fro, and their daily diary meetings were now purely functional exchanges with none of the cheerful banter she had become used to over the years. It was almost as if he was blaming her for Nathaniel's departure. But she knew in her heart that she had only acted as any long serving loyal employee would have done.

Today, CK seemed in a particularly foul mood. An unscheduled meeting at 1pm with two representatives of the Guild of Weavers, Fullers and Shearmen had meant that Sophie had to frantically re-schedule the rest of that day's appointments, and Kennaway's disappointed clients had had no qualms about giving her a hard time. She wondered whether it was too early in the day for a restorative sip of vodka.

As her hand crept towards the bottom drawer of her desk almost of its own volition, the front door of number fourteen was opened with a bang. Without a word of acknowledgement, the slim black figure she had always known only as Marcus swept imperiously past her and straight in to CK's office.

Charles Kennaway was standing with his back to the double height Georgian window with its view of Southernhay Gardens. His two visitors were perched uncomfortably on Georgian library chairs, briefcases on their laps.

One of them was asking, 'So can you assure us that the summary dismissal of Mr Barton was in no way connected to the Guild?'

All three turned to Marcus as he strode across the office to the high bookcase. He ran his eyes rapidly over the shelves, found the volume he wanted, pulled it out and briefly examined the back cover. With a disdainful sniff, he threw the book on the floor, turned on his heel, and strode back through the office door.

The three men looked at each other in dumb amazement and then looked as one through the open door to see Sophie holding a half bottle of vodka to her lips. There was a muttered '*Me hercule!*', the front door of the building slammed and Marcus was outside once more.

The Southernhay Gardens that Marcus saw before him was a long narrow expanse of grass and tasteful planting that ran along the line of the old city wall down to the remains of the old South Gate. The parallel rows of Georgian buildings on either side were interspersed with the occasional modern building, each marking a hit for the Luftwaffe during the Exeter Blitz seventy years before. Marcus remembered it all too well but preferred not to dwell on the past. The present demanded all his attention.

He took a seat on a bench under an ancient beech tree and reflected on what he had just confirmed. Two days ago, he had had to dispose of Nathaniel Barton and to recover the apparently inoffensive leather bound volume Nathaniel had been clasping firmly as he slept.

Marcus' first reaction had been one of relief. While he had no direct knowledge of what this book had looked like or contained, the principal concern was that it was a loose end. Neither he nor anyone else in the Guild appeared to know of its existence, let alone its contents. In truth these had turned out to be harmless and uninformative. Yes, there had been a hint of something 'not quite right' in the final journal entry, but nothing that should have prompted alarm. These were after all the ramblings of an obscure eighteenth century solicitor which had lain undiscovered in an even more obscure Institution.

It was hard, then, to see what harm The Book could have caused, especially now that Marcus had eliminated the last of the Nathaniel Bartons. And yet...

The Nathaniel Barton who had recently led Marcus such a merry dance had meekly surrendered and gone to bed with The Book in his hands. It didn't seem to make sense. Marcus knew that the meek conveyancing solicitor was no hardened warrior or experienced plotter. So had he just given up?

The other mystery was that much of The Book had consisted of empty pages. This much he had known since reading the entry in the Institution's Acquisitions Book.

He had tested those blank pages for invisible inks and secret writing, but that had yielded nothing. So how could The Book have posed a threat? Marcus did not know, and this lack of knowledge troubled him.

It was as he had sat pondering these same imponderables yesterday with The Book on his lap that his fingers had started idly picking at a corner of the cover. When Marcus had looked down, he realised that he had unconsciously teased out the end of a long black hair, not a stout bookbinding thread. He had thought little of it at the time and he'd been relieved to hand the book over to the Guild.

Then, waking with a start at three in the morning, he'd remembered.

Some years ago (was it 1993?), the senior partner at Kennaway's, CK's father, had wished to mark the bicentenary of the practice with a lavishly bound history of his predecessors. Against his better judgement, Marcus had been present at the drinks party held in celebration of the anniversary. He recalled being cornered by the small rotund craftsman from Salisbury who had been commissioned to carry out the binding work – to a standard, Marcus recalled, many times greater than the self serving text it housed.

Klein had been the name, and he had spoken, tediously, of his family tradition, stretching back through generations in Ulm, of incorporating into the binding a hair of the craftsman who had carried out the vanity project for Kennaway's.

The twenty year old memory had now been confirmed by inspecting a copy of that same commemorative volume in CK's office, and Marcus was now in possession of an uncomfortable fact. The book which he had thought represented the end of his mission and which he had passed to the Guild was merely a copy. He now needed to go to Salisbury in search of the original.

It was unlikely that Reuben Klein himself was still alive, but *someone* had carried out that work for Nathaniel Barton, and someone would pay dearly.

Saturday 20 April 2013

Chapter 46

The day after Faith and Natty arrived in Austria was spent entirely in a bubble. They didn't leave the hotel at all and spent most of the time in their room. Faith took the opportunity to unwind after the roller coaster ride of the past few days. Natty seemed relaxed and self contained, but slipped away a few times to make phone calls or log on to the internet using the hotel's facilities in the lobby.

At breakfast on Saturday morning, Natty had broken the bad news.

'I've got us train tickets for ten past one this afternoon. We're travelling light, so we'll need to jettison everything we can't fit into rucksacks.'

Seeing the glum expression on Faith's face, Natty tried to reassure her.

'Remember we'll be able to replace everything for you in the land of Prada, Dolce & Gabbana, Armani, Valentino, Gucci, Fiorucci...'

'Stop, stop, stop,' spluttered Faith who had been sinking her teeth into a particularly luscious Sachertorte. 'I get the message!'

Half an hour later, Faith had concluded that apart from 'basics' – which for her simply comprised her ipad along with the two changes of clothes – she only needed to take the new shoes she had picked up during her all too brief stay in Exeter, for sentimental reasons if nothing else.

Natty kept the rucksack he had travelled with from Exeter. The most precious item it held was The Book.

As they left the hotel, Natty had a final word with the concierge and some more cash discreetly changed hands. As their cab took them first to a charity shop where the cases of clothing were gratefully received and then to the railway station, Natty explained what that conversation was about.

'The hotel booking was for four nights. I 'persuaded' Heinrich to overlook the fact that we are checking out early. If the Guild *do* manage to trace us this far, that might just confuse them a little.'

With their train for Venice leaving a little after one, Natty and Faith tackled hot beef rolls with lashings of pickles and sweet mustard washed down with litres of lager. This might not be Germany, but the Austrian cafe owners shared the same predilection for extravagant portion sizes as their more northern cousins.

When Natty commented on how well Faith was managing to keep up her consumption of oversized food, she reminded him that she had spent the last couple of years in New York, the spiritual home of the gargantuan sandwich.

As she wiped the last crumbs and mustard from her chin, Faith reached across the table and gently touched Natty's wrist.

'I haven't asked before now. It's been such a whirl and also, whenever I think of Nath-, of your father...' She fell silent for a while.

'The thing is, Natty, did you call the police before we left Exeter?'

'Well, yes, and it was a bit strange. I thought the best thing would be to say that I lived across the street and had noticed the front door opposite was swinging open and wondered if there was anything wrong. I was transferred to someone who asked me if I was the same person who'd phoned before with the same story. I began to get worried. It sounded as if they were trying to keep me talking while the call was being traced, so I rung off.

Then last night, I used a computer in the hotel lounge to check a news website. Yes, Nathaniel's – my father's –

murder *has* been discovered and the police are investigating. That's all I know.'

The two sat silently for a while. It was good news (of a sort) that Nathaniel had been found and that he would now be cared for. As to where any police investigation might lead, they could only hope it would not involve them.

The rail journey from Kitzbühl through Innsbruck provided a series of bland picture postcard views and the twenty miles spent in the tunnel under the Alps was downright boring. But the spectacular scenery of the Brenner Pass, followed by the less dramatic but achingly beautiful vistas of the northern Italian lakes and the Venetian lagoon, kept Faith's face almost permanently glued to the panoramic windows of their first class coach.

Natty too was, to his own surprise, swept up in the thrill of the journey. All his previous trips to Italy had been by plane, a method of moving from A to B that efficiently replaces the real experience of travel with an unappetising blend of tedium and discomfort. Now, for the first time since he had left Exeter, he found himself starting to relax. He was beginning to like the feeling he got just hanging out with Faith, and he wondered whether it might lead to anything more.

The trip by water taxi from the Santa Lucia station to their hotel on the Grand Canal passed Faith by in a blur. Frustrated at the news that they would be leaving again in less than twenty four hours, she was consoled by Natty's promise that they would return and spend some more time there together. She could not help wondering whether that would be as friends or lovers.

What they could not know then was that they would indeed be back in only a few weeks, but as fugitives, running for their lives.

Sunday 21 April 2013

Chapter 47

The next morning, as Faith made short work of her packing for the final leg of their journey, Natty was on his mobile, this time chatting in very plausible Italian. She wondered whether there was any end to her companion's talents

The flight from Venice to Pisa was longer than Faith expected, but uneventful. She spent most of the flight absorbing an Italian phrasebook and dictionary she had bought at the airport. She was determined not to depend entirely on Natty when they went out and about over the coming months.

As Faith set off for the taxi rank opposite the Pisa airport terminal, Natty called her back.

'Sorry, girl, we've a bit of walking to do now.'

With clear blue skies and a temperature at a very comfortable 18 degrees, Faith shrugged and followed Natty down one of the featureless roads that seem to surround every small European airport. Within minutes, they were, almost, in the countryside. But increasing numbers of light industrial buildings confirmed that they were entering an area of Pisa that few tourists got to see.

Faith could no longer contain her curiosity.

'And the reason for this charming detour is...?'

'Simple. We're almost at our destination, and Toscano is going to be our home for a while now. So we need transport; and what better than...'

They had arrived in the Via Augusti Righi and were standing in front of a car dealership. Natty gestured grandly at a gleaming dark blue Land Rover parked on the forecourt.

'There she is – our very own chariot of fire!'

As Faith walked cautiously round the vehicle which looked like a more angular version of her father's old Jeep, an impossibly handsome figure in a pale grey suit emerged from the building.

As the two men caught sight of each other, they both crouched, slapped their chests with their hands and cried out, 'Panza! Panza! Panza!'

Before Faith could ask what on earth all *that* was about, the two had embraced and kissed each other on either cheek. Natty made the introductions.

'Faith, meet Salvatore Amati – dorm mate at school, one-time partner in crime, and now Signor Respectable in Pisa.'

'Natty always had a talent for spotting beautiful women. Good to see he hasn't lost it.'

Before Faith could lose it, Natty had handed Salvatore a small brown envelope in exchange for the keys to the Land Rover. He helped her to mount the high step into the passenger seat.

As Natty pulled out into the road, he called back through the open window.

'You never saw us, Salva!'

'Never saw you? I don't even know you!'

Faith settled into her seat as the Land Rover merged into the busy traffic on the superstrada for Florence.

'So what's with the Panza business?'

Natty smiled.

'Salvatore, our friend Hugh and I were room mates at school. We all moved on to Oxford and remained very close. So close that Salva and I went into, er, business together after graduating. Hugh was the goody goody. He joined the police for heaven's sake. One of our school set books for A level was *Don Quixote* and we realised that if we put our initials together, we could spell 'Sancho'.'

Faith recalled that Don Quixote's fiercely loyal (if slightly dim) companion was called Sancho Panza.

'So 'Panza' was kind of your war cry?'

'Very much so. We swore an oath in blood (schoolboys eh?) that we would always, *always*, come to each other's aid if we used the magic word. And that's what happened with Salva. I phoned him from our hotel in Venice and, although we hadn't spoken for maybe two years, he was ready to help in any way he could.'

Natty stopped talking for a few minutes as he negotiated a queue of traffic behind an oil tanker. 'I'd do the same for him; and I guess, if it came to it, we'd lay down our lives for each other.'

The couple fell silent for a while. While Faith had no real understanding of the English public school system and the bonds it could create, she had to be impressed by the strength of feeling in Natty's words.

It would be some time before they truly appreciated what that bond would lead to.

Chapter 48

Halfway up the deeply rutted track, Natty halted, turned off the engine and wound down the window.

'Listen to that,' he said.

'What?'

To begin with, Faith could hear nothing. It was the first real silence she had experienced in their mad dash across Europe. Then, as her ears strained, she began to make out a subtle symphony of interweaving sounds. The muted croaking of a pond full of frogs, the occasional chirp of a small songbird against a background of gently stridulating crickets. A gentle warm breeze rustled the leaves of a nearby olive tree.

'Nearly there,' said Natty after some minutes. He restarted the engine and the Land Rover resumed its lurching progress up the hillside.

So, here they now were, just entering the small estate that Natty said had belonged to the Codringtons (*his* family, not hers) for nearly sixty years. Nine hundred miles from Exeter, Devon, four thousand miles from Exeter, Ontario. Suddenly she felt very alone, adrift.

'Natty – why are we here?'

'Why are we *here*? Or why are we here *here*?'

'Don't go all clever and philosophical on me. We've come so far, so quickly. I know we're running away, from the people who killed your father and who would probably kill us if they found us. But what are we running to? And why have you come with me?'

'I can see why you're a historian. You ask the right questions...'

Faith shot him a hard stare.

'And I expect the right answers!'

'The quick and simple answer is – I like you, and I'm sure I would like you more if I got to know you better. But there's more.

You knew my father, in some ways better than I ever did. I'm not looking for detail, but would like to know what you knew of him.

There's simple chivalry as well, maiden in distress and all that. There's someone out to get you and I'm determined to stop them.

And then there's The Book. It's not just a history of my family, for better or worse; there's real history in there, stuff that the world doesn't know, and I think you're the person who can get it out there. And here's the place we can do it...'

The Land Rover took them over a crest from which they could look down on a sprawling tiled farmhouse. On one side, a pergola covered in an ancient vine provided shade. On the other, a winding path led towards a small swimming pool artfully set in level ground above disused terracing. The ground sloped steeply away on two sides, giving fine views of the woodlands in the valley and of the hilltop village of Casole d'Elsa beyond.

For once in her life, Faith was at a loss for words. This was a miniature paradise. The distant village aside, there was not another house in view. Given a decent internet connection, she could write and study here to her heart's content and yes, perhaps she and Natty *could* come to know each other better.

While Faith was distributing her few belongings around her new bedroom and Natty was compiling a list of items they would need to buy from the nearest supermarket, they were naturally unaware of what was being broadcast on the early evening news in the UK. There had been a shocking murder in the Cathedral Close in Salisbury. The police were giving little away. A national redtop had acquired some details after a conversation with a constable who needed some 'help' with his gambling debts, but they were far too gruesome to publish.

Unsubstantiated reports on the internet spoke of a bookbinder's tools being used against him and of white walls spattered with blood. Whatever the full story, the long saga of the Klein family had come to an inglorious and painful end. Police were following up reports of a white van seen in the vicinity, but as time passed it was clear that those responsible would never be found.

Whether Faith and Natty would be found was a question they tried hard not to think about. Their focus was now to be The Book, the documenting of its secrets, and each other.

Tuesday 23 July 2013

Chapter 49

They were beginning to get used to the constant heat and humidity. Perched on the terracotta rooftop, they felt as if they were immersed in lukewarm water, even as the sun began its descent. The dusk light was almost luminous, clear enough for them to pick out a small sounder of boar rootling at the wood's edge. Crickets chirped; frogs croaked; somewhere a cuckoo called. Behind them, the lights began to twinkle on one by one in the hilltop town.

'Are we safe here?' she asked.

'Are we safe anywhere?'

'We have each other...'

'And The Book.'

They kissed, slowly, and one by one the stars twinkled too.

Outside the terminal building at Pisa Airport, a short man clothed in black and holding a small black leather bag was standing completely still. He sniffed slowly and the ghost of a smile played around his thin lips.

The white scar that ran from his forehead to his chin appeared to glow in the setting sun. He sniffed the air again.

After more than two thousand years, he was home. He would find them. He would find The Book.

If you have read this far, you will know that the story of The Book and of Faith and Natty is far from finished.

It continues in 'Brother Martin's Library of Unreadable Books'. *Here is the first chapter.*

Chapter 1

The first time Faith went down the well she had wanted to die. The impenetrable blackness was bad enough; but when she flicked on the little light attached to the stupid elasticated band round her head, it somehow made matters worse.

Darkness is darkness, but light brings shadows. And shadows hide ugly black nameless things that can jump out and get you. However many times Faith went down the well – it must have been ten or eleven times by now – it never seemed to get any easier. Yet Natty insisted on it; once a week, at different times and on different days, but always beginning with that long slow climb down a rusting iron ladder into an unseen void below.

She had to admit, though, that the repetitive, tedious scary process was necessary. It was two months now since they had arrived in what had been Natty Codrington's family holiday home in the heart of Tuscany. The former farmhouse was perched on a low hill overlooking woodland on three sides and, in the middle distance, the hilltop village of Casole d'Elsa surrounded by fertile plains. The interior of the building had been restored with a combination of excellent taste and significant amounts of money, the former provided by his artistic mother, Sally, and the latter by his stepfather, Tristram. But while the setting and the farmhouse itself were both beautiful, it was the remoteness and anonymity of the location that meant most to Faith and Natty.

Earlier that year, Natty's natural father, Nathaniel Barton, had discovered a book – *The* Book – that told the story of generations of Nathaniel Bartons who had acted as assassins for the Exeter-based Guild of Weavers, Fullers and Shearmen. That discovery had cost Nathaniel his life – and the lives of others who had helped him. Faith had befriended Nathaniel, although at first she had been engaged by a man called Marcus to spy on him. Now Nathaniel was dead and Faith – who now had The Book - was on the run.

Fortunately, she had Natty Codrington on her side. An artist and poet, heir to a large fortune but with the feral skills and cunning acquired through a period as a drug dealer in his early youth, Natty had ferried Faith through Europe to this idyllic Italian hideaway.

The kitchen was the heart of the farmhouse and it was the room in which Faith and Natty spent most of their waking hours when indoors. In the centre was an imposing oak table flanked by benches and with a high backed chair at either end; at a pinch, a good two dozen people could have sat round it. Across one end wall ran a long marble worktop with two deep sinks inset. There was an open fireplace with a log store on one side and a wood fired oven on the other. Next to the oven was the curved wall of the well; its opening was covered with an oak worktop which continued round two walls above cupboards and shelving. Two generous windows gave views of the vegetable plots and the fields beyond.

It was during the second evening after their arrival that Natty had told Faith the story of the well. They sat at the oak table, their plates cleared of pasta but with generous glasses of Chianti in their hands. The early summer temperature was low enough to justify a small fire and the logs glowed and crackled cheerfully.

Natty was relating the history of the farmhouse.

'No-one knows how old this building really is. I remember a pal of mine who stayed with us one year was convinced that it is on the site of a Roman villa. What *is* true is that dad – Tristram, that is – uncovered some mosaic pavement when they dug out the swimming pool. And as a boy I was always able to find mysterious pieces of rusted metalwork and odd parts of statues without much effort.'

Faith, who had carried out a bit of her own research on arriving at the farmhouse, chipped in. 'It's probable, isn't it, that the old pilgrimage route in the valley below was Roman too?'

'I'm coming to that', said Natty. 'When Tristram bought this place, it was owned by a family called Moretti. In fact, Maria Moretti, the matriarch of the family was our housekeeper.

Towards the end of the Second World War, when the Italians had pretty well given up but the Germans were determined to hold the line against the Allied invaders, the Moretti brothers were part of a resistance movement, taking pot shots at Germans, sabotaging trucks, generally being a nuisance.'

Natty went across the kitchen to the old well; with something of a flourish, he released a catch under the countertop and lifted it up to reveal the opening beneath. A waft of cold damp air came into the kitchen, and Faith recoiled.

'And this was the Morettis' escape route. They planned that, if ever they were attacked here by the Germans, they would scoot down the well shaft and out through an old water course to emerge in the bushes alongside the valley road.

And you're right. It was a pilgrims' way known as the *Via Francigena* – the road from France, though it's usually thought of as starting from Canterbury. And it follows the line of an older, Roman road.'

'And you're telling me this because?'

'Isn't it obvious? We've just spent five days zigzagging across Europe to this (we hope) safe haven where you plan to write up everything we can discover in The Book. You're then going to publish, destroy the Guild, and become a rich and famous historian.'

'Unless the Guild get to us first.'

'Quite. That's why we need this well. From what little we know, the Guild is powerful and has powerful friends. Despite all the precautions we took, it is entirely possible they may find us here before your work is complete, so we do need to be able to leave the building quickly. The well shaft has a ladder and the cave at the bottom leads us out to the salt road, which is where I'll be parking the Land Rover from now on. I suggest we keep an emergency bag down there too in case we have to make a quick getaway, and I shall insist we rehearse the procedure every week.'

Melodramatic as this seemed, Faith only had to recall the dead look in Marcus' eyes to appreciate that they needed to keep out of his clutches. If that meant risking a return of all her childhood fears of darkness and confined spaces, so be it.

End Notes

These notes are intended to be read only after you have read the story. Otherwise, you will find a combination of plot spoilers and distracting snippets of information that could spoil your enjoyment.

If you have any further questions or comments, I am very happy to be emailed at ivereadthebook@gmail.com.

The origins of this story

Temperamentally, I have always been an only child, even though reality compels me to acknowledge the existence of two significantly younger brothers. I was raised in a working class family which valued words, reading, literature and creativity.

I believe that one consequence of these two factors has been that at very regular intervals I have, with no conscious effort, been presented with what I have felt (modestly) were brilliant ideas for works of fiction.

These have been very diverse in terms of subject matter and tone. One was based on the idea that the Roman emperor Nero did not commit suicide in 68AD but fled to the Middle East where he underwent a spiritual renaissance and became a prophetic figure. Another book that never saw the light of day was a murder mystery set in a dystopian future where a rich tourist could holiday by transferring his brain to the body of a third world peasant farmer.

These 'ghost books' never found their way onto the page, for whatever reason. I was too busy, I lacked the confidence to work the idea into a proper story, the ideas themselves could not be developed.

This story is something else. It appeared in my head in broad outline one April morning, and it arrived at a fertile time. Though I am constitutionally lazy, I have always thrown myself into my work. But in April 2013 this was no longer the case. I found I had the head space to pick this story up, to turn it round and to twist it in the light. A long holiday in an idyllic but extremely hot retreat in Mallorca (thank you, Claire) gave me the time to put a few thousand words down on paper, or at least up in The Cloud. Then, finding my full time job had disappeared in my absence, I now had the time to complete the task.

This experience has been delightful. I have experienced a phenomenon that previously I had ridiculed, that the characters in a book could determine what happened next. As I transferred words to paper, I found that some key elements of my original conception were discarded and that new characters and plot elements came to the fore. But the story itself survived.

The end result is one that I find myself pleased with. What is even more pleasing is that, following the publication of this first volume, I now have the opportunity to write more about the legacy of the Bartons and the machinations of the Guild.

The fact that you are now reading this is my greatest reward.

The Nathaniels

The first name for the central character that came into my head was 'Nathaniel Bowden'. I don't know where that came from. The only Bowden I ever knew was a fellow sixth former I haven't seen for almost fifty years.

After drafting the first chapter, it then occurred to me that there was an issue about the way 'Bowden' should be pronounced. It reminded me of those interminable debates in the seventies about David Bowie. Was it 'bow' to rhyme with 'slow' or with 'how'. I felt this might get in the way of some readers' enjoyment of the story, so switched to 'Barton'.

Why 'Barton'? It has a vaguely historical feel, and it may be echoing a TV drama that made an impact on this author in his youth ('Vote, Vote, Vote for Nigel Barton'). For 'Nigel', read 'Nathaniel'.

But just as the bare bones of this story appeared in my head one morning, the origin of the hero's name is also mysterious. Frankly, I'm not bothered.

The Book refers to eleven Nathaniel Bartons; brief dates below.

1) Nathaniel Barton, fuller, b. 1654(?), d. 1685

2) Nathaniel Barton #1, lawyer, b. 1720, d. 1780, m.(1) Anne Spry 1739; m.(2) Mary Kennaway 1766

3) Nathaniel Barton #2, clerk, b.1767, d. 1829, m. Elizabeth Jeffery 1798

4) Nathaniel Barton #3, merchant, b. 1799, d. 1880, m. Emma Baring 1820

5) Nathaniel Barton #4, merchant, b. 1823, d. 1881, m. Fanny Blackall1846

6) Nathaniel Barton #5, importer, b. 1848, d. 1908, m. Emily Tucker 1870

7) Nathaniel Barton #6, banker, b. 1871, d. 1914, m. Hannah Thomas1909

8) Nathaniel Barton #7, stockbroker, b. 1903, d. 1973, m. Edith Brock 1930

9) Nathaniel 'Johnnie' Barton #8, estate agent, b. 1931, d. 1983, m. Sarah Milford 1953

10) Nathaniel Barton #9, solicitor, b. 1957, d. 2013, m. Sally Burn 1982 (divorced 1985)

11) Nathaniel Codrington (né Barton), poet and painter, b.1981

It should go without saying that all Nathaniels lived in Exeter and each (except for the most recent) had at least one son.

The surnames of the various spouses are all shamelessly taken from the roll of Masters of the Guild of Weavers, Fullers and Shearmen.

The Organisations

The Guild of Weavers, Fullers and Shearmen

Throughout my fiction, this body has for consistency been referred to as the Guild of Weavers, Fullers and Shearmen, usually abbreviated as 'the Guild'. In fact the name of the organisation at the time of writing is The Incorporation of Weavers, Fullers and Shearmen, a title conferred in 1620. Before that date, it is variously referred to as a Company or Guild (or Gild). The first documented references date from the fifteenth century, but it almost certainly existed in some form before then.

For those interested into looking at Guild records, it should be noted that they are <u>not</u> held in the Devon & Exeter Institution as stated in The Book. Some are retained by the Incorporation's company secretary, some are at the Devon Heritage Centre, and there is an exciting project to digitise the minute books, thus making them far more widely available to interested parties.

http://tuckershall.org.uk/index.php/history

http://www.exetermemories.co.uk/em/_buildings/tuckers_hall.php

The Devon & Exeter Institution

This is a magnificent though little known organisation situated in Exeter's Cathedral Close. It was founded in 1813 with the aim of '...promoting the general diffusion of Science, Literature and Art, and for illustrating the Natural and Civil History of the county of Devon and the city of Exeter'. Its history and current state are broadly as described in The Book, though there are a number of significant differences between the Institution as portrayed in this fiction and the real thing:

- The people who work there are different
- The relationship with the University is slightly different
- There is no *Major* or *Minor* Library – they are *Inner* and *Outer*
- There is no map table in the centre of the room
- The cataloguing system is somewhat different

The need for urgent restoration of the building's fabric *is* genuine, as is the news story that alerted Nathaniel Barton to the Institution's existence.

http://www.devonandexeterinstitution.org/

Kennaway & Partners

This is of course an entirely fictitious legal practice, bearing no relationship whatsoever with the firm of lawyers that, in the real world, currently occupies numbers 13 through 15 in Southernhay, Exeter. Although, as they say, 'other solicitors are available', Crosse & Crosse (www.crosse.co.uk) is particularly worthy of note, having supplied the southwest with its first female partner in a solicitors' practice.

The Places

Bishop Blaize Inn

The Bishop Blaize Inn, dating back to 1327, was the first public house to be built outside Exeter's city walls. Saint Blaize is the patron saint of weavers and the pub is conveniently situated next to the fields where weavers and fullers stretched their cloth on racks with tenterhooks. It was only natural that this should have been the meeting place of the Guild of Weavers, Fullers and Shearmen until 1471, when that function was taken on by Tuckers Hall in Fore Street.

Equally it was an obvious rendezvous for the eighteenth century Nathaniel Barton to meet his anonymous drinking companion before his untimely drowning in the nearby river.

Casole d'Elsa

This is a living Tuscan hilltop town. The property where Faith and Natty are staying is based on one that used to be let by the fine villa lettings company, Invitation to Tuscany: http://www.invitationtotuscany.com

Combe House

This is an award winning country house hotel where the quality of the locally sourced food and the intelligently selected wine list is exceeded only by the warmth and professionalism of the managers and staff.

Exeter, Devon

Exeter is the county town of Devon and has a long and proud history stretching back before its time as the Roman garrison town of Isca. From the early middle ages onwards, its wealth derived largely from the manufacture and export of woollen materials. Much of this wealth was then diverted into banking and finance, and this economic background frames the events described in The Book.

http://en.wikipedia.org/wiki/Exeter

Exeter, Ontario

Exeter – 'Home of the White Squirrel' – is a town of some 5,000 souls in Huron County, Ontario, Canada. It was founded in the nineteenth century, and the original settlers were supplemented by numbers from Exeter and Devon. There is indeed a South Huron District High School although it cannot claim Faith Codrington as one of its alumni. Genuine former pupils include Tim Long, executive producer of *The Simpsons*, and Harriet Brooks, a remarkable early nuclear scientist who worked with Ernest Rutherford. A potted history of Exeter can be found on: http://en.wikipedia.org/wiki/Exeter,_Ontario

Mol's

A little artistic licence here. Mol's was a famous coffee house in Exeter's Cathedral Close from 1726 to 1837. It is no longer trading, although its name is still proudly displayed at first floor level along with a grand coat of arms. Its function has been replaced by the estimable Tea on the Green in the same building.

http://www.exetermemories.co.uk/em/molscoffee.php

Phoenix Arts Centre

The Exeter Phoenix (as it is properly called) is a long established venue in Exeter's historic centre – just off the street that is believed to have inspired J K Rowling's Diagon Alley.

It houses galleries, a learning centre, studios and performance spaces. As yet, it does not retail Mayfair spirits, nor are its staff, performers, visitors and studio theatre exactly as described. This is a *story*, remember. The real Phoenix, though, is well worth a visit; find out more on http://www.exeterphoenix.org.uk/

Rose and Crown, Salisbury

This is a thirteenth century coaching inn located at the edge of the water meadows that border the cathedral. The descriptions of the staff, facilities and rooms are entirely fictitious and bear no relation to the high standards that actually apply.

http://www.legacy-hotels.co.uk/legacy-roseandcrown/

Rusty Bike

Nathaniel Barton's local. Formerly a decrepit boozer, it was revived by Hamish Lothian, pub proprietor, pig farmer and generally stout fellow. It provides excellent beers along with a varied and changing menu, often based on their own pigs.

http://www.rustybike-exeter.co.uk/

Tuckers Hall

Since 1471, Tuckers Hall has been the home of the – real – Guild of Weavers, Fullers and Shearmen; 'tuckers' is an alternative name for fullers. The Guild in its modern-day incarnation could not be more different from the evil conspiracy described in The Book. The mediaeval building is worth a visit in its own right and it has been supplemented by a series of excellent displays in a sensitively designed modern extension.

Now an Incorporation, the Guild has moved into the twenty first century with an ongoing project to digitise their unique collection of records. They also have a fine website on http://www.tuckershall.org.uk

Well House Tavern

A recently refurbished pub with an unequalled view across Exeter Cathedral Green, the Well House is an offshoot of local chef Michael Caines' small but perfectly formed empire. It is the haunt of many more locals than Nathaniel Barton and keeps a fine cellar. See more on: http://www.michaelcaines.com/taverns/exeter

The Assassinations

This story alludes to the murders (or attempted murders) of various prominent people through the past four centuries. The *official* history of these deaths is tabulated below.

- **King Gustav III of Sweden**, assassinated in 1792 by person or persons unknown

- **Jean-Paul Marat**, French revolutionary leader, murdered in his bath in 1793 by Charlotte Corday

- **Spencer Perceval**, British Prime Minister, shot in 1812 by a disgruntled John Bellingham

- **William Huskisson**, a Member of Parliament, who has the unenviable distinction of being the world's first victim of a steam train 'accident' in 1830

- **Nathan Mayer Rothschild**, prominent financier who is reported to have died of an infected abscess in 1836 while attending a wedding

- **Prince Alfred,** Duke of Edinburgh and second in line to the British throne, shot in the back in 1868 while in Australia by one Henry James O'Farrell, a recently discharged lunatic who believed he was being directed by the Fenian Brotherhood, an Irish Republican movement. Alfred survived and eventually died in Germany in 1900 of heart disease exacerbated by alcoholism

- **Czar Alexander II of Russia**, killed in 1881 by one Ignacy Hryniewiecki

- **President Carnot of France** (1894)...

- **Prime Minster Antonio Canovas of Spain** (1897) and...

- **Empress Elizabeth of Austria** (1898) – all supposedly killed by 'Italian anarchists'

- **King Umberto of Italy** was assassinated in 1900 by a native born Italian, Gaetano Bresci, who had emigrated to the United States. As chance (?) would have it, Gaetano was a weaver

- **William McKinley**, President of the United States, was shot in September 1901 by Leon Czolgosz, an anarchist who claimed to have been influenced by Bresci

- **Jean Jaures**, a leading French leftist and an anti-war campaigner, was killed in 1914. The man convicted of his killing was subsequently pardoned

- **Leon Trotsky**, an architect of the Bolshevik Revolution, was the victim of Ramon Mercader, a Spanish-born agent of Josef Stalin

- **Victor Cazalet** was a British Member of Parliament accompanying the Polish war leader Sikorski in 1943 when their plane inexplicably crashed off the Spanish coast

- The murder of **King Abdullah of Jordan** in 1951 was assumed to be perpetrated by a clique of army officers

- UN Secretary General **Dag Hammarskjold** died in an air crash in 1961; there continue to be different explanations for the incident

- ...and of course the conspiracy theories about the assassination of **John F Kennedy** in 1963 continue to flourish

- **Pablo Neruda** was a figurehead for South American leftist movements when he died in hospital in 1973, apparently of heart failure

- **President Anwar Sadat of Egypt** was another statesman killed, allegedly, by an amorphous clique of army officers in 1981

Miscellanea

Bays

Bays Brewery has been a family-run business in Paignton since 2007. In the fine tradition of Devon's production of excellent food and drink, they supply a range of ales, beers and lagers to pubs, bars and shops across the country.

www.http://www.baysbrewery.co.uk

Bob's Jerk Shed & Bistro

Sadly, an entirely fictitious restaurant chain in Canada. If it existed, I would surely want to eat there!

Mayfair Vodka

This boutique producer of London-distilled spirits currently offers a gin, a vodka and rum. Their products are found in a small number of prestigious establishments on both sides of the Atlantic. Unfortunately, they are not (at the time of writing) available in the Exeter Phoenix. Find out more on

http://www.mayfairbrands.com/

Picpoul de Pinet

Picpoul de Pinet is a delicious lemon-scented full-bodied white wine from the Languedoc region of France (*not* recommended with ice). It used to be quite difficult to find but is now more widely available from a range of large and small retailers.

Ruinart

This is the oldest champagne house still trading, founded in 1729 (when Nathaniel #1 was but a child). Its sparkling wines are not to everyone's taste but they deliver a refined and elegant tribute to the Chardonnay grape. Visit http://www.ruinart.com

Tariq Ali's *1968 and After: Inside the Revolution*

Always thought provoking and often spot on in his analysis, Tariq Ali is well worth reading, especially by those who know nothing of the *soixante-huitards*. Bliss it was in that dawn to be alive.

Trewman's Flying Post

Trewman's Exeter Flying Post was a weekly newspaper published in Exeter between 1763 and 1917. A complete sequence from 1769 to 1917 is held in the excellent Devon Heritage Centre.

http://www.devon.gov.uk/index/councildemocracy/record_office.htm

The Original Backers of The Book

This story would never have been published without the generous support of individuals who, through the Kickstarter crowdfunding website, each pledged £10 and upwards to help me cover the costs.

I hope that they are pleased with their investment, for which they have received numbered and personally dedicated copies of The Book and inclusion in the list below:

A Nony Mouse (Devon)
Aileen & John Despard
Alex Thorn
Ali Archer
Andreas Gustafsson
Andy Woodhead
Anne Oxborough
Anonymous (Canada)
Anonymous (Devon) x 5
Anonymous (Dorset)
Anonymous (Exeter)
Anonymous (Hampshire)
Anonymous (US)
Avery L Heart
The Biggs Family
Caroline Romijn
Catherine Gregory
Chloe Smith
Chris Franklin
Chris Lorimer
Corinne Thomas
Damian Oldham
Dan Lockton
Daniel Bosgraaf
Daniel Porter
Darren Herd
David Shearmon
Davyd Coe
Doug Sheppard
Eileen Jarman
Einstein Tremeer
E D E Bell
Frank Pike
Gary Price
Geoffrey Dawkins
Hattie Brember
Heidi Watson-Jones
Isabel Virden
James Barker
Joe Marshall
John Madigan
Jon Barlow
Kathleen Seed
Kathryn Rendell
Liz & Brian Norman
Liz Byrne
Liz Georgeson
Lynda Swalwell
M Crawshaw
Margaret Seed
Marilyn Small
Mark & Fiona Lovell

Martin & Sally Nunan
Paul & Ardene Hicks
Peter Hoskin
Peter Walker
Phil Davidson
Phil Skipper
Rachel Iles
Rebecca Clifford
Richard Belcher
Richard Day
Rob Laine
Rob Targett
Roger & Mimi Hatfield
Roselle & Daniel Brenchley
Sam Freeman
Sarah Boxall
Serena FitzGerald
Simon Cohen
Spencer Brint
Stephanie & Tim Darrie-Laye
Sue & Tom Westgate
Sue Edwards
Sylvia Jarman
Tracy Austin
Vivien Leigh
Will & Mel Freeland
Yvonne Hensman

A further 103 people made cash donations.